KILL ME

The Harpur & Iles series

Bill James

KILL ME

W. W. Norton & Company
New York   London

First published 2000 by Macmillan Publishers Ltd.
Copyright © 2000 by Bill James
First American edition 2000

First published as a Norton paperback 2001

Manufacturing by Courier Westford

Library of Congress Cataloging-in-Publication Data

James, Bill, 1929–
  Kill me / Bill James.—1st American ed.
    p. cm.
  ISBN 0-393-04920-5
  1. Harpur, Colin (Fictitious character)—Fiction. 2. Iles,
Desmond (Fictitious character)—Fiction. 3. Police—
England—Fiction. 4. England—Fiction. I. Title.

PR6070.U23 K55 2000
823'.914—dc21
                                                    00-025050

ISBN 0-393-32166-5 pbk.

W. W. Norton & Company, Inc., 500 Fifth Avenue, New York, NY 10110
www.wwnorton.com

W. W. Norton & Company Ltd., Castle House, 75/76 Wells Street, London W1T 3QT

1 2 3 4 5 6 7 8 9 0

1

Suddenly this June night there were faces here that should not be here. She knew them from briefing photographs only, some taken furtively and not very good, but good enough. Two. Yes, she had picked out two. That was not right. If two of them had made it this far, there ought to be a third. Where was he, the third? Where? She tried not to look about too frantically for him, and kept on trading and checking for forged twenties whenever a customer approached.

She did look for him, though, and knew from half a dozen of the dimmish, over-enlarged pictures viewed repeatedly during last month's briefings what she was looking for. It would be a thin face on a thinner body. To mark the lack of meat, the trade and everyone else, except probably his mother, called this lad Corporeal. If it came to shooting, was he too thin to be hit, but not too thin to hit her? And of course it would come to shooting. And of course Corporeal would show in a minute to reinforce those two, despite the operation scenario which said that neither Corporeal nor the other pair should ever get this far.

The plan, like so many police plans, lay dead or dying, and she could be next. True, Iles had told her at the very first of the briefings five weeks ago that although the project had a brilliant likelihood of success it might need some adjustments on the day. 'What Harpur would probably call "fine-tuning", given his flair for a shagged-out phrase,' the assistant chief had said. Well, this was the day and on the day the project did need some adjustments fast: a total but swift retune. Because Corporeal was not in sight, and because of what Iles had told her about him she found herself thinking of Corporeal as the most lethal. Stupid? All three were gifted. And to cope with the threat the three might offer there had been three principal briefings during May.

2

THE BRIEFINGS

Briefing One, 5 May

Iles said: 'Naomi, you're going to be central to an operation that should eliminate permanently all threat of invasion by this fucking arrogant London gang into our drugs scene. Things are shaping for us. Naturally, although the plan has a brilliant likelihood of success, it might need some adjustments on the day. What Harpur would probably call "fine-tuning", given his flair for a shagged-out phrase. Isn't that what you'd call it, Harpur?'

'They shouldn't reach you at the Eton, but we have to provide in case they do,' Harpur replied.

Twelve blown-up photographs, most black and white, were laid out on a trestle table. They each showed one of three men.

Iles said: 'Colonizers. This is the pattern now. Things in London and Manchester and Liverpool get tough for them because of good police work there, or competition from other dealers, or more likely both. So they look for new markets. They'll try for ultimate control of all drugs pickings here and in any other biggish urban orchard. Best you familiarize yourself with their faces. Oh, yes, it's more than possible they'll be stopped a long way from the Eton on the night, much more than possible. However ... look, here's the boy they call Corporeal, as slim as the Book of Jude.'

Iles passed an elegant finger over a group of the photographs. 'They've done six pictures of him – above his share – compensating for lack of body weight. Real name, Digby Lighthorn, specialist pusher to the wealthy, and hence a fierce interest in that select floating restaurant and trading centre, the Eton Boating Song, where you'll be attractively in place and trading. Corporeal handles mostly coke, but some H, and Amyl to gays, inevitably. He does know guns, but we're not sure to what proficiency, are we, Harpur?'

'From where you'll sit you can watch the whole bar area, and, naturally, we'll have protective people all round you,' Harpur told her. 'You just behave as if you're what you're supposed to be – established and esteemed supplier to the Eton's prosperous users.'

Iles said: 'Notice, Naomi? This sod, Harpur, never actually answers a question, which is why he's eternally bogged down at detective chief super. I mean, that's one of fifty reasons he's stuck at detective chief super. Ever seen more subordinate eyes than Harpur's, Naomi, or more cringeing teeth?'

Harpur said: 'Perhaps we should stick to Angela Rivers, her cover name, now, sir. Accustom Naomi and ourselves.'

Iles said: 'So very, very right, Col. Forgive me. Have you ever seen more subordinate eyes than Harpur's, Angela, or more cringeing teeth?'

Naomi said: 'When you tell me none of these three should get to me at—'

'Harpur has information that they'll certainly set out for the the Eton Boating Song that day – or rather, night – but might be intercepted some distance away by a shooting party, isn't that so, Col?'

Harpur stepped to a room plan fixed to a large cork board on the easel. He pointed to a small mauve circle. 'You're here, Angela, in the Eton bar. This is the recognized pusher's seat.'

'It's a bothersome tradition I'm in,' she said, 'both previous holders slaughtered: Eleri ap Vaughan, Simon Pilgrim, Si one of the best throat-cut jobs the doctor ever saw, I heard.'

Iles said: 'Eleri and Pilgrim were folk who did not have our backing.'

Harpur indicated on the room plan all the middle area of the Eton bar. 'Yes, we'll have officers at most tables in this part. And I'll be close to you here, with Peter and Siân.'

'Harpur's surprisingly capable in this kind of blood-all-over situation,' Iles said. 'His talents are heavy talents. Less nifty with the paper clips.'

'We pull you out at the first threat of gunfire,' Harpur told her, 'probably through this door here' – he pointed at a yellow rectangle on the diagram – 'yes, out of that door, onto the deck, then down the gangway to a car we'll have waiting. But I stress it should not happen because they'll be stopped.'

'Intercepted?' she asked. She tried to keep her voice unnervous, but knew it must sound thin. 'Who'll intercept them?'

Iles said: 'It's possible – oh, probable, yes, probable, yes, extremely probable, if Col's tip is right, that a local crew . . .'

She did not like the way both Harpur and Iles spattered yesses in the forecasts, wanting to make things sound positive; *needing* to make things sound positive, because they might not be. 'A police local crew will intercept?' she asked.

'No, no, no,' Iles replied, with what seemed to her a very rounded law-and-order laugh. 'Would the police prepare an armed ambush in such circumstances? That would be intolerably improper, Naomi. Angela. Oh, yes.'

'Armed?' she said.

'Corporeal and his London chums are trying to annex one of the most profitable sites on our patch, Angela – The Eton Boating Song's famed cocaine station,' Iles replied. 'These are large-scale business manoeuvres. Yes, there'll be talented gunfire – from rivals.'

'You mean a local crew of dealers?' she asked.

'We understand it's a possibility,' Iles replied. 'This is some of Col's rather shady information – you know what he's like. Harpur hears more fucking voices than Joan of Arc, all of them slippery and bought. Now and then they get things right, and now and then is an exceptionally high rate of return from informants.'

'You're saying a local firm will gun down Corporeal and the other two when they're on their way to finish me at the Eton?' she asked.

Iles laughed again, though this time it seemed more a refined chuckle. 'Gun down? Gun down? These are rough-edged words, Angela. Who knows who will hurt whom? We can only tell you what the outlook appears to be.'

'But a gun encounter somewhere on the dockside?' she replied.

Iles said: 'The dockside does look a likely site. This will upset Chiefy and Mrs Chiefy. They believe the sweet new marina development should have abolished violence there.'

'And if Corporeal and the other two London people aren't expecting a trap, they're the ones likely to get knocked over, aren't they?' she asked.

'I don't think Colin would dispute that reading,' Iles replied. 'You'll ask why we're not trying to stop that happening.'

'No, I won't ask that. I think I can see it. You want these three eliminated and these locals look likely to do it for you.'

'It would be for *us*, Angela – if that were a fair reading of things. But it isn't. The information is uncertain – inevitably. Not enough to justify an Armageddon operation by our people.'

'Oh?' she replied.

'No, indeed,' Iles said. 'That's so, isn't it, Col?'

'You might wonder why we're not arming you personally, Angela,' Harpur replied.

'Oh, this is the chief's ruling,' Iles said. 'Now listen, folk, I hope I would never speak a word against Mr Lane in the presence of career underlings like you two, Angela, Colin – that would be grossly indiscreet – but you know what a total fucking wanker he is about guns. I'd have kitted you way back, Angela. I'm only the dogsbody, though, and there'd be no point in arguing with the chief. It's *Mrs* Lane one would have to convince, and I'm permitted few audiences.'

'To get you up to real proficiency in the time would not have been possible, Angela,' Harpur said. 'And in any case, once you'd gone undercover you couldn't come in and practise on the range. It might be a giveaway. You're supposed to be an upper-echelon pusher in Mansel Shale's fine firm. You must not be seen near any police property.'

'You really think they don't know who I am?' she asked.

'But most of us around you at the Eton will be carrying something,' Harpur replied.

Iles said: 'Harpur's a beautiful shot, although he's nearly as palsied-neurotic about weaponry as Lane. Col *will* fire, however, if things are very, very bad, and I think even he would regard things as very, very bad should it appear you might get killed, Naomi. Angela. Isn't that right, Harpur? You could force yourself into effectiveness in those circumstances?'

'Our best marksmen will be scattered all around the Eton, waiting for my orders,' Harpur replied. 'We're determined to minimize hazard to you, Angela.'

Briefing Two, 18 May

The sessions had taken place in what Iles referred to as a 'safeish house' rented for six months in the name of a woman he knew. Naomi was not sure who she was: Harpur had told her it might be one of the ACC's revered Ulster great-aunts, or a seventeen-year-old ethnic whore Iles revered very frequently in his car and so on. The house was at a decent end of the city and Naomi had to travel there by two taxis: hailed taxis, never picked up at ranks. She would go into the city centre first from her newly provided hideaway flat, then switch after a bit of a look around behind her. Harpur and Iles arrived separately at the house, driving partway and then a walk. She always left first. She had the idea that neither Iles nor Harpur would trust the other not to try something if one to one with her. But since Harpur was her undercover controller she would have to work alone with him eventually, suppose it came to eventually. Iles liked having the house in a rich district; regarded high-calibre suburbia as a good disguise. Harpur had decided it would be unwise to meet in her flat or in his place or Iles's.

Harpur brought the pictures, diagrams and sketches in a holdall and displayed them fresh each time. He also brought three pistols each time and matched them at the beginning of every briefing with the three London men. Corporeal always used a 9mm eight-round Parabellum Walther, and the other two Browning FN 140DA automatics with twelve-round magazines. She did not understand why it was important for her to know this. If someone, or more than one, started banging off at you in the small space of a restaurant bar, you would not be interested in what type of weapon, weapons, were cutting you in half, nor in how many bullets were available to do it. But she listened, nodded, memorized.

Iles stacked the pictures of Corporeal. 'We've got him fixed in the mind, I'd say, wouldn't you, Angela? Shall we look at the other two now?' He displayed the six remaining photographs. But then he suddenly went back to the half-dozen of Corporeal and fanned them out again. 'I'm glad there are more of him, and not just because he's so damn lean. I want to stress that if there were to be any danger to you – very, very if but *if* there were – suppose somehow they dodged the ambush – in that case it's from Corporeal the peril would most likely come. He will feel the Eton is so *him*, the way Thatcher *knew* she was right for Prime Minister.'

'You mean that if I'm there, apparently trading, Corporeal's going to see me as the opposition, to be removed?' she asked.

'This is a possibility,' Iles replied.

The house was furnished in real upper-management opulence, though the old, splintered easel and the cork board had been imported from headquarters, plus the trestle table. If you thought about that kind of stuff being brought in from a van, you had to wonder about the anonymity of this safeish house. She and Harpur were seated now, in wide cream-beige armchairs, while Iles stood near the table, occasionally holding up one or more photographs. They drank tea which Iles had made and served in delightful, fine flower-decorated china. 'You've planned it like this, haven't you?' she asked Iles. 'I'm bait. Have you actually agreed it with Shale and his partner, Panicking Ralph – their fortunate interception? There's a little blitz alliance? That's why I asked whether they know who I am. It would be a nice operation, wouldn't it: get rid of the London invaders and everything reverts to the healthy, peaceful scene where Shale's and Pan-icking's combined firms are tolerated?'

Iles chuckled at this. 'The chief is entirely opposed to such blind-eye arrangements with the police, even in the interests of peace,' he replied. 'That would totally offend his notion of the right.'

'The chief doesn't run this domain,' Naomi replied.

'Well, Angela, *Mrs* Lane plus the chief are a very compel-ling influence,' Iles replied.

'*You* run the domain, Mr Iles,' Naomi replied. 'Doesn't he, Mr Harpur?'

'Here's the one they call Lovely Mover,' Iles replied, a photograph displayed for her in each of his hands. 'Delightful clothing on supple limbs. Lincoln W. Lincoln, who came on ahead of the other two to our region. Path-finder. Explorer. Business emissary. Carries the automatic in a left-mounted shoulder holster under this gorgeous, gener-ously cut jacket. Yes, probably did one of your predecessors as queen of the Eton bar – Eleri, that lovely old rogue. Might have done Si Pilgrim too, though we don't have LWL down as a throat guru. Perhaps he's been on a course lately.'

'Timberlake's still doing good work on the Pilgrim case,' Harpur said.

'It's just that we never get witnesses on that kind of killing, Angela,' Iles said. 'Or we do get witnesses, but not witnesses who will talk like witnesses in the box.' Iles put the photographs of Lovely Mover down and made a fan of the remaining four. 'Tommy Mill-Kaper. Excellent family. His grandfather was a distinguished thinker and servant of the state. Full of high convictions. Won the VC with Wingate out east in the Second World War. A lot for Tommy to live up to, and he seems to be on a different career route altogether. So far. He *has* convictions, but not the same type as Grandad's. Tommy traffics mostly grass and Ecstasy, plus some crack and coke. He's your boy for raves and taprooms. All three are sent from London by Everton Evas Osprey and the Rt. Hon. They will be expected to produce gains. And they *will* try. Everton sees us as patsies, and Shale and Panicking as patsies too. That south-east London confidence. Shale a patsy, I ask you, Angela! Or even Harpur. One feels quite sorry for them.'

Briefing Three, 30 May

Harpur said: 'Could you wear something dark on the night, Angela?' He unrolled a piece of upper-body armour on the table, all ribs and straps. 'They don't do these in light colours, and best not have it showing through.' He brought a folded Marks & Spencer carrier bag from the holdall and put the body armour in it. He covered it with tissue paper, also taken from the holdall, then handed the carrier to her. 'You won't *need* the armour, and it will make you hot on a June night, but do wear it. Yes, we'll stick with regulations on *Protection in Possible Gunfire Incidents.*'

Iles said: 'Corporeal. Watch for Corporeal – that is, if any of them at all turn up, which, of course, they won't. Would we put you in there if we really thought they'd get past the convenient interception, Naomi?'

'I'm Angela,' she replied. 'I don't know. Would you? Would you, Mr Harpur?'

'Care for one final run over the details of these pistols before I pack them, Angela?' Harpur replied.

3

And so tonight, when she was not craftily looking about for Corporeal, or doing discreet coke deals with the Eton's gilded faithful, she managed a swift eye survey of Lincoln W. Lincoln's left shoulder, seeking the shape of a holster and a Fabrique Nationale Browning 7.65mm automatic under the lovely loose cut of his tan-to-gold jacket. There were difficulties. Part of the time he had his back to her and when he did not she might be busy with a customer. He was standing at the bar with Mill-Kaper, possibly watching her in a mirror behind the bottles, and occasionally turning around and seeming to glance amiably about the room at anyone but her, but now and then at her just the same, and not amiably. She did not want any eye-to-eye with him, and it was tricky avoiding this when you were scrutinizing so far up someone's body as a shoulder, even when the someone pretended not to be looking at you. Eye-to-eye could tell tales, her nervy tales, his agenda tales. One of LWL's tales, readable in his gaze if she had met it, might be that he was there to kill her in due course tonight – clear a route for his chieftains into the Eton – and she feared that when she did read this the few bits of poise and disguise and mental order she had kept going so far would leave her. God, Harpur was right – the heat of this damned armour! Was Lincoln W. Lincoln casing her chest for evidence of defence, the way she cased his shoulder for evidence of attack? What use shielding your chest when your face and head were nicely on show for a Fabrique Nationale Browning 7.65mm automatic, still, thank God, cosy in its cot under the wide tan-gold lapel? People of Lovely Mover's sort were not taught to shoot only at the chest, as police were. She felt like screaming at him, 'You're not supposed to be here, you fucker. You and your fucking jacket should have been tidily waylaid. What about the ambush?'

Harpur was somewhere close, but out of sight. She wished he was closer and she wished she could see him. He had the sort of features that had obviously taken a lot of damage during his career without killing him, and she wanted someone else's features to attract the damage tonight, preferably without killing him, but, in any case, to get between the damage and her. Possibly, though, he had met Lovely Mover before this evening and would have been recognized. She could see plenty of other work friends, all of them striving to look thoroughly unpolice in smart-casual gear and acting a good night out, though decorously in such a select, panelled setting as the Eton bar. But they would be as familiar with the blow-up pictures as she was, and very alert now, ready to outmatch any Brownings or Walther when Harpur yelled his warnings. He had told Naomi he always shouted, 'Armed police!' three times: one for the targets, one for luck and one for the editor of the *Guardian*. Harpur would be a *Daily Mail* man, at least.

You could see what Iles meant about the arrogance of these London people: they hung about in the bar, sizing her up, apparently careless of being noticed and remembered. But, of course, they weren't all here. Lovely Mover and Tommy Mill-Kaper might be only diversions. She tugged her eyes away from LWL's jacket shoulder and looked for Corporeal again, more urgently now, and perhaps more obviously.

Instead, she saw . . . she saw . . . but, Christ, how was this possible? Had she started to hallucinate after all, shoved haywire by the stress? This job was too big for her? She saw . . . thought she saw . . . wanted to see . . . did see, did see, didn't she? – thought she saw . . . saw two men who until not many weeks ago had between them been her whole recent love life. Perhaps they still were, if they were really there and she was really seeing them – not just longing to see them, because to her panicking soul and busy subconscious they had come to stand for ease and safety and the old clear-cut and unthreatened Naomi Anstruther life, not this perilous A. Rivers life. One of them was Donald McWater. She had loved and shacked up with Don until this damned undercover assignment split them: that final terrible quarrel and coldness on holiday in hot Torremolinos, because he thought the work she would move into on return was idioti-cally dangerous. Had he been right? The other . . . even stranger . . . impossible . . . the other was a lad called Lyndon Evans, a fling, that was all: just a couple of days' comforting rebound romance after Donald flew home early in a rage from Spain. These two, Don and Lyndon, were here now . . . weren't they? Weren't they . . . near the main door to the bar? They were separate, not together. She tried to will them not to approach her, and for a while that seemed to work. Donald had stopped just inside the bar and was staring at her, but apparently without recognition. He might have sensed he must not show he knew her. There were other people behind him, and then Lyndon, his fair hair and unfledged Welsh face just visible, peering around them. Donald might not know he was there. Lyndon kept gazing at her too, when he could, but grinning and making small, would-be discreet waves. Somehow he did seem to realize that she could not acknowledge him, and that he must not visibly acknowledge her. She thought he had seen Donald. Had they followed her here somehow – if they were here at all? This was part of the operation? She wanted to squeak at Harpur and ask him what was happening, but she could not see Harpur, and knew she must not call to him anyway – that much of her brain still functioned.

Lyndon's patience seemed to go. This lad worked on a factory production line: no undercover skills or training needed there. Suddenly, he pushed through the group of people around him and started to run towards her, still grinning like a groupie, still waving, and now calling her name above the noise of the chamber quintet-quality Muzak: 'Naomi, Naomi, Naomi.' Donald saw and heard him, went startled, and then also began to run. It was like a race and she was the winning post and prize. She was doing a £200 coke deal with a couple of Old Etonian Etonians, but quickly half stood from her chair, momentarily conscious above all of rage with Lyndon for blaring her real name like that, ditching precautions. After all, he was only a pleasant South Wales lad she'd comforted herself with a few times in a resort hotel, and in the aircraft toilet once on the way back to Britain. The old Etonian Etonians howled a protest as a couple of coke sachets and their money slid to the floor.

She did not even glance down. She did glance at an abrupt movement behind Donald and Lyndon, though, and now saw Corporeal in the doorway, that famous super-thin face and spectral neck, and that famous fat 9mm Walther in his meagre hand. He, also, was running towards Naomi, the gun out in front, meant for her. She heard Harpur bellow from the left, 'Stop! Armed police!', but only once before the firing began, and then she could distinguish nothing above that din. She glimpsed Lovely Mover, his jacket wide open now, the holster on view and empty, his Browning in a two-handed grip but aimed to the side of her, maybe at where Harpur's voice had come from. Mill-Kaper seemed no longer next to LWL at the bar. He might be down. Then Lovely Mover seemed to swing the Browning away to a different target.

Still half upright, she was hit to the side by the body of a falling man, perhaps Lyndon, perhaps one of the Old Etonian Etonians, perhaps anybody male. Her left shoulder and breast felt suddenly warmly wet, in the holster region, if she had been wearing one above the armour. A second later she was flat and a second after that was pulled by her ankles very fast along the floor. The firing had stopped and the Vivaldi strings or whoever it was could be heard again urging fussy refinement. At least two people tugged her, and possibly three. She was being dragged towards the door that had been marked in delicate yellow on Harpur's room plan. Yellow? Her skirt rode up and almost covered her face. She was skating across the board floor on her thighs and knickers. The armour straps were pulled tight by the friction and cut into her shoulders. A few seconds after this, she was on her feet and running down the gangplank, her skirt respectable again, the body armour skewed to one side under her dark blue blouse and probably ineffective. Someone helped her into the rear of a car parked there, its engine running. Siân Sampson and Peter Liss took places in the vehicle with Naomi, Peter in the passenger seat, Sampson alongside her. They had been part of the closest protection group with Harpur. Although she thought she might have seen him during that confused rush along the deck and down the gangplank, he was not present now. 'You're going to mess up the upholstery, Naomi,' she said, 'but it's Mr Iles's car, so the back seat is used to rough treatment. Here he comes.'

Iles got in behind the wheel. He was wearing some sort of buff-coloured dungarees and a check cheese-cutter cap, as if he had been to read gas meters. 'You keep a wonderfully powerful hold over your men, Angela. Naomi,' he said. 'They die for you. Mind, I believe there are certainly women who would do that for me. Shall I drive you to where you can clean up? You're not hit, only bloodied by the fair-haired lad. I've no role at this kind of messy incident – shouldn't be here at all. Harpur's gone back to inventory.'

4

On her way into the funeral Naomi was more or less pleased to run across a girl called Esmé who had been with the same package holiday party as Lyndon in Spain. Donald and Naomi had done some grand club outings with their group around Torremolinos and Malaga. Esmé could be a pain – so damned clever – but on the whole it was nice to see her. They took their places in a pew up near the middle of the church and whispered together, waiting for Lyndon's body. It had been brought back after the Eton to his home in Cardiff. 'He was my lovely friend, Naomi,' Esmé said. 'Lately, that's all he was. What he had become, just a lovely friend. All right, I fucked him once. That is, not just *once* – not a one-night-stand – but I mean once upon a time for a while. But you had him later, in the hotel, the Boeing, so you're closer to him now, I see that. You've got the responsibility.'

'Responsibility?' Naomi replied. They were whispering. 'Oh, at the time I just needed someone who – I needed some solace.' Yes, that. She had refused to give up the undercover work, so goodbye, Donald. And then – yes, for solace – hello, Lyndon.

Esmé said: 'Lyndon's the far past for me now, but I still know we've got to find the savage London sods who sent that trio. Find them, get them. Just you and me, Naomi, we handle it. It's plain. They would have killed you. Instead, Lyndon. And Donald. You owe them all ways.'

'*Get?*' Naomi asked. It was a small, damp-smelling, pretty church in a Cardiff suburb, crowded today: nice to see the turn-out for Lyndon. The chief, Iles and Harpur were further towards the front, just behind what Naomi took to be Lyndon's family, the chief and Iles in dress uniform. It was to be a modified service for the dead and Iles would read a lesson. Protocol said senior police officers might attend the funerals of those slaughtered by criminals – even *should* attend – but not if the victim was himself a criminal. Lane, Iles and Harpur would not go to Corporeal Lighthorn's or Tommy Mill-Kaper's in London when the coroner released the bodies. About them there was some query.

Esmé said: 'You know. *Get* them, those London magnates. Sort them out. It's how we do things here.' To Naomi it sounded absurd, this slender, pretty girl of her own age talking vendetta in a church. Now and then, as her anger took over, Esmé's voice rose almost to ordinary speaking level. Naomi frowned, put a finger to her lips. 'Yes, get the swine,' Esmé said.

'We—'

'You'll say that two of the bastards have been got already – Lighthorn and the VC progeny.'

'Well, yes, and—'

'I know. And the third, the one they call in the press Lovely Mover, he dodged away somehow and the reports say he is being "urgently sought".' Esmé sneered the last words and then sneered them again. ' "Urgently sought". You're a cop, believe in cop things, so you think people who are "urgently sought" get found. Me? No, I *don't* believe it.'

'Yes, he'll be found. We know him.'

'Anyway, I'm not very bothered about some low-rank soldier in the Eton bar that night flashing a gun. I mean the chieftains. You're a cop, you'd know who they are. Or could find out.'

Naomi heard the tiny purr of fat rubber wheels behind. They stood. 'Don't keep telling me I'm a fucking cop,' she muttered.

'Knew as soon as you spoke on the aircraft out to Spain, though you never let on – tried never to let on.'

Yes, too damn bright. Naomi turned her head. Lyndon's coffin came on a gleaming little trolley. Walking ahead of it in his dark robes and dark hat, the vicar spoke the required words, which she found did not do much for her: '*I am the resurrection and the life, saith the Lord: he that believeth in me, though he were dead, yet shall he live . . .*' Naomi began to weep. She felt she might pass out and staggered slightly, bumping against Esmé. Had she caused this death, and Donald's? Esmé gripped her right arm, just below the elbow, steadying her. Esmé was weeping too. The coffin moved slowly up towards the altar.

'Kill? You're talking about very big people,' Naomi said.

'Which?'

'Who sent the three.'

'Of course. Good, you agree.'

'To what? We'd never even get close,' Naomi said.

'What?' Esmé put her head nearer Naomi's mouth. The

vicar had continued to proclaim the prayer book formula. He was an old, tall, broken-nosed man with a majestic voice, used to funerals.

'We'd never get close to the masters in London,' Naomi said, 'even if I knew them and where to find them.'

'We've *got* to get close,' Esmé said. 'They send thugs who kill Lyndon and your long-time steady. This is all your love life for the time being. Probably. Don't you *want* to get to them, for Christ's sake? Two lovely lover men who put themselves in the path of bullets meant for you.'

'Yes, they did that,' Naomi replied.

'There you are, then.' Esmé had stopped crying but began again now and pushed her face against Naomi's jacket to stifle the noise.

'It's why I go to the funerals,' Naomi said. 'Gratitude. Don's yesterday back home, now Lyndon's here in Wales.'

Esmé pulled herself clear and glared at Naomi, the swimming green eyes ferocious. Again she spoke almost at normal pitch, trying to be heard above the vicar: 'Gee! Somebody saves your life, so you turn up with a wreath and it's all square.'

'But, like you said – I'm a cop.'

'Meaning courts, trials, all that, for the devils who did it? Hopeless.'

And the service began. There were good hymns and solid prayers, standard prayers, prayers which might have consoled some – those who could be consoled by the sing-along words. As a special adaptation to the service, the vicar called on Iles and he went to the lectern and read what she knew the family had suggested, a piece from Psalm 130. He had rehearsed it in the car this morning as he, Lane, Harpur and Naomi drove to Cardiff. The family had asked that the chief constable himself should read. They wanted to line up themselves and their dead son with lawfulness, and the chief was its prime symbol. But Lane had decided the stress would be too much for him. In the car, Iles had said: 'These are folk who could not know the impressive depth of your sensitivities, sir.'

The ACC read in a conversational, almost offhand, style, and yet at times his voice wavered, as if he might not be able to continue; as if, after all, the stress were too much for him as well as for Lane. There was showmanship to it, naturally. This *was* Desmond Iles. But Naomi also heard real anguish, perhaps even real despair, as he spoke the verses.

Out of the deep have I called thee, O Lord: Lord hear my voice.
O let thine ears consider well the voice of my complaint.
If thou, Lord, will be extreme to mark what is done amiss: O
    Lord, who may abide it?'

Iles never looked at the text. A couple of readings in the car and he had everything held in his head. He divided his gaze between the coffin just beneath him and Lyndon's family on his left. To Naomi, the rich blue of that ceremonial uniform seemed somehow to set off the ACC's manically unpredictable looks: like a master of ceremonies who had been snorting something top-rate, or supping leftovers at a champagne party. Recently, he had given up the *en brosse* barbering adopted for a while after a season of Jean Gabin films. Now, his grey hair was longish and at one stage it fell onto his brow when he leaned forward over the lectern. Naomi had seen something like that happen in the days before *en brosse*. Then, he used to push it fondly and languorously back. But apparently he once saw the politician Michael Heseltine make such a move on television and he at once abandoned it.

When the reading was over Iles stared about the church for a bit but did not leave the lectern or look like leaving it. Naomi felt the congregation grow nervy. Possibly she caught the sound of an appalled sigh from Mark Lane, heavy with terrified anticipation. The vicar, who had sat down in the pulpit almost out of sight, stood and coughed. It was probably a breach to allow someone lay to read any part of the funeral service, and now the ACC seemed set on making the irregularity worse. Iles turned and gave him his personal stare portion. He twitched his hand slightly, signalling that vicars should keep out of church things.

'Christ, what *is* this?' Esmé muttered.

'Only Ilesy,' Naomi replied.

The ACC said: 'Ladies and gentlemen, you'll look at me in my regalia, you'll listen as I caress the Scriptures, and you'll wonder what sort of game this is for a policeman. You're right. And I'm not just *a* policeman today. I am *all* policemen. If my chief weren't subject to dire humility he'd be standing here, and you'd see the symbolic role more clearly. Things are slipping away from us. We used to be known as "pigs", because we scavenged, cleaned up, efficiently dealt with all those dirty complexities the rest of you wouldn't touch.

Today, we are not even capable of that. We are near defeat, and our function now is to get to funerals of the butchered innocent and read ancient soothing wisdom over the corpse. The fight's gone out of us because the fight's lost.'

Naomi heard the chief cry desperately, 'No, no,' like a mugged duchess. He half stood, as if to go and displace Iles at the lectern microphone. But then Lane seemed to falter, his head fell forward and in a moment he sat down again. Iles smiled forgivingly and ignored him from then on.

'I'm here – I and my colleagues are here – because your grand lad, Lyndon, was in our care in another city and you know what happened to him,' he declared. 'We failed to look after Lyndon Evans properly. True enough, we blasted the life out of two of the derelicts responsible for this.' He gestured feelingly towards the coffin with his thumb. 'But let me ask you now what will happen when we catch the rest of them and have to take the louts to trial – the third gunman and the godfathers? Has anyone ever told you about our bent, bribed, frightened, blind courts and our—'

Naomi saw Harpur stand now, but fully stand, not like Lane. Harpur was in a dark reach-me-down suit that did not do too bad a job. He pushed out of the pew and walked to the side of the lectern.

Iles watched him unmatily and seemed to lose his narrative. He said: 'Yes, this lad Lyndon came sniffing into our area, looking for a girl called—'

Harpur approached Iles, put a hand on his shoulder in friendly style and tried to reason with him. All the same, it looked like a sort of arrest, attempted arrest. The microphone picked up some of Harpur's words: 'Sir, it would be much better and more usual now if—'

Naomi was not sure how things went after that. The ACC seemed to lurch a little to the left, as if going onto one foot. He might have used the other to kick Harpur's legs away from under him. Iles knew all kinds of dire martial-arts tricks and had once head-butted a drunken detective into subjection at a leaving party. Or perhaps Harpur was simply put off balance by Iles's sudden movement and stumbled. The lower woodwork of the lectern made it impossible for her to see. At any rate, Harpur pitched back against the church wall under a statuette of Christ doing a blessing and sat down heavily on the flagged floor. His legs were bent beneath him awkwardly, but he seemed still conscious.

Iles smiled and continued: 'Yes, looking for a girl called Naomi – one of my colleagues, who is here today, as beautiful and brave as ever. His wish to find her could not be more understandable. But he could *not* find her, because—'

Harpur stood slowly, then bent down and pulled out the lectern microphone plug. Iles raised his voice: 'Because, as is now generally known, she had been ordered into secret work. However—'

Harpur began to sing in a powerful, throaty voice: 'The Lord's my shepherd.' After a moment, the vicar joined in. The organist caught the tune. The congregation took up the hymn. Iles gave Harpur a noble little bow and came away from the lectern.

In a while, the service proper continued. The vicar resumed from the prayer book: '*But some man will say, How*

are the dead raised up, and with what body do they come?
Thou fool, that which thou sowest is not quickened except it
die.'

'Oh yeah?' Esmé muttered.

After the burial there were sandwiches and tea in the church
hall. Esmé introduced Naomi to Lyndon's parents. 'He spoke
about you a great deal, my dear,' Mrs Evans said. 'I understand you had many interesting conversations in Spain and
on the aeroplane about topics such as the European Mon-
etary System and bullfights.'

'Oh, yes indeed,' Naomi replied.

'Lyndon always longed for good discussions,' Mr Evans
said.

Iles approached. 'Gallantry in others is always liable to
unnerve me, Mr and Mrs Evans,' he said. 'And Lyndon was *so*
gallant. I mean, a nobody kid from a nobody place and yet he
could deliberately sacrifice himself, though admittedly for a
prime girl like Naomi. Always in the face of such bravery, I
find myself wondering whether I can do justice to it – quite
literally wondering whether I can do justice, retributive
justice, along properly legal lines. Hence my little prose poem
just now.' Reassuringly, he raised both hands in blessing
mode, like the statuettes. 'Thanks be that poor Col didn't
injure himself. Do you know, one of the press people in the
church was going to report that I'd attacked him. Oh dearie
me! Wanted a comment. But we've put that right – made
it clear Harpur simply grew unsteady in his rather boyish

excitement. They won't dare. Plus, I'm going to ask the chief and holy Joe to disregard Col's disgraceful vandalizing of my little homily. Mercy follows naturally from such a good service, I think. Ah, here *is* the chief now.'

Lane and Harpur joined them. 'He was a wonderful son, Mr and Mrs Evans,' the chief said. 'He and McWater gladly interposed themselves between Naomi and a gunman when they saw she was in danger.'

'That's like Lyndon,' Esmé said.

'I'm sure it is,' Lane replied. 'I'm sorry to say we're not certain yet, Mr and Mrs Evans, how Lyndon came to be aboard the Eton Boating Song at all.'

'He grew fond of Naomi during their holiday meeting in Spain and came from Cardiff looking for her,' Harpur said. 'She had not given him an address. We assume he followed McWater to the Eton, sir. McWater was searching for Naomi himself, perhaps to seek a reconciliation, as I understand things. McWater suspected Naomi was doing undercover drugs work, and he might have heard of the Eton's reputation as an upmarket dealing centre. He would hope she was there.'

Lane paled more than he was already pale and then cried out: 'Reputation? An open reputation? Upmarket drugs emporium? How can this be? I will not have these tolerated criminal businesses on my ground.'

'Oh, you know how it is, sir,' Iles replied.

'No,' Lane said. 'No, I do not know, *will* not know.'

'Oh, you know how it is, sir,' Iles replied.

'Donald told us where he worked – when we were in Spain,' Esmé said. 'I expect Lyndon tailed him from there.'

'Resourcefulness, Mr and Mrs Evans,' Iles said. 'This was a fine boy. This was the kind of boy we want in the police, isn't it, Chief?'

'Oh, he would never have joined the police,' Mrs Evans replied. 'Too ungovernable.'

'I suppose we are,' Iles replied.

Naomi drew Esmé away from the group. 'Yes, you're probably right,' Naomi said. 'That's how it will have to be handled. *We* do it. If Iles thinks the police can never get these people legally, they can't be got legally.'

Esmé grinned: 'You *do* see your responsibilities, then.'

'I'm an ACC groupie, not a chief groupie.'

'Do you know, in the church I thought Iles might be mad,' Esmé replied, 'yet now I believe he's—'

'Oh, yes, he's mad,' Naomi replied, 'but with lapses.'

5

During the undercover duty, Naomi had been moved out of her flat into an anonymous apartment in the Valencia Esplanade district. She returned permanently to her own place now: what had been her own place and Don's until the split. Undercover was finished. Her name – two names – had been in the media, and pictures. Anstruther-Rivers was known. She would be shifted to some other kind of work after a rest and counselling. Lane believed in counselling, for others.

Not long after she was back in the flat, Naomi had callers.

Mansel Shale said: 'No way I could rest without coming over to tell you total regret for that mix-up at the Eton, my dear, and to give you my own and, indeed, the whole firm's sympathy. Of course we knew you were police, an undercover officer, but this we saw as the beginning of a proper arrangement with your senior men later. But then this tragedy at the Eton. This is two lads shot who been dear to you, and it's terrible. Take my fucking word for it, Naomi, it should never of happened and *would* never of happened if all parties had behaved as ordained.'

'What the hell *is* this, Mansel, coming to my home?' she said. 'You're out of your rut.'

'I did want to see you and explain things. How see you? Could I go to the funeral of your two friends, Donald and Lyndon? Not on. Decorum. Decorum's what I prize above all, and what I had to think, advised by Alfie, was maybe you would not care for the presence of someone at these obsequies who seemed to have . . . well . . . through fucking up been the cause of the deaths of your friends. So here I am to tell you them London trio should of been taken out a long way before the Eton. Some weak brother put us in the wrong place. I'm here to apologize for him, as well as for myself.'

'Decorum is a word Manse lives by, Naomi,' Alfred Ivis said. 'It will certainly form part of his escutcheon in the event of a title.'

'We'll be taking up Ralphy Ember's bit of a lapse with him at our next business meeting, naturally, Naomi,' Shale said.

'Taking up?' Naomi said.

'We not bugged here, are we, my dear, in this pleasant room, probably full of memories of Donald McWater?' Shale replied. 'Have a quick look for eavesdrop fitments, Alf, would you? They might of installed stuff without you even knowing, Naomi, pre your undercover job. They like to know the lot about officers going into that work.'

Ivis stood and did a careful tour of the room.

Shale said: 'I expect you heard Panicking Ralphy was the one who messed up our ambush. Only stuck us in the wrong fucking place for it, that's all – because he's scared or got some private scheme. This is a partner, but you can never tell with Panicking. That ambush should of been perfect and sweetly final, but let Panicking into a project and look out for snot in the beluga. So, you'll say, why partner him? I got to admit I'm asking myself the same for the time being. Well,

Ralphy might be able to show us a reason for it in a full formal meeting. I better not pre-judge.'

'One thing Manse never does is pre-judge, Naomi,' Ivis said.

'Alf, don't tell me you heard of many situations where a superb girl like this sees two of her finest – and one of them sharing this property for months . . . two of her men knocked all ways. Search Naomi's person as well for extra ears, would you, Alf? Do you mind, love? Alf will de-sex his fingers for the nooks. He got a flair at that.'

Ivis crossed the room towards her, the big meaty face amiable. Naomi stood and held up a fist. What else did she have to hold up. 'Sod off, Alf,' she replied.

Ivis stopped and looked at Shale. Shale pulled a cigar from his top pocket and put it unlit in his mouth. Then he removed it and held it between his fingers. He said: 'All right. Oh, certainly all right. I think we can trust Naomi. Haven't we all been mutual in an operation?'

Ivis returned to his chair.

'Is that why you're here?' Naomi asked.

'What?' Shale replied.

'You want a trusted messenger?' Naomi said.

'Who to?' Shale asked. 'Saying what?'

'To Harpur and Iles. Especially Iles. You want him to know you stood by the ambush agreement. That it was Ralphy who faltered.'

Ivis said: 'Please let me assure you, Naomi, that Mansel's only motive for this visit was sympathy for you at a time of distress. A wish to console.'

'I should think Manse wanted to kill me himself when he first found out I was going to infiltrate,' Naomi replied.

'Enemies, friends, they change, Naomi, dear,' Shale said. 'Think of the Soviet Union in 1941. Until June it was the opposition. Then Adolf invades and Russia's suddenly our grand ally.'

They were in Naomi's living room. She and Don had bought most of the furniture together from second-hand and antique shops. It was one of the things they had agreed on – a liking for oldish stuff. There had been many things they agreed on. Of course. But also that one central catastrophic difference. Perhaps he had been right about undercover. It *was* stupidly dangerous, and it *was* impossible to run things efficiently and securely. But it had been Don, not herself, who died because of the danger and inefficiency and no security.

Shale said: 'I think it's pretty famed that what I'm interested in is peace. I don't think "famed" is too strong a word.' He replaced the cigar in his pocket.

'Not at all too strong, Manse,' Ivis replied.

'I got to ask, very very simple, what was the object of that ambush, if only it had come off as it should of?' Shale said.

They seemed to wait for Naomi to reply. She stayed silent.

'Plainly peace, Manse,' Ivis said. 'Peace is probably another word for that Mansel Shale escutcheon eventually – in the Latin form, *Pax. Decorum . . . Pax.*'

Shale said: 'If we could of only done them three nice and neat on the dockside – then no carnage at all at the Eton. No

34

innocent and lovely comrades of Naomi hit. Plus, as result, a continuing peace. That is my objective – our objective.'

'Manse has tirelessly sought to cooperate with the police in establishing and maintaining a happy and settled state in which decent business can be decently conducted, Naomi,' Ivis said.

'You want me to tell Harpur and Iles that you – you personally, Manse, maybe not Panicking – that you personally and your firm are still worth an alliance despite the Eton chaos?' Naomi asked.

Ivis leaned towards her in his chair, his voice fierce with thanks. 'Manse thinks such a recommendation to Harpur and Iles coming from you, Naomi, would be immensely effective. True, you're not of great rank. But you were very central to that incident and could have suffered. This would be the voice of perception and of experience. It would be the voice of a star.'

'Plus they're both tit men,' Naomi replied.

Ivis held up a hand: 'Oh, please, Naomi, don't depreciate yourself.'

Shale said: 'Harpur is for sure.'

'Can't you talk to Harpur or Iles yourself?' she replied.

Ivis said: 'Of course one certainly could. Manse has a well-established and warranted relationship in that direction, particularly with Mr Desmond Iles. But—'

'It been fucked up a degree, naturally, by the Eton episode,' Shale said. 'We could be seen to of missed on our side of things. Your kind of help would be priceless, Naomi, totally priceless.'

He nodded to Ivis, who pulled out a wad of unfolded twenties from the inside pocket of his jacket.

Shale said: 'I would like you to regard this only as compensation for the distress caused you by my firm and Panicking's. All this is, Naomi, is an ordinary business transaction, the kind of offer any enlightened company would make when it knows itself at fault.'

'It is to offset what has happened in the past, not to influence your behaviour in the future,' Ivis said.

He stood and brought the money over to her. She ignored it. Was there anything in her anywhere that wanted to accept? Might there be one day – a couple of years on, ten? Would she grow into worldliness, more worldliness? Maybe. Not today, thanks. Would she have accepted if there had been more – say enough to refurnish, replace the pieces that said too much about Don and made her edgy? Well, there wasn't more. For a second she did think of asking them instead for the names and whereabouts of the people who had sent those three Londoners here, and for the whereabouts of Lincoln W. Lincoln. They would certainly be able to answer the first part. Those London kings were sure to be familiar throughout the trade. But here, at home, and with the funerals into the past, that agreement with Esmé had come to seem a bit mad. How the hell could they manage such a vengeance mission?

Evas put the money back in his pocket. He looked smug. Perhaps he had told Shale she would never touch a bribe but been overruled.

KILL ME

Shale said: 'I know that in some way and soon we'll be able to help you, Naomi.'

6

Shale felt that was all right, the meeting with Naomi Anstru-ther. You could not expect an officer to pouch money right away on the first flash of notes, especially a girl, and especially if the quantity did not flatter. There was no happy tradition of women officers taking. Shale thought it might of been better after all if they had caught her at one of the funerals, and made a money approach there, when she would of been even more opened up by sadness. The thing to do was to come along with a bit more next time, say reaching the grand, and a glorious hint that there would of course be follow-ups.

Personal relationships, personal relationships. These were so crucial in business. Soon after that visit to Naomi, Alf told Shale that the owner of the Eton Boating Song wanted a confidential interview. Ivis stuck this on the end of their company talk today, like it was such a nothing matter he had almost forgot, and he brought out a bucketful of reasons why Mansel better refuse.

'I've no feelings at all against Jeremy Littlebann, Manse, believe me,' Ivis said, 'but is it smart to risk closer association in view of events? Taint. Due distance is needed, Manse.'

'I'll see him,' Shale replied.

'With respect, Manse, have you thought he will be under surveillance now, almost certainly?'

Clearly, Littlebann was not an employee of Mansel Shale Inc., not a bit – not someone to be looked after like personnel – but his fucking restaurant was a hulk without Shale. Mansel Shale Inc. set up all the drug dealing there and it was drug dealing that kept the Eton hearty. Or did until that gun play. Naturally Littlebann would want a discussion and advice. Four people shot dead in your bijou restaurant bar could slur a reputation. This sort of thing would be rare at the Savoy. Even folk who liked the Eton for a downtown thrill would get bothered by such out-and-outness.

Ivis said: 'The thing about Jeremy and his wife, Manse, is that—'

Would you fix it, then, Alfred?' Shale replied. 'I'll see him at the rectory.'

'At home, Manse? Is that . . .'

Their conversation today was in the yard of Ivis's place. Alfred lived in a converted lighthouse on the headland. Cold lumps of sea spray flew all ways and hit you in the neck and ear. Anyone could tell the fucking oceans would eventually pull down this cliff and get everywhere, swamping. How it was sure to be in, say, a million or two years – there would be no pylons or Disneyland, just fucking water. This spray flinging itself around here up over the top of the cliff now was only reconnaissance. Shale fixed his cycle clips and mounted the 1930s Humber two-wheeler that he often used when visiting Ivis. Shale could bike up here through back lanes and not be observed. The Jaguar was too well known, and Denzil, Shale's chauffeur. He cruised off. Shale knew he did not actually need cycle clips, because this Humber had an all-round metal chain guard – part of a solid style – but he had been raised by his mother in the clip habit. He did not mind discussions with Alfred, but obviously these were best when they finished.

Ivis brought Littlebann that evening. 'One is baffled, Manse. More, one is hurt,' he said.

'We got you very much in mind here, Jeremy,' Shale replied, 'Alfie as much as me.'

'It's remarkable how Manse's mind and my own so often run in parallel, Jeremy,' Ivis said. 'And yet perhaps—'

'It's Ralph Ember who caused one all this prime shit and dwindling fucking business,' Littlebann replied.

Shale hated the name Jeremy. It was a name for acne squeezers and TV smartarses. 'You're troubled about Panicking Ralph?' Shale replied.

'He's your associate, so quite possibly you don't want to hear,' Littlebann replied. 'But Panicking—'

'Mansel is not one to ignore a grievance – a possible grievance – against a colleague, merely because that person *is* a colleague.'

'Don't tell me you can't see Ember's game plan, Manse,' Littlebann replied. 'One doesn't say you're in on it, would never say you're in on it. How could you be – it betrays you. But you'll have spotted traces of it, I know.'

'Betrays?' Shale asked.

'Ember wants to kill the Eton, that's clear as fucking clear,' Littlebann replied.

Ivis did another laugh. 'Why? So he can steal your customers for his club, the Monty? Can you imagine the Eton's distinguished clientele wanting to transfer to—'

'The Monty's a shit heap, Mansel, and no competition, agreed. Not what one means at all. But Ralphy's quick, he's a long-term schemer. He wants destruction of the Eton and the rise of somewhere else in its place, where he'd be big. Not the Monty, no But somewhere else. Why he fucked up that ambush and filled a mahogany-panelled room on the Eton with deads and blood. This was very much a commercial ploy, Manse.'

'Well, they reported it in the news pages of *The Times*, not the business section,' Shale replied.

The three were talking in his den. He loved this room, and did not mind letting even someone like Littlebann into it for a short period. Shale's house had once been St James's rectory and he had bought a lot of the furniture when he moved in. There was a Salem bookcase and big leather-topped desk, and Shale had an idea the rectors would do their sermons and write testimonials for folk going for jobs as vets at that desk. He felt this put him into a kind of decent succession. They were drinking gin and pep from quality glassware. He was fussy about that kind of thing.

Littlebann said: 'As one understood it, Manse, that gun party were never supposed to reach the Eton. But Ember notices a lovely chance to fuck up my operation, destroy my place's image.'

'The only image it got is a floating fuel station for snort and jab folk,' Shale replied.

Littlebann had a twitch about that.

Ivis said: 'Our own view, Manse's and mine, was not some deviousness from Panicking, but rather that he acted from one of his quite standard terrors, Jeremy. We think he opted himself and the rest of us out of a gun attack. Manse is certainly going to take up the matter with Ralph.'

'Panicking got other pluses,' Shale said, 'but matters needing guts will always find gaps.'

'We're certainly going to speak to him,' Ivis said.

'Speak to him?' Littlebann yelled. 'Christ, Alf, the Eton was a beautiful developing business and now it's shattered.'

'This will be a real speaking-to,' Ivis replied.

'I don't see it like that,' Littlebann said. 'And nor does Inga.'

Littlebann was the sort whose wife *would* be called Inga.

'I seen her on TV news with you after the shooting,' Shale said. 'You both did brilliant – that fine shock to find drugs were traded there.'

'So moving,' Ivis said.

'I don't say she sees more than you, Mansel,' Littlebann said. 'But we don't think the Eton will ever recover. I mean ever. These were patrons able to afford a good pattern to their lives. They could come to the Eton for a fine meal and wines and they knew there would also be opportunity to make a discreet purchase from a dealer they recognized and respected. Well, then these dealers start disappearing and there are terrible aftermath reports – Eleri ap Vaughan murdered, Si Pilgrim murdered. But, thank God, this was a faithful clientele, Manse. They took time to adjust from Eleri to Simon, but they *did* adjust. Business was back to what it was in her day. Inga and I were congratulating ourselves on this, when suddenly Pilgrim's gone also, and then we hear about an agreed project to install an undercover officer as means of eliminating potentially grave London opposition. I'll admit this project seemed likely to benefit all, so one accepted.'

'I really appreciated that,' Shale replied, 'and I know Harpur and Iles did also. But it would not of mattered whether you agreed or didn't, Jerry,' Shale said. 'Who the fuck *are* you? This would of gone ahead regardless.'

Ivis refilled the glasses.

'Central to our reason for accepting was the belief that there would be no violence at the Eton,' Littlebann said. 'Inga and I could not bear the idea of strong-arm arrests, all that kind of heaviness in such a setting.' He gave a sad little groan. 'Little had we fucking realized, Manse: it was not a matter of mere arrests, but an appalling fusillade causing deaths and injuries in one of the Eton's most comely public areas.' He drank, using a special birdy style of his, head back to help it down. 'Inga and I know – know as fact – that at least forty established customers have said they will never return to the Eton. It is not simply that the risks are too great. Possibly we would have been able to reassure them on that. But it is the character of the Eton which is irrecoverably fucking soiled, Manse. This was a gathering place where discreet drug dealing in high-quality materials appeared to be sensibly tolerated by authority. Police gunfire puts an end to that. Even if Manse came down and gave assurances to remaining regulars at the Eton that there had been no substantive changes in the police blind-eyeing policy, we don't think it would make enough difference.'

'Mansel is certainly not going to do that, in the circumstances,' Ivis said.

'Which circumstance, Alf?' Littlebann replied. 'The circumstances are that my fucking business has been throttled. When I say forty clients have gone already, I mean forty *buying* customers – coke customers, or H or the gay stuff. Obviously there's nothing in the actual drugs profits for us, except a nominal rent percentage as venue holders, but that forty would be present on the boat in parties of four, six, a dozen, twenty, especially the gays, they love the communal side. That's a lot of meals and drinks, Manse. We're talking fifty, sixty quid a head on average, even allowing for non-drinking old ladies with weak stomachs.'

Littlebann had a pause and another swallow of gin and pep. He was bald, very tall and thin, with a face that did not seem to believe much of what was said to it, and especially not what *you*, whoever you were, were saying to it now. Mark Lane, the chief, had a similar expression, but Littlebann's face was more the sort Shale would expect to be running a false-leg centre or a pottery shop. There was redness under his nose. He looked like he used to have a moustache but then lost his nerve and scraped it off. It was that kind of face – a sort of bareness, too many big spaces. You could put marquees up on it.

Abruptly, Littlebann said: 'Yes, well, what I hear is that Ember's gone over to the London outfit – Osprey and the Rt. Hon. Went over a while ago.'

Shale had wondered about it, of course. That sort of slipperiness and the metropolitan connection would be so right for Panicking. But Shale had heard no reports or even rumours.

Ivis wagged his big face and did bafflement. 'With respect, Jeremy, are you saying that Ralph Ember is acting secretly for Everton Evas Osprey and the Rt. Hon., yet puts three of their people into a police ambush on the Eton?'

'It leaves just Ralphy to partner them here. He'd like that,' Littlebann said. 'Plus it destroys the Eton. I hear they want to set up an operation in Noisy Graham's place, Seconds, instead.'

Ivis said: 'But Everton and the Rt. Hon. are not going to like Ralph for—'

'For getting two of their boys killed and almost a third?' Littlebann asked. 'Perhaps they don't know he arranged it. Do they care about losing two or three gun-fodder troops as long as they smash the Eton and get a big local entity like Ralph cooperating?'

Yes, Shale had wondered about all that.

'Why, here come those two terrorists!' he cried. His children, Laurent and Matilda, were back from their private school by bus and breezed into the den, still with satchels and in their blue uniforms trimmed with black. Kids had to cope with all sorts of people as they grew up, so he did not mind them meeting someone like Littlebann. Shale introduced the children.

'Oh, I suppose you're all busy again, are you?' Laurent said sadly. 'Always busy, meetings.'

He liked Ivis to tell him about the Royal Navy. Alfred was an expert on this and the structure of the human body. He could talk about the history of warships – Jutland, up the Yangtze, Glorious First of June, anything – or the way the bones of the foot worked. Shale did not mind Alfie getting close to them. It was probably all right. The thing was, their mother had gone off permanently for fulfilment and you had to get them attention here and there to make up for it.

Shale said: 'Alfred can do a real Navy session with you one day soon, Laurent. He's going to give you the Western Approaches.'

Matilda said: 'Daddy, we can wear earrings and bracelets Friday afternoons.'

'Friday afternoons is when earrings and bracelets look best,' Shale replied.

'Did Mum leave any?' Matilda asked.

'I'm sure she did,' Shale said. 'I'll have a look for suitable pieces.'

Sybil took every fucking thing, of course, and a bit more. He'd send Alfie out to buy something decent and Shale would tell her he had found the stuff in Sybil's dressing table. You did not want kids thinking their mother was a grab-all when she was. Alfie would choose just right. He was good at that sort of thing as well as the Navy and foot bones.

When the children had gone, Ivis said: 'They hope to draw the ex Eton clientele to Noisy Graham's?' He chuckled a bit heavily. 'That's almost as hard to believe as getting them to the Monty.'

'They'll upgrade, obviously,' Littlebann said.

'Noisy?' Shale said.

'Well, with guidance from Ember,' Littlebann replied. 'Ralphy knows clubs. He's always wanted to improve the Monty but was scared of losing his rough-house members. Here's his chance.'

Shale said: 'You're telling me a partner of mine is with the opposition?'

'You had an idea, did you?' Littlebann replied.

Ivis said: 'What Manse has to bear in mind is—'

'What do you want me to do?' Shale asked Littlebann.

'Plainly, one doesn't intrude on whatever happens between you and Ralph Ember. That's private.'

'What do you want me to do?'

Littlebann said: 'Well, Mansel, your firm wouldn't like Seconds to proceed, would you? That would be a competing London operation right at the centre – worse than if they'd taken the Eton. They want monopoly. Can you see Osprey and the Rt. Hon. happy with less?'

Shale stood and had a pace. Then he sat on a straight-backed chair. He liked this position. He felt solid. 'Christ, I see it. You want me to knock over Ralphy, and then you buy the Monty at a giveaway.'

'Inga and I think we must have a total change of location,' Littlebann replied. 'You would, of course, be able to put a franchised dealership in there to the standard fashion. I'd get rid of the villainy element, first thing. It would suit us both, Manse. The Eton buyers might come. This would be new ownership, a new standard for the club – the way it used to be years ago, I gather, but still with the required slumming buzz. It would take a while, yes, but what else, Mansel? We've got to act.'

Shale hated that, the 'We', like they were confederates already.

Littlebann said: 'If Ember were in a terrible tragedy, the price of the Monty is going to come down, I'd say. What's his wife know about running that sort of place? She'd rush to sell. And if the proprietor was slaughtered, it would look a risky spot, nearly as bad as the Eton.'

'It *is* a risky spot,' Shale said.

'These are inconstant fucking times, Mansel,' Littlebann replied. 'Shifting alliances.'

'Oh, please don't tell Manse what the times are like, Jeremy,' Ivis replied. 'If there's one factor Manse is famed for being in touch with, it is the times.'

7

A master-mind called Andrew Rockmain turned up at headquarters and Harpur had a call to the chief's suite to meet
him. Remeet him. When Harpur arrived today Lane and his
guest were seated in easy chairs at the conference end of the
suite.

'May I stress that this is very much a confidential visit
and, as it were, off the record, Colin?' the chief said.

That probably meant he did not want Iles told. Occasionally there came these spells when the chief longed to be
chief. Harpur felt he knew Rockmain pretty well – or as well
as anyone would ever know him. And Rockmain knew *him*
pretty well too, or thought he did. This lad had a police rank,
but did little that would be recognized as police work: no
traffic direction or lost dogs. He was a psychology wizard
and lorded it at a centre named Hilston Manor, available for
special requirements to all British police forces. Rockmain
was an expert in assessment and training of officers selected
for undercover duties. Naomi Anstruther had been sent to
Hilston before infiltrating the drugs business, and, as Anstruther's controller for the operation, Harpur had also been
ordered to see him: apparently it was necessary for Rockmain
to gauge how two officers might function together under
exceptional stresses. As Harpur understood it, Rockmain had
thought a lot of Naomi and not much of him.

'It's about Naomi Anstruther,' Rockmain said.

'Andrew is uncertain how she will behave from now on,' Lane said.

Rockmain replied: 'This is a girl who has seen two . . . well, two lovers . . . I don't think this is overstating it . . . although, as I am informed, one was a comparatively casual relationship . . . but none the less two men dear to her in different fashions shot down in her presence, and, perhaps most important, shot down apparently shielding her.'

'Oh, yes, shielding her,' Harpur said.

'Exactly,' Rockmain declared. 'This is a girl confronted not just by deaths, but by sacrifice. This is trauma.'

'There are problems we might well be able to head off,' Lane said. 'I'm grateful for Andrew's time.'

The Home Office gave Rockmain the rank and presumably the money of a Metropolitan commander. He did something now that Harpur remembered from the Manor: arched his back slightly in the chair, a kind of cower, as an indication of humility. He was very slight, almost frail, with a flimsy neck. Altogether, he looked wonderfully vulnerable, but wasn't.

'I deem her very able – in undercover work. But that work is over, isn't it? The infiltration of the Shale syndicate ended with the Eton incident. She's been named in the press.'

Rockmain was very smooth-faced, and kept his fair hair a bit long, probably to proclaim boffin status. Generally, he wore expensive denim but had put on a yellow-to-beige lightweight suit today, perhaps because he was off home ground.

'Andrew does not know how the distress will take her, Colin,' Lane said. 'Naomi might turn to private vengeance.'

The chief sounded anxious but decisive. The setting possibly reassured him. Invitations to his suite were rare. Normally, the Lane liked to saunter into people's rooms and talk about whatever was troubling him. Often, he would be in shirt sleeves and have no shoes on. Formal meetings had always seemed to unnerve him, and he loathed smartness, feared it: feared anything to suggest the police were not utterly civilian. Lately he might have grown more assertive, more power-conscious.

'You've arranged bereavement counselling for Naomi, sir, haven't you?' Harpur asked Lane.

Rockmain went very respectful and spoke to the chief: 'Obviously, I say nothing, absolutely nothing, against such counselling. I have people at Hilston who offer such a service. But this is not quite the essence, as far as Anstruther is concerned.'

'Andrew thinks Naomi is of an unusual psychological type, Col,' Lane said.

'Very unusual,' Rockmain replied. 'Not unique, but, yes, very, very unusual. May I try to explain?' He arched himself for self-effacement once more, but there was only push and certainty in his voice. 'I fear a possible . . . well, unpredictability – to use a lay term – in the girl's personality,' Rockmain said. 'This was an officer supremely suited to undercover work, possibly the most suitable I ever encountered. I won't oppress you with trade gibberish, but Jung deplored what he termed the "eternally fixed" or "hopelessly petrified" in someone's make-up. The point about Anstruther is that she has always sought by instinct to escape from a fixed, frozen self. She hated definition, was always seeking "the other self or selves", as we may call them. Hence, perhaps, the moving between two boyfriends. Obviously, this is a wonderful qualification for an undercover operator, where the main requirement is to drop one's actual police role and become something else.'

'Commander Rockmain sees a danger that Naomi will not be able to resume that conventional police role,' Lane said. 'He's afraid Naomi may lose belief in law and order and—'

There was a single rap on the chief's door and then it was pushed open. Iles said: 'Ah, is this a private clambake or can anyone join in? You'll recognize the line, Chief – *Some Like It Hot*, when Jack Lemmon's got Marilyn into his sleeping berth on the train and they're interrupted by the girl trombone player with the big mouth. Rockmain, isn't it? I hardly recognize you out of French sewerman's gear. But you're looking damned fecund, ideas-wise. Damned fecund.'

'Ah, Desmond,' the chief muttered, 'I'm so pleased you could look in. Commander Rockmain happened to be—'

'Educational,' Iles said. 'Anyone from Hilston – sure to give us an eye-opener, and Rockmain above all. I always think, Chief, and perhaps you do too, that the word "guru" was specifically sculpted for Andrew.'

Iles closed the door and came and took a chair opposite Rockmain. The ACC had on one of his fine-cut navy blazers and narrowly tailored grey flannel trousers. He wore a tie of dark blue background with silver shields, perhaps a rugby club, though Iles had become sickened by rugby union since it turned professional. He despised money, especially everybody else's.

'Andrew was talking about otherness, Desmond,' the chief said.

'Ah, here's a theme indeed,' Iles replied. 'I can understand why he'd want to get into his car and belt over to discuss a topic like that with you.'

' "Otherness" in the sense of a fluidity of self,' Lane replied.

'Is this that John Updike shit, Andrew?' Iles asked. ' "I have the persistent sensation in my life . . . that I am just beginning." Was it Miroslav Holub who said, "Our ego lasts three seconds?"'

'Commander Rockmain's scared Naomi Anstruther will turn avenger, I think, Mr Iles,' Harpur replied. 'That she'll say, "Fuck the police effort on this. They'll never get anyone for the deaths of my beaux, so I'll do it myself. I'll move out of the legality realm, go for justice, instead." '

'Didn't Bacon call revenge *wild* justice?' the chief asked.

'Someone like that,' Iles said. 'Triteness is a very old game, same as tennis. Myself, I certainly see a startling difference between the lawful and the just, and a bit of freelance revenging is often understandable, even praiseworthy – though I don't believe you would accept that, Chief.'

'The very opposite of the police role,' Lane cried.

'Yes, I believe Naomi might suffer acute and very dangerous uncertainty of function in the circumstances,' Rockmain said. 'I think her police training, indeed her training in conventional morality and restraint, could be, as it were—'

'Put on hold,' Iles said. 'Discarded as useless.'

'Put on hold,' Rockmain said. 'Discarded as useless.' He switched his mean little gaze to the ACC. 'This seems to be a state you understand exceptionally well, Mr Iles.'

'Would that be so, Desmond?' the chief asked.

Once or twice, or oftener, famed local villains had died violently after court acquittals. Harpur knew the chief wondered whether Iles had done private adjustments of the trial results. As a matter of fact, two thugs the ACC believed had murdered an undercover officer were themselves found murdered not long after their Not Guilty verdicts.

'I've always been very fond of Naomi,' Iles replied, 'though not in a pussy-craving way, I trust, Chief. As a colleague, yes. That kind of unlibidinous affection is quite possible, isn't it, Col?'

Harpur said: 'I—'

'Oh, what the fuck's the use of asking a shag-around like you?' the ACC remarked.

'You must all look after her,' Rockmain said. He stood. 'I do not want this meeting minuted, Chief.'

'It's easy to imagine you were never here, Andrew,' Iles replied.

8

Naomi had given her address and phone number to the girl called Esmé at Lyndon's funeral, and wondered afterwards whether this was intelligent. Naomi was not really into revenge, even when the cause looked so damn reasonable. So damned irresistible? Resist it.

And then Esmé turned up at the flat, full of hatred and joy. 'I thought it was best not to phone,' she said. 'I was sure you wouldn't like it. Security.'

'Nobody's going to tap a police officer's phone,' Naomi replied.

'No.'

'No.'

'No?' Esmé said. 'Look, you don't *mind* me coming, do you?'

'Not a bit. Pleased, really pleased.'

'I thought you would be.' She gave a vast grin, glinting with more hatred and joy. 'And I've got great, great news. I've identified one of them. Well, half identified – one of the sodding bosses. We're on our way.'

'You've seen him?' Naomi asked. How the hell would a girl from Cardiff put the finger on Everton Evas Osprey or the Rt. Hon?'

'Not *seen*, but I dug out a name,' Esmé replied.

'Dug out?'

'A cover name. One of them is called the Rt. Hon.'

'The Rt. Hon?' Naomi said. 'Like MPs and so on?'

'What he calls himself,' Esmé replied. 'Not an MP, I don't suppose, but just a name he fancied, I expect, like a joke.' She grew crestfallen suddenly. 'But perhaps you'd already heard of him. He's famous in the trade. Must be, or how would I have discovered him.'

'How did you?' Naomi replied.

'Oh, I asked around.'

'Asked around where?' Naomi said.

'In London. Of course. That's where he is – what they say, anyway.'

'Who says?'

'All sorts. You people must have heard of him. He's on file – dossier pictures?'

'You just went to London and asked?' Naomi said.

'I asked the right people, obviously. Not the Archbishop of Canterbury.'

'Which right people?'

'Well, naturally, people doing drugs,' Esmé said.

'Which people doing drugs?'

'Friends of friends of friends. You know how it is, Naomi.'

'Where? Which parts?'

'Peckham, New Cross, Lewisham. That area.'

'You went around south-east London asking people you didn't know questions about who controls the drugs business?' Naomi had a mind-view of this round-faced, pert-looking girl in her twenties hanging about corners and doorways in some of those unfriendly streets, angling for inside chat.

'Not that I *totally* didn't know. Like I said, druggy pals in Cardiff had druggy pals up there. I had a sort of way in.'

'God, Esmé, you were lucky to get a way out.'

'I was pretty careful.'

'How can you be careful if you're asking.'

'I was sort of roundabout.'

'People on drugs, Esmé – they talk a lot. Everything's loosened up.'

'Exactly. One of them talked to me, with the name.'

'I meant talk about being asked. But all right. Your informant – a user, a dealer?' Naomi asked.

'Bit of both.'

'Man, woman, age?'

'A man, about twenty. Student type. Does it matter?'

'Some people shoot their mouth off more than others.'

'What sort of people?' Esmé asked.

'Men about twenty, student types. The younger the worse. No street savvy.'

'But I needed someone without street savvy,' Esmé said. 'The rest were all uptight.'

'Yes, you said.'

'But you don't seem to get it, Naomi.'

'I get it. It's dangerous – if you go back. Even if you don't go back. They could trace you via this friend of a friend of a friend, couldn't they?'

'They wouldn't say who I was, where I was.'

'Anyone will say if they're scared enough,' Naomi replied.

'But why should the Rt. Hon. or anyone else get so bothered? The name must be known all over the place. Even the
police must know it. I think you knew it. Yes?' She made it
sound as if she would forgive Naomi for playing dumb.

'Knowing it is different from asking questions about him
on his patch, Esmé, and sounding like South Wales –
sounding like Lyndon. People can make guesses.'

'Who'd guess an out-of-town kid like me might want to
do the Rt. Hon. and whoever else?'

Yes, who would? The notion was mad, wasn't it? This girl
needed looking after. This girl took control. Naomi made her
a meal. Esmé would have to stop the night, maybe more than
one night. Looking at this slight bright visitor seated on the
scarlet chaise-longue in her long, nightie-type off-white
dress and black boots, Naomi felt enormously wise and
experienced about the ways of drugs traders, and enormously useless. She felt like the embodiment of all police:
she knew a lot – a lot more than Esmé, probably – but was
hemmed in by legalities and hesitancies and sensible fears
and sensible certainty that evil would always be around and
would probably prevail. Esmé's vengeance mission was pre-
posterous and inspired. It could grip Naomi. Oh, yes, it could
grip her. It had more to it than that dirty arrangement Shale
wanted her to broker: an alliance between his outfit and the
law. She had done nothing about that. Would do nothing
about it? She cooked chops and potatoes. They drank the
remains of a bottle of Pigassou, sitting on the floor to eat.
Naomi did not want to do a properly laid table: too orderly.

Esmé said: 'You've had undercover training, Naomi. I

thought you'd probably be able to handle all that sort of thing – the sussing out – much better than me. And maybe you've got access to papers.'

'I'm on the sick – trauma.'

'Oh, good. So you're free. I'm free too. I'm a Civil Servant, you know. I've taken leave.'

'I'm having trauma counselling, grief counselling,' Naomi replied.

'I think you keep your grief inside. It's there, but it doesn't show.'

'That's what the counsellor says.'

'You should let it come,' Esmé replied.

'That's what the counsellor says. I don't think I'm like that.'

'What we'll do is better than counselling. It puts things right.' Her face tightened up while she thought about this and tried to be fair. 'Half right, anyway. Lyndon and Don will stay dead.'

'Can you stay over tonight – or for as long as you like?' Naomi replied.

'Thanks.'

'We could go clubbing later,' Naomi said.

'I haven't brought any clothes.'

'Some of mine might do.'

'Fine,' Esmé said. 'How far have the police got with it?'

'It takes a while.'

'What I mean—'

'Yes, I know,' Naomi said.

9

Later, in the Chiffon club, Naomi spotted two men watching her and Esmé. Well, that was all right, wasn't it? If you went clubbing with another girl you expected some interest. It might not be the whole point of going, but it was some of the point. You could soften grief in all sorts of ways.

There was watching and watching, though. This seemed to Naomi the wrong sort, too intent, too unaware of anyone else. It was directed mainly at Esmé. So, had jealousy got to Naomi? Could be. The men were presentable: twenties, both dark-haired, both decently built and decently dressed, neither ugly. Was there something about them that did not look local? Crazy thought. What the hell did local look like? This was a big town. It had all sorts. Occasionally, the two men did seem to notice Naomi. One or other of them would eye her as she danced or sat out at a table with Esmé, as if trying to read who and what Naomi was. Or that's how it seemed to her. From far back, when she first agreed to under-cover work, she had begun to worry about whether people could look at her and spot cop. Perhaps this explained her jumpiness now: she hated that kind of typecasting – the incarceration in a profile. The two were certainly not Everton Evas and the Rt. Hon. Yes, those *were* on file and Naomi had seen dossier pics. They were older and Everton was black. Everton Evas Osprey and the Rt. Hon. would not handle this kind of work personally. Which kind of work? Well, tracing someone who had been asking intelligent questions in London SE streets. And making sure there were no more. Of course, it might not *be* work at all, just a couple of lads looking to score, and why not?

To back up its name, the Chiffon had lots of bits of bright and blurry light materials hanging in strips on the wine-coloured walls and in the doorways. The aim was to give a drifting, winsomely fragile look to this basement brick and plaster. Plonk cost four pounds a small glass, and Latvian champagne seven. If you were early there were saucers of peanuts and crisps on the bar. It was a class spot for this street. The group were playing a Chris Bowden soul jazz number, maybe from *Time Capsule*, Naomi thought. She liked it: slow, a bit funky, not a blast. She and Esmé went out and at first, anyway, took it how it should be taken, laid-back, contemplative, complicit.

'What do you think of them?' Esmé asked, quitting that half-gone mood for a moment and flicking her spicy glance towards the men.

'Maybe.'

'Maybe what?'

'Maybe,' Naomi replied.

They might have traced Esmé to Cardiff, then followed her to see what her contacts were, what her game was. Perhaps they had been outside Naomi's flat, then come on behind them to the Chiffon. It was a big night in the club, a lot of people, and Naomi lost sight of the men for a while. That troubled her, but not as much as if she had lost sight of Esmé. She hadn't. There was Esmé, dancing in the nice minimalist style Naomi remembered from club outings in Spain, and wearing Naomi's gold and scarlet velveteen blouse and one of Naomi's black miniskirts. She was grinning contentedly now to the music, though occasionally her eyes would swing towards the bar again, looking for the pair, but looking for them because she thought they seemed promising, not the way Naomi looked for them.

And suddenly the two were alongside, dancing in that same save-yourself style as Esmé, and getting between her and Naomi now. They stayed deadpan. Nobody talked. No eye-to-eye stuff. The music was not loud, but too loud for easy talk. The one with Naomi was crew-cut and very white-skinned, maybe a Finn or a baker. He had hooded dark eyes which might have done something for her if she had not been so frightened, a smallish, bolshy, heavy-lipped face, like the James Dean legend. She could see now why she had decided they were not local: they looked like conquerors, a touch of the swashbuckles. The music had changed to a Deep Breaths number, 'Call Me Collect', still relaxed, still dreamscape. She could have really enjoyed herself here tonight. He mouthed-shouted something and she cupped a hand to her ear.

'I think I've seen you before somewhere.'

'Oh, yes?'

He smiled, passable small teeth. 'No, I mean it.'

'Here,' she said. 'Wednesdays, Saturdays.'

'Must be. I'm David.'

'Naomi,' she said.

They might already know it if they'd been hanging around the flat, quizzing residents, returning Esmé's tactics. He wore a quite heavy grey-wool jacket flecked with silver. His mate was in the same sort of coat, but navy. The Chiffon was always hot and it was hot outside. Quite heavy wool jackets were brilliant at concealing shoulder holsters whatever the weather – nearly as good as that lightweight coat Lovely Mover had been wearing at the Eton.

'Naomi' he said, 'rare but nice.'

'I love this number,' she replied, taking her hand from her ear to prove concentration on the music. It was 'Top Bunk Bottom Bunk', a complete load of shit, full of go-nowhere guitar and palsied sax. She spread wow-me-baby rapture across her face and made sure she knew exactly where every door was.

When the music finished and Naomi and Esmé moved towards the bar the men came with them. 'Lee, this is Naomi,' David said. 'Lee.'

'And this is Esmé,' Lee said.

'What are we drinking?' David asked.

'Pepsis,' Naomi said. 'Replace the moisture.'

'True,' Lee replied.

Their accents were from nowhere, not local, not southeast London, not Birmingham, not the Royal Academy of Dramatic Art. Lee was a bit bigger than David, school-prefect haircut, wide-eyed, heavy-chinned, thin-nosed, thin-lipped, less tasty than David, but tasty enough. Esmé seemed to think so.

'We heard of the Chiffon from all over,' David said.

'Are you new here?' Esmé asked.

'Not very.'

'But you're new here too, aren't you?' Lee asked her. 'I hear Taff, don't I?'

'I used to live in Cardiff,' Esmé said.

'Not now?' Lee asked.

Perhaps Esmé had picked up Naomi's worry. 'Oh, no, not for a while,' Esmé replied. But Esmé had not done a proper think on it: if these two were tracking her, they knew about Cardiff. Naomi watched her grow more and more nervy.

'Let's sit, shall we?' Lee said. 'Esmé, you look half dead.'

'I look what?' she hissed.

'Only half,' Lee replied. The four of them found a table. 'I love it, the Chiffon,' Lee said. 'Tasteful.' He pointed at some of the hanging strips of stuff. 'Like a theme.'

'Lee's into all that – mood,' David said.

'Interior design,' Lee said.

'That your work?' Esmé asked.

'Just amateur,' Lee said.

'Have you got jobs?' Esmé asked. 'Can I guess what? I'm good at that.'

Yes, on their holiday plane she had guessed Naomi was the police, the devastating little cow.

'I told Naomi I thought I'd seen her before – not a line. I did, do, think so,' David replied.

'I said we come here Wednesdays, Saturdays, Esmé,' Naomi replied.

'Oh, yes,' Esmé said, 'always.'

'We wondered what your . . . well, *interests* were,' David said.

'Which?' Naomi replied.

'Both of you, naturally,' he said. 'Well, Esmé.'

'Interests?' Esmé said. 'I'm in the Civil Service. It grips you.'

'Yes, but *interests*,' Lee asked.

'Well, the Chiffon,' Esmé said. She waved a hand to take in the bits of wagging stuff and the rough walls. 'Is that an *interest*?'

'Of course,' David replied. 'And?'

'What is it, an interview for a post?' Esmé asked, with a big laugh. 'You want me to say, *Reading good books and helping the elderly*?'

'We're from London way, as if you couldn't tell,' Lee said, 'but we know someone who knows some people in Cardiff, as a matter of fact, don't we, Dave?'

'Oh, you mean Dick Meyer, do you, Lee?' David replied.

'Do you know a lad called Dick Mayer, Esmé, I wonder?' Lee asked. 'Or sometimes Rick, never Richard.'

Esmé did a fine face-full job of registering no recognition and took time as though to give the name a couple of runs through her memory. 'Don't think so,' she said.

'About thirty, shortish. Snorts a bit when he's got cash.'

'No, I don't think so,' Esmé stated.

The group went into what sounded to Naomi like that early 1990s Uphill River tune 'Where Does It Hurt?' but rearranged into fifties rock-around-the-clock. 'Now you two sit here,' Naomi told David and Lee. 'This is one Esmé and

I always do together Wednesdays. Change of mood. Only together, absolutely no intruders.'

'You a couple, then?' Lee asked. It was suddenly half snarl. He and David both looked troubled that the girls were going from the table.

'We're a couple for "Where Does It Hurt?",' Naomi said. 'We have a special bond with Uphill River from way back.' It was the kind of thing a girl in the Chiffon might say after a few Pepsis. They left their handbags under the table. On the floor and yelling to beat the din, Naomi said: 'We get out. No return.'

Rocking there, Esmé stuck a communicative nod in among the routine head-jerking. She looked very scared and all at once dependent, as if she longed to call a police officer. Unnecessary: she had one, and they would find another. There might be no need, anyway. Dave and Lee could still be just two lads out prospecting, two lads who happened to know another lad in Cardiff. If they were, they might hand in the girls' handbags to the management. If they did not, no tragedy: clubbing, you took only make-up and entry money, condoms, drinks money and taxi money. They would sort out the taxi somehow when they got to Harpur's house. He was still her undercover controller, wasn't he? She was entitled to call on him with her liabilities and terrors.

They edged over towards the main exit. God, but the intention was so fucking plain, wasn't it? She expected to see one or both of them waiting there. Not yet, so go. Naomi barged quickly past half a dozen dancers and then turned and grabbed Esmé's forearm to make sure she kept up. Esmé was the one in peril. Esmé she must not lose, yet had the idea that some day not far off she would. They were into the bit of vestibule and then past the bouncers and reached the street. She saw no taxis. 'Run,' she said. 'There'll be cabs outside the hotel.' Even if not, there was always a comforting little crowd of comers and goers around the Martyr. And the lighting there was friendly, maybe protective.

She thought she heard running behind, perhaps more than one pair of feet, shoes crunching broken glass: this was the city's busiest entertainment area, after all. She did not turn to check whose shoes they were but kept sprinting. A cruising taxi idled across the junction in front of them and they both screamed at it, real screaming, no playing about. For a second it looked as though he might not want to get involved in this, whatever it was. But then the old Granada stopped and Naomi pulled the rear door open and they fell in. 'Arthur Street,' she said, '126.'

'Mr Harpur's place?' he replied. 'Things are *that* bad?' He gave the accelerator a bang. When Naomi looked through the back window she saw David still twenty yards away. He was holding the handbags out in front of him in one hand, like a good deed. Lee was a long way behind, not really rushing. Perhaps he thought the girls would return to Naomi's flat and could be cornered there. Naïve, these Londoners.

10

'Colin, I'd like to know more about this girl Esmé Carpenter-Mace from Cardiff,' Lamb said.

'Cardiff's a long way off, Jack,' Harpur replied.

'You haven't heard what happened to her?' Lamb asked. 'They've got an ID now. It will be in the media tomorrow or the day after.'

Pack Lamb was the world's greatest informant and he belonged to Harpur, exclusively to Harpur. It was a fine arrangement, but occasionally Lamb would behave like this, asking the questions as though Harpur were the grass and Lamb the detective. Jack enjoyed stringing out the time before he disclosed what he knew, and this was his way. Or *one* of his ways. Lamb yearned to be valued – *was* valued, but wanted to be valued more. 'I did think you might know all about her,' he said, 'seeing what had gone on here.'

If Lamb thought you knew something, the chances were you did and that he knew you did, not thought you did. Lamb was right, as ever. 'Say the name again,' Harpur replied.

'Esmé Carpenter-Mace,' Lamb replied. 'Fairly distinctive. I understood she was at your house very late Wednesday night, or rather Thursday morning, and went back to Cardiff not long after. This girl's a pal of your undercover officer, Naomi Anstruther, star of the Eton gun games. Naomi was with her at your place on that night, morning. Again, as I understand things. This is via a voice that talks intimacies to me now and then from a club called the Chiffon. Heard of *that*, Col? I wouldn't be surprised. And there's a taxi driver gives occasional nuggets too. Didn't you pay for the cab? The girls had lost their handbags. Recall that?'

It was unlike Lamb to disclose sources, even when Harpur asked for them. Now, here they were unprovoked. Harpur felt troubled.

'As I'm told it, Col, two men, twenties, probable handy firepower under the standard sort of jacket, were doing an interrogation on the girls and then giving them plenty menace. I mean serious, gang-style menace. You must be asking yourself, should you have let Esmé go back unprotected to Cardiff.'

'I'm not asking myself that, Jack.' Yes, he still asked himself that, and asked and asked, and always got the answer, No.

'Two men chasing the taxi on its way to your house around 1 a.m., one of them holding the girls' handbags like bait. That's my information, Colin. I've only guesswork identification on these two. One crew-cut. Know them?'

'The Chiffon's in a rough bit of the town,' Harpur replied. 'All sorts about there late.'

'How did the girls explain it, Col? I gather you went looking for the men immediately afterwards. That's my tip, from the club neighbourhood.'

Well, of course he went looking. Those two might have told a tale. But they had obviously realized someone would come, and Harpur did not find them. 'Girls alone in a place like that – short cut to aggro. But you'll ask, why should that be? Why can't we police more efficiently, so women *can* go out unescorted, even to a pit like the Chiffon?'

'No, I wouldn't ask that,' Lamb replied. 'This was not just two girls getting themselves accosted by local yobs, was it? This has depth – and death for Esmé Carpenter-Mace in Cardiff. An unseemly death. They followed her back there?'

'She's dead?' Harpur replied.

Lamb did not answer, disregarding Harpur's routine show of ignorance.

Harpur said: 'Are you telling me there's a connection between the Chiffon incident and what happened later to the girl?'

Lamb gave him a bit of a gaze, a Lamb-style contemptuous gaze, as though this question also were idiotic. Certainly it was. They were talking at a new rendezvous point tonight, behind a dockside tea and wad stall, closed now until morning. Not far away was moored a Royal Navy frigate, used for training reservists. Lamb had chosen this spot. He liked meeting places with some link to the armed services. Often, they used an old concrete defence block-house on the foreshore; and sometimes a Second World War anti-aircraft gun site which had once tried to protect the city. Usually, Lamb would wear clothes that harmonized with the particular location: military garments bought in surplus stores. Tonight, he had on a short-sleeved white open-necked shirt with three thick gold rank bars on the shoulders: hot-weather wear for a commander in the Mediterranean or Far East. With it he wore an informal, long-peaked mauve cap, the mode publicized by American admirals on TV. To Harpur, it always seemed nuts that Lamb would select these remote meeting spots for secrecy, then turn out in grotesquely memorable clothes. But things had to be done the way Jack chose: *he* lived with the hazards.

Lamb did some pacing about for a while behind the tea-break stall, walking with a roll, as if on deck in heavy weather. Harpur felt he should salute him as he passed each time, or talk in semaphore. 'So, you'll be asking why I brought you out here, Col,' he said, taking a pause and a lean against the stall.

Too fucking right. 'It's always great to see you, Jack, regardless,' Harpur replied.

'Clearly, not just to tell you stuff you already know or to ask you questions you don't answer, in your ebullient little way.'

Harpur said : 'Jack, when I get a call to a talk with you, I know I'll—'

'Try to see things the way *they* might, Col.'

'The girls?' Harpur asked.

'The men who sent them – Everton and the Rt. Hon.,' Lamb replied.

'You *know* they sent them, Jack?'

'How do you think they would view this girl, Esmé?' Lamb replied.

'How *who* would view them?'

'Everton Evas Osprey and the Rt. Hon. Or their troops.'

'You *know* they were their troops, Jack? Didn't you say you had no real identification?'

'These are lads called David and Lee, as I get it from a voice at the Chiffon.'

'Yes.'

'Ah, the girls would have told you that on the night. And you – brave and bright as you are, Col, no question – you go out, unarmed despite their cover-all jackets, and ask in and around the Chiffon if anyone has seen David and Lee. When I say brave and bright, Col, I mean brave as in foolhardy and bright as in animal intuitive. You knew these two had to be more than casual pick-ups. And, of course, you knew their names would not be David and Lee, but David and Lee would do for the time being.'

'You *have* got something on these two then, Jack?'

'As I said, no categorical identification, but the descriptions, I'm told, fit a couple of talents working for Everton and the Rt. Hon. Replacements for those done at the Eton. This would be Brian Bernard Rayne – crew-cut, heavy lips – and Gordon Lusse, bulkier.'

'You've put in a lot of work on this, Jack.'

Lamb was staring out across the dock, in case some enemy dreadnought leapt the lock gates and sneaked up on the frigate. When he felt satisfied things were safeish, he said: 'Obscene murder of a helpless pretty girl, Col. Can I ignore that?'

He lived with a very pretty young girl himself, in a manor house, Darien, and this would sharpen his disgust at Esmé's killing. Almost always at these meetings with Harpur, Lamb would try to justify his activities as an informant. He hated to seen merely an all-purpose grass. Jack stressed that he informed only when the behaviour of villains outraged him by its needless cruelty or surpassing dirtiness. Harpur would stay dutifully attentive while Lamb expounded his snitch gospel. Jack was, of course, a bit of a villain himself, or how would he know so much about villainy? He ran a magnificently successful art business, and Harpur never asked about *how* Jack ran it: *quid pro quo*, the foundation of all fruitful informing.

'I come back to my original suggestion, Col,' Lamb said. 'Try to see things the way Everton or the Rt. Hon. or Rayne or Gordon Lusse might regard Esmé.'

'How would that be, Jack?' Harpur replied.

'This is a kid who's been up in London asking significant questions. Asking questions in the right areas – New Cross, Peckham, Lewisham, that kind of unrelaxed community.'

'I thought some were *very* relaxed. You've voices reporting to you from so far off, Jack?'

This Lamb seemed to regard as another halfwit question and discounted it. 'I don't know her motives – asking about Osprey and the Rt. Hon.' His voice thickened into resentment, even self-pity: it would be pain for Lamb to admit to gaps. 'It's the kind of thing Everton and the Rt. Hon. would soon hear about, and they would dislike it. These are folk wedded to privacy.'

'Like yourself, Jack.'

'I wondered if it was some sort of revenge mission,' Lamb replied. 'Perhaps Esmé knew the lad called Lyndon, shot at the Eton. He was Cardiff too, wasn't he? Plainly, they would not tell you something like that on the night they came to your house. A revenge plan by some kid Civil Servant clerk – it would look not just daft but potentially criminal. Yet it's possible. And Naomi involved? Have they both dropped belief in police procedures?'

Harpur laughed: 'Naomi *is* police, for heaven's sake, Jack. She's not likely to turn away from—'

'Naomi even more than the other girl might see the law as useless: she knows from inside how hesitant and hamstrung you lot are. It would not suit her needs, or Esmé's. Naomi is a girl who lost a lover in that shooting and who was a target herself. Might she feel a debt to Donald McWater, one to be paid by personal actions, in alliance with Esmé Carpenter-Mace?'

'Mad,' Harpur replied. Yes, it was possible. Anstruther could go like that. Didn't she take pride in a personality that shifted with circumstances? This is what Rockmain said. Hadn't he forecast a switch to private vengeance by Naomi? Harpur said: 'I tell you again, Naomi's a trained police officer, Jack. She's not going to drift into the sloppiness of vendetta.'

It began to rain. They stood alongside each other with their backs against the wall of the tea stall for shelter, like conspirators before a firing squad. 'Yes, revenge, as in one of those old-fashioned plays, Col. Heard of the Jacobeans by any chance? Or maybe *Hamlet*? It seems crazy to you, does it? And it would probably sound crazy to Osprey and the Rt. Hon. I ask again, how would they see it?'

'How, Jack?'

'Those two underling heavies, Rayne and Lusse, come down here to check, and spot Esmé apparently hand in glove with Anstruther – sharing her flat, I believe, and out clubbing together. They ask some local questions and discover Naomi is a cop. Perhaps they discover she is an undercover cop. Perhaps they already knew. The press did Naomi big. What would that make them think of Esmé, Col?'

Harpur saw the answer, naturally, but he said: 'Well, they might think almost anything. They might—'

'It would make them think Esmé and Naomi are part of a covert police operation. Oh, you'll say they'd know Esmé was not a police officer.'

'For fuck's sake, don't keep telling me what I'm going to say, Jack.'

'All right, they'd probably know she was not a cop. But they'd think she had agreed to act spy, for her own reasons – those revenge reasons, maybe. Yes, she might have been fond of the dead boy, Lyndon. *Had* Esmé agreed to spy for you, Col?'

'We don't use civilians in that kind of work. Everton would know this,' Harpur said.

'Of course you use civilians in that kind of work. We're called finks or narks or touts, remember?'

The rain was over and Lamb had been at his captain-on-the-bridge pacing again, that measured, swinging amble, but now he came and stood close in front of Harpur and stared down at him. Lamb would be around 260 pounds and six foot five. Harpur was big enough, but Jack made him look minor. People thought of informants as small, slinky and furtive. Not Lamb. Harpur was conscious of the massive stretch of white wardroom shirt, blocking out everything around and for a moment flattening his capacity to think.

Lamb said: 'I know you never expected to hear Jack Lamb refer to himself as fink, Col. Well, you'll never hear him do it again. I had to show that you people will use anyone.'

'You're not anyone, Jack. You're someone.'

'Kind.' Lamb drew away again, now obviously getting ready to leave. 'The injuries to that girl,' he said. 'The eyes and ears and so on, quite apart from the death wounds: not necessary – O God, what a farcical fucking word about such abuse – "necessary" – but no, not necessary at all. Just intended to give a little message about trying to see too much, hear too much, discover too much.'

'What too much, Jack?'

'Those two are going to move in here in person, aren't they, Col?'

'Everton and Basil Cope – the Rt. Hon?'

'Absolutely. Maybe joining up with Panicking Ralphy.'

'Ralph Ember? He partners Shale, for God's sake.'

'Did. *Apparently* still does. Yes, apparently. What I'm told is Everton and the Rt. Hon. see the Eton as finished now, and they're right. Customers will never return in the old numbers – too violent even for the frisson seekers, and on the police target list. Perhaps Panicking sees that too. Shale's sort of stuck to the Eton, isn't he, Col? It was his prime outlet. Panicking might be cutting him adrift. Ralphy Ember's got one of the most brilliant business heads in your realm. Trends, Col: he can spot them before most. That's why he owns a place like Low Pastures and his club, while former colleagues are doing decades of time or are crippled or dead.'

'He could run faster and earlier from fucked-up robberies, that's all,' Harpur replied.

'I hear Everton and the Rt. Hon. will put their distribution centre in some other restaurant. This is a delicate move, so they'll handle it themselves, with Panicking's advice and possible middle-manning. It might be Noisy Graham's Seconds or possibly the Calaboose – Wankers, as some call it, after the quality of the patrons. Now you get all the implications, do you, Col?' Lamb asked considerately, like to the remedial class.

Harpur said: 'Tell me, Jack, oh, tell me, tell me, do.'

'Bollocks,' Lamb replied. 'Everton and the Rt. Hon. would be afraid you and your people were on to this project and had started a counter-operation through the spy, Esmé, and the cop, Anstruther. It's quite possible Everton and the Rt. Hon. imagine you and your colleagues are sharp and well informed, Col, the silly sods, and thought they had to stop your operation. But you are now – well informed, anyway, I don't know about sharp – well informed because you've got a top-quality fink.'

'Jesus, Jack, you said you'd never—'

'A top-quality fink,' Lamb said.

'That's an injustice to you, Jack.'

'Which? Top-quality or fink.'

'You know which,' Harpur replied.

'Of course I do,' Lamb said.

'How's art?' Harpur asked.

'Wholesome.'
'Yes?'

11

Harpur went home. His daughters were playing simple poker with their boyfriends and Denise in the sitting room, maximum stake ten pence each hand. There was a smell of ganja, but not enough for a passive high. He asked them to deal him in. Harpur fancied himself as a poker player. He considered that when he wanted to he could show an unreadable face, made for bluffing. They read him with ease, and after an hour he was losing heavily – sixty pence, most of it to his daughter Hazel. Jill, his younger child, looked sorry for him, ashamed for him, and tried to help Harpur when it came to her deal, working him a couple of aces or kings by some deftness she had learned at Sunday school or in the youth club. Harpur was not sure whether the others noticed. Jill managed it skilfully, but perhaps they were all sorry for him, ashamed for him, embarrassed by his uselessness, and let it go. After another hour his losses were up to almost a pound, the bulk still to Hazel but some to Jill's boyfriend, Darren. Jill withdrew for a couple of hands and went to make tea. When she came back with the tray she said: 'You've got all muck and cobwebs over the back of your jacket, Dad. Have you been leaning against something grubby in a secret spot listening to your fine fink finking again?'

Darren said: 'You shouldn't talk to your father like that, Jilly, when we're here. You should show respect.'

'My name's Jill, Darreny,' she replied.

Hazel's boyfriend, Scott, said: 'My mother says nearly all detective work is to do with informants. But she calls them Bertie Smalls because he was the first supergrass. She said this sort of work can get . . . well . . . like what she calls "grey areas", being, well, you know . . . like shady . . . although, obviously, Mr Harpur, I don't mean every—'

'Who's your mother?' Jill replied.

'What?' Scott said.

'Who is she?'

'She's my mother.'

'Exactly,' Jill replied. 'Family stupidity.'

Hazel said: 'We were just talking about those two girls who came here the other night, Dad.'

Harpur laid down a full house, aces and jacks, but Denise had four tens and raked in. Harpur said: 'You shouldn't even have been up when they called.'

'We weren't up,' Hazel said. 'We were asleep. But we heard them banging at the door, which is more than you and Denise did. If we hadn't let them in . . . well, I don't know what. So frightened.'

'You and Denise drink too much at night, Dad,' Jill said.

'Like blotto. Denise is only young, you know,' Hazel said.

'Old enough,' Denise replied.

'Oh, old enough for . . . old enough in some ways, yes,' Jill said. 'A relationship. But not used to so much booze. I shouldn't think so.'

'We'd been celebrating, that's all,' Denise said.

'What?' Jill asked.

'I got a first class in one of my modules,' Denise replied.

'Dad would expect you to,' Hazel said. 'I don't mean because he's a slave driver. Because he thinks you're tops by nature. "A star undergraduette" he calls you.'

'Of course she is,' Harpur said.

'He's always saying it, Denise,' Jill said.

'One day he'll be disappointed,' Denise replied.

'Nobody here thinks so,' Jill said.

'What happened to them, Dad?' Hazel asked.

'Who?' Harpur said.

'Those two women – the cop girl, Naomi, and her friend, Esmé,' Hazel replied. 'I like it. I wouldn't mind being called Esmé.'

'You wanted to be Anita,' Jill said.

'Esmé, Anita, same sort,' Hazel replied. 'It's not Hazel. Is she all right?'

'This girl was *so* scared,' Jill said. 'Well, Naomi was scared, but this other girl was *really, really* scared. I could smell the sweat.'

'Are they all right, Dad?' Hazel asked.

'Would this be a matter of sexual harassment, Mr Harpur,' Scott asked, 'such as in the press?'

'Like that,' Harpur replied.

'And more,' Jill said. She poured tea in mugs and cut slices from a big shop cake.

'Was this like *significant?*' Scott asked. 'What I mean – this girl, Naomi, also in the media, wasn't she? The Eton. This girl was undercover, Yes? The Daily Telegraph explained it all and said about undercover and said she would have a controller. I wondered if you were her controller, Mr Harpur, which is why she would come here, you being of high rank.'

'Denise didn't like it, did you, Denise?' Jill asked. 'Two women, not bad-looking and in smart dress, two *girls*, really, coming to the house for Dad in the middle of the night. Well, not many undergraduettes sleeping with a man regular, at least since the death of Mum *would* like it, would they? Oh, at least since then.'

Harpur said: '*Regularly!*'

'Sleeping with a man very regularly,' Jill replied.

'Denise knows those callers were work,' Harpur said.

'She didn't look like she knew they were work,' Jill replied.

'*As if* she knew they were work,' Harpur said.

'Of course I knew it was work,' Denise replied. 'Am I going to get jealous about every female your father has to see in his duty, for heaven's sake?'

'About most of the young ones, I should think,' Jill replied.

Scott said: 'my mother says—'

'Says what?' Jill snarled. 'She ought to shut up. My dad can have a girlfriend if he likes, can't he, a student or whatever he likes – because *our* mother is dead? Hazel and me, we're old enough to understand these things, nearly sixteen, Hazel, thirteen me. This is a house of grown-ups, tell your nosy mother, right?'

'Hazel and *I*,' Harpur said.

'I wasn't going to say anything about Denise,' Scott said.

'Well, your creepy mother would.' Jill said. 'But Denise is

nice. And Dad is entitled. If he can get a lovely girlfriend like that somehow, it doesn't matter what he looks like himself, the age and his skin, he's entitled. Even Hazel says Denise is nice, don't you, Haze?'

'And when you went out looking for the men, Dad, Naomi was really tense,' Hazel replied. 'She asked me were you armed, and she wanted to dial 999 and get them to send gun-trained heavies to look after you. Were the men armed, Dad?'

'Armed, no,' Harpur said, laughing a bit. 'A couple of disco Romeos.'

'How do you know?' Jill said. 'You didn't find them, did you?'

'*Were* you armed, Mr Harpur?' Darren asked. 'A .44 Magnum, something like that?'

'Of course he wasn't armed, dumbo,' Jill said. 'Where do you think we are, the Bronx?'

'This was brave, going out,' Darren said.

'He's supposed to go out, idiot,' Jill replied. 'He's police, isn't he? Do you think all a detective chief superintendent is supposed to do is cuddle up to a girl student?'

'Especially if he was officer Anstruther's controller,' Scott said.

'And Denise was very worried about you too, Dad,' Hazel said.

'Of course she was. She loves him,' Jill replied. 'Naomi was worried, being a police officer worrying about another police officer – what's known as the culture. But Denise was worried about him because of sex and so on.'

'Right,' Denise said.

'Are they safe, Naomi and Esmé?' Hazel asked. 'Perhaps those men are still looking for them.'

'Should you of let Esmé go back to Cardiff, Dad?' Jill asked. 'So exposed.'

'*Have* let. How could I stop her?' Harpur replied.

'I worry about that Esmé,' Hazel said. 'When you were out, Dad, really weeping, shaking, saying she wished she'd never started it.'

'Started what?' Darren asked.

'Saying to Naomi if she got out of this, that's if Esmé got out of this, she was never going to do anything like it again,' Hazel replied, just forget it and leave it to the police.'

'Anything like what?' Darren asked.

'How do they know each other, if she's from Cardiff?' Hazel asked.

Denise said: 'I agree with Jill, Colin. The girl called Esmé was terrified of something. She thought she'd made some appalling mistake, but she wouldn't tell us what. Jill did ask. Can you find out if Esmé's all right? *Is* she?'

'To me this sounds like a gang thing,' Scott said. 'Perhaps they'd got mixed up with extra-dangerous stuff through undercover and the Eton. My mother says drugs gangs run Britain now and the police can only watch. She says the gangs just kill anyone in their way and nothing is done about it. Maybe this girl Esmé was in their way. Is that how it was, Mr Harpur? And maybe the cop girl, Naomi, is in their way too.'

'Hark at the chief of detectives,' Jill replied.

12

Naomi thought she would drive to Wales and look once more at the spot in Cardiff where Esmé was killed, get it under her feet and against her palms, the firm exactitudes of tarmac and brickwork. She needed detail: needed nearness to the little triangle of meagre grass where Esmé was sitting that night, legs sexlessly and lifelessly apart, and the window above with a blind part down, stuck at a mad slant. This urge to examine it all again had nothing to do with detection. She did not expect to make discoveries, find clues. She sought something to centre on, and something to give her a centre: something solid and as ordinary as a street surface, garden railings, an end-of-terrace wall. Probably there would still be bloodstains. She wanted the geography above all, though, and when she had the geography of this death she could put it alongside the geography of Don's death and Lyndon's, which were already precise and terrible in her mind. With all these locations brightly mapped in her memory, she might know which way to go. She liked open options, but eventually you had to opt, at least for a while. Get a route.

Naomi went early in the morning and reached Cardiff by 10 a.m. She parked a distance off, then returned on foot to the hellish spot. Perhaps it was wrong to say Esmé had been killed there. Naomi had found her at this spot and she was dead; no knowing where it had happened. This morning

Naomi could not get close: there were police about. She could see, not touch. A gaudy, small blue-and-white-striped tent covered one area of grass where she remembered blood. It was in a little side garden of an end-of-terrace house. When Naomi had come running, searching the other night, Esmé's body was folded in there behind the railings, and hardly noticeable except to someone frantic to find her: back against the brickwork, legs stretched out in front on the grass, her face nearly unrecognizable in the dark, and nearly unrecognizable whatever the light, probably. There had been blood at her head height on the side of the house as well as on the patchy would-be lawn. Naomi had been able to see the glint of that under streetlamps. She did what was required in a police officer confronted by a possible death and went to look for Esmé's pulse. No pulse. The rest of it was unforgivable in a police officer confronted by a possible death: she gave an anon. call for an ambulance from a pay-phone and then disappeared.

Most likely it was not bright to come back here sight-seeing now. But she walked past only twice, once as soon as she arrived this morning, and once from the other direction early in the afternoon, as if she lived close and had been somewhere. Police in dungarees were grubbing about in the garden near the striped tent and in neighbours' gardens. At the end, she went back to her car and sat there for a few minutes, getting her ideas into a kind of shape, then left. She did not think she would come back for a third view.

She reached home just before 7 p.m. and found an answerphone message from Harpur saying he would call around. An hour later he arrived. 'I don't know if you've kept in touch with the girl you were with at my house late the other night,' he said.

It had been strange at Harpur's place: that student in his dressing gown, so jealous, and the loud daughters so helpful and nosy.

'You mean Esmé?' Naomi replied.

'*Are* you in touch with her?' Harpur asked.

'Off and on, obviously. This was just a holiday friendship. What about her?'

'Well, look, Naomi, she's dead,' Harpur said. 'Am I telling you something?'

She stayed quiet. They were both standing in the middle of her living room, surrounded by the bits of furniture she and Don had bought together. Soon, she'd have a purge of them – they made her sad, sadder. After half a minute she sat down.

'Dead how?' But she went on in a rush. 'Don't tell me – I bloody know it – she's been killed. Murdered? My God, three people close to me. Three. What the fuck goes on, Harpur?'

'You really hadn't heard?'

'Has this been on TV, in the press?'

'It's taken a while to trace relatives. There was a mention in some papers, but no name before they were notified.'

'I think I saw it somewhere. This happened in Cardiff, did it? Christ, Harpur, I read about a woman there who had her—'

'There was some defacement,' he replied.

Yes. Some. Enough. There would have been plenty of time

for it. On the night, Naomi lost her for best part of an hour. Esmé rented a lock-up garage and they had left her car there and hurried the couple of hundred yards on foot towards her flat in a spruce Cardiff suburb. Of course, her tails had observed her doing that before, knew the procedure, logged it, and suddenly there was a vehicle slowing alongside them and Esmé pulled into it, Naomi shoved aside, stumbling in those fucking useless disco shoes, then righting herself and running after them, not even bothering to read the number plate because it would be stolen or false, concentrating on her breathing and keeping up some sort of pace – in those fucking useless disco shoes. Couldn't she have done more to stop that snatch – done *something?* The night had been going on eternally and perhaps around 4 a.m., or whatever it was, her alertness had failed. After more than another half an hour's running, walking, hobbling – maybe forty-five minutes – Naomi had turned a corner and by some sharpness or fluke saw the body against the wall in a less spruce Cardiff suburb.

Harpur said: 'Her parents will be located soon and told. The media will get the name and so on then. I thought I should let you know before that.'

She sat with her head down, staring at the knees of her jeans, and wept. This was no act. She knew about the death, but to hear it told now still hit her. There was fright in her crying too. She might be on someone's list with Esmé. And if she was not already on someone's list, she could be soon: all she needed to do was go on from where Esmé had been stopped. And she would. Well, she thought she would.

Christ, was there really a choice, even for someone as avid for freedom of purpose as herself? *Herself?* What did that mean? Who was herself – a between-roles cop, an avenger, an ex-lover, a woman driven half nuts by triple loss, triple grief, triple trauma? Because she did not know the answer yet, or for how long it would be the answer, she played ignorant with Harpur and wept as at a first hearing.

He waited for her to recover, then said: 'We wondered about a possible connection with the two men at the Chiffon.'

'Which?'

'The men you said you—'

'No – I meant which "we" wondered.'

He skipped this, of course. 'Do you know whether Esmé had any—'

'She didn't recognize those two, I'm sure of that.'

'Did she have any contacts in south-east London?'

Yes, she had contacts in south-east London, but contacts who contacted someone else about her and her questions.

'Contacts?'

'Business acquaintances,' Harpur replied.

'What business? Business like in *The Godfather*? Criminal dealing? As far as I know she was a Civil Servant.'

'Perhaps she mentioned other interests,' Harpur said.

'Not to me. Look, Mr Harpur, I'm grateful for . . .' She did not finish it. You did not offer a controller gratitude. He was obliged to do what he could for you, and Harpur had merely done it. He would have done more. They could have stayed at his house. He had pressed them to wait there that night.

But Esmé seemed to feel she would be safe only back at home. She had to go. Naomi travelled with her, might have stayed in Cardiff with her for at least a day or two, keeping an eye, though that was not something to tell. 'Mr Harpur, you did everything anyone—'

'You're distressed,' he replied. 'Naturally. You need a while to take it all in, steady yourself. I do understand. We can talk later, when you've—'

There was a knock at the door. She went to open it and Iles came unhesitantly in. He had on a brilliantly cut green-to-tan country suit and brogues, a combination she had never seen on him before. Maybe he was going home from a rural-pursuits class at the town hall or hare coursing. He fondled the Edwardian music cabinet and gazed about affectionately at other pieces of furniture, then chuckled sweetly for a while and turned to stare at Harpur with deep rubbishing energy:

'Col, I don't know that I'd have bet my entire patrimony on it, but I had a notion I would find you here. I went to your house with some information and your daughters said you'd left in a hurry. I assumed this could only mean an urgent duty call. That left me to settle which would be the *most* urgent, and I decided it might well be to someone of your sort, Naomi. When Harpur goes out and sniffs the air for priorities it's most likely he'll get a whiff of someone built like you, skin like yours, vim and suppleness like yours.' The ACC's voice changed. 'There was a period, as you probably know, when Harpur's most pressing duty calls were to my wife, at times when I was out serving this realm and so on.

Yes, as you probably know. As every bugger knows.' Iles began to shout, almost scream, his chuckling gone and gone. O God, her neighbours. The ACC's face had paled, all wrong for a hearty outdoor suit. 'My wife hardly remembers you now, Harpur,' Iles declared. 'Naomi, my wife hardly remembers him. I say to her, "Harpur this" or "Harpur that", recounting little work tales, and she will say, "Harpur?" And I reply: "You know, darling, the Harpur who used to betray me with you during one autumn into winter." And she will say, "Oh, *that* Harpur, Des. The one with the complexes. Anthony Harpur, was it? Bob Harpur? Is he still around, then?" That's the kind of impression he leaves with women, Naomi. That's the kind of impression you leave with women, isn't it, Harpur?'

Iles, nowhere near frothing, reached out towards Naomi as though to signal he was an unforgettable alternative, but did not actually put his hand on her.

How *is* Sarah, sir?' Harpur replied.

'Brilliant, Col. At the nub of my being and, Naomi, only those one really esteems reach one's nub. I hear a woman dead in Cardiff with crude post-death disfigurement had some link with our Cardiff boy killed at the Eton, and therefore with Naomi. Why I'm here.'

'Is it?' Harpur replied.

Iles sat down on the chaise-longue, stroking its scarlet material with fingers apart. 'I'm not right for this kind of elegant flashiness,' he said. 'I see myself as muted, oh, pathetically workaday. Don't you ever think of the effect your pussy-mania might have on Hazel and Jill and that nice undergraduate you get cohabitation with now and then, Col? This is the student who burnishes Harpur's ego and so on, Naomi. Met her? South Wales police have just told us of the girl Esmé's murder. I went to your house, wishing to discuss this, Harpur, but, of course, you—'

'I came to forewarn Naomi, sir,' Harpur replied.

'You didn't know about it, sod. We've only just been informed of the tie-up.'

'It's been in the press, sir.'

'But no name,' Iles said. 'No background.'

'One deduced, sir. That, after all, is what detection's about,' Harpur said.

Naomi watched Iles take a moment with this. 'You've had some private whisper from some private voice, have you?' he replied. 'You sit on stuff that should be available to at least myself and possibly even to the chief. O Naomi, such a team man is Harpur, aren't you, Col?'

'Naomi was very upset to hear of the death,' Harpur replied.

Iles smiled beautifully and hugged himself, stretching back on the scarlet, so that to her he looked for a second like a butch courtesan in gamekeeper's tweed. He said: 'But don't you love it, the marvellous generosity of women, Col? Here's two of them banging the same lad pre-Eton, as I understand it, yet Naomi can grieve at her death. They're different from us, Harpur, finer, nobler, emptier. Rockmain tells us you might turn avenger, Naomi. He diagnoses no consistency of persona, or something akin. Sounds like total bloody madness. Naturally, one wonders about one's own consistency of persona and nearness to total bloody madness.'

'Rockmain's a prick,' she replied.

'Of course he is,' Iles said. *'Are* you into vengeance, Naomi? Was little Esmé? Revenge is an art, not for half-baked kids who lose chunks of themselves in a swamp like Cardiff.'

13

Now and then Mansel Shale would forgive Alfie all that non-sense stuff such as living in a fucking lighthouse and his lopsided kids. The thing about Alf was research. Shale had taught him all businesses needed information, and Ivis could get it and put together lovely files. Like today, he would often come up with useful new aspects of a situation, and some of the long-time dossiers he had were full of fine secrets for screwing top sods. Maybe, after all, it was handy Alf had a lighthouse, because there were spare rooms he could keep the archive in where they most likely used to store wicks. Leadership he would never reach, but Alf did get items. He said: 'I'd like to mention a few aspects not covered by the media about this girl murdered in Cardiff. The one with links to the dead lad in the Eton.'

'The girl face-butchered?' Shale replied.

'Unfortunately, yes, Manse.'

'I'm opposed to that kind of thing,' Shale said.

'I know you are, Manse.'

'I see the body as sacred. Often. There's something in the Bible about that, you know.'

'The temple of the Holy Ghost,' Ivis replied.

'You won't get no fucking argument from me,' Shale said.

'I learn the girl, Esmé Carpenter-Mace, was in these parts immediately prior and seen with the famed lady cop, Anstruther, perhaps even staying in her flat. This is from friendly folk here and there.'

The friendly folk would get a place on Alfie's expenses form as 'tips to special contacts, £300', or around that, but all right, insights did cost. Yes, insights cost, say £50 or maybe £100 max., but all right, Alf had a lighthouse to finish converting, and eventually get some decent furniture into.

Shale said: 'Esmé? That supposed to be her name? I don't fucking believe it. Most likely Siân, Julie. Every girl is Siân or Julie now, so they calls themselves Esmé.'

'Perhaps handed some menace in the Chiffon and subsequently, Mansel,' Ivis replied.

It was a dry day and they were walking the cliff path near Alfie's place. You would think from how he went on out there that this whole slab of environment, sea included, was Alf's. Every so often he stopped and stared out at various waves or genuine seagulls or vessels. He put a grand smile on, like he had given the OK for it all and was pleased the way things were shaping.

'Menace by who?' Shale asked.

'This could be London,' Ivis said. 'This is two lads who could possibly be called David and Lee, or who could be called anything. For instance, they could be called Brian Bernard Rayne and Gordon Lusse. That's where the descriptions lead.'

'These are Everton people, Rt. Hon. people?'

'As ever, you get there fast,' Ivis replied.

'They hit Esmé?'

'Likely, Manse. I have them as that calibre.'

'Eye people, ear people?' Shale inquired.

'If they had a special request. Oh, look, Manse.' He pointed lovingly towards some sea blob. 'Seals. A pair. Always they look so relaxed and playful. Not so, of course. Ask the fish they swallow!'

Shale gave a comradely nod towards whatever it was, probably a couple of tree trunks. 'I don't mind seals, Alf,' he said. 'These are creatures that can swim miles underwater, eyes open the whole time, no goggles, obviously. This is a triumph nobody can't take away from them. Crew-cut?'

'Rayne, yes.'

'Who else knows this?'

'About him and Lusse? It's possible one or two.'

'What? Some grass to, say, Harpur?' Shale asked.

'On the cards. A lot of talk about.'

'That's OK. It might be a help.'

'Right,' Ivis said.

He could be like that, Alfie. He would find out useful aspects but did not always see what they meant or even often. This was the difference between troops and a commanding officer. If Shale said certain matters could be a help Alfie would say, Right, or if Shale said they was a pain Alfie would say, Right.

'So, is the girl cop next?' Shale asked.

'This is certainly the question, Manse,' Ivis replied.

'I'm disappointed with this girl. I hoped she'd try to get that friendship arrangement for us with Harpur and even Iles and the chief. I hear nothing.'

'A definite shortcoming in her, Manse.'

'But this death and the gouging and so on could be useful,' Shale replied.

'Oh, certainly,' Ivis replied. 'I felt you'd be pleased.'

'I'd say this girl, Anstruther, will go to that Esmé's funeral,' Shale said. 'I'd say she was that kind of full-power girl.'

'She did go to the dead boy's from the Eton mishap, Manse. I think I've got a note.'

'She struck me as the sort who would have big sympathy for people shot like that and sculpted, although she's police. Wanting to make a decent gesture and not just flowers.'

'There seemed a lot to be said for her,' Ivis replied.

They turned and walked back towards the lighthouse. Shale did not mind going in there as long as Alfie's children were at school and his wife shopping, despite the chairs and dud carpets.

'You and I know she'll go to that funeral, Alf. *They'll* probably know she'll go to that funeral, Alf. I think we better be there.'

Ivis stopped agreeing then. Shale knew he would. Alf had such a down on funerals. About funerals he would be independent and sometimes fucking cheeky.

He said: 'Oh, Manse, I know you're always very concerned to attend occasions of that sort, but—'

'They might come looking for her, like "Next, please!" We better be there, Alf – take out this crew-cut and Lusse, if necessary.'

'But, Manse—'

'I don't want to see some further girl face-carved like that,

even police. This is a girl I've spoken to in her own home, for
God's sake.'

'It's a credit to you, Manse, definitely, but—'

'Plus, there's a business point, isn't there, Alf?'

Sometimes you had to lay it all out with neon arrows to
the important bits before Alfred would understand. 'Well,
quite a few business points.' They went inside and Alf
brought out the gin and pep and mixed drinks in a couple of
Brer Rabbit mugs. 'We knock over B. B. Rayne and G. Lusse
and we got Naomi Anstruther's thanks, wouldn't you say,
Alf? Plus, maybe Harpur's and Iles's thanks, even Mark
Lane's, for saving their girl. And another plus, when we
knock over them two we're telling Everton and the Rt. Hon.
they're not dealing with no out-of-town nincompoops, we
got resolve. So, they back off our realm? I think so.'

'I'm sure Everton Osprey and the Rt. Hon. know you're
not a nincompoop, Manse,' ivis replied, with quite a laugh. 'I
don't think anyone is going to refer to Mansel Shale as in the
nincompoop category.'

'We could get our fine agreement with the law out of this,
Alf,' Shale said. 'There'll be obligation to us, saving an officer,
and a recognition of things as they are – and things as they
are will be *us*, Alf, just us. Everton and the Rt. Hon. will see
this area is sweetly sewn up – us and the police. That's going
to piss on their schemes, Alfred. They'll think of looking
somewhere else – forget Noisy Graham's place, forget Panicking Ralphy Ember's filthy secret work for them here – if
dear Jeremy Littlebann's got it right. Fucking *Jeremy.* You
ever heard of anyone running a snort centre called Jeremy,

Alf? We can have our talk with Panicking then, really give him some quiz. Maybe that bastard's suddenly going to find he been ditched by his London allies and he's on his own. It could be satisfying to chat with him then, Alf. Find out about the funeral, would you?'

Ivis was sitting in a sort of armchair that had been through at least two world wars but might of been reupholstered in some kind of material around 1920, probably old no man's land uniforms.

'Manse, have you thought that if they had wanted her as well as the girl, Esmé, they could have done her at the same time?'

'Possibly,' Shale said. 'But these boys had orders, didn't they? Get this Esmé and make it like noticeable, with the bonus injuries. Esmé, Alf. Them two, the crew-cut and Lusse, are just ordinary employees. They do what they been told to do, and that's all. But then they go back and tell Everton and the Rt. Hon. that this girl they dealt with was good pals with an undercover cop. This could worry Everton and the Rt. Hon. This could look like these two girls are in something conjoint. A revenge thing? Did they both think a lot of that lad dead in the Eton, from Esmé's home town? So, Rayne and Lusse get a second helping of orders – go and finish Anstruther too. Where's the easiest place to find her, and so meaningful? At her friend's final send-off. Get us to the funeral, Alfred. Find out the place and time.'

'Manse, you're saying do it in a church? Gunning folk in a church? This would be difficult and very eccentric. This would not be like the Eton.'

'Yes, like the Eton in some ways – the same because it's about people coming for Anstruther.'

'We'd be identified, Manse. This is going to be a church full of people, many of them reputable, probably. Witness material.'

'I mean get them *near* the church, not *in* the fucking church, obviously, Alf. Somewhere quiet. Yes, like it was supposed to happen on the way to the Eton. We just get them, so they never reach the service or Anstruther. She'd appreciate who done it for her and so would Harpur and Iles, even the chief – like intuition. But they would not want to push for detail. They'd want to give some recompense, and that means silence from them and a welcome to our business plan because we're so clearly their friends, Alf.'

'With respect, Manse, this killing—'

'Killings, if we're lucky.'

'These killings will not be on this ground, and Harpur, Iles and the chief will not be running the inquiries. The funeral's Cardiff, I expect. This will be South Wales police.'

'Mark Lane will have a brotherly word with them. *Go easy on this one, boys, this one's just what the doctor ordered.* And, in any case, we're not going to leave any evidence about, are we, Alf? This is a straightforward interception. You must of done similar many a time.'

'Yes, but Manse, I—'

Shale looked at his watch. Those cracked children would be home here any time now with their flit-about eyes and funny ways of walking. He stood and went out to his bicycle. The thing about Alf was he was entitled to say what he thought – of course he was – but Shale was entitled to get home while Alf was thinking about saying it.

14

Ralph Ember drove down to Hampshire to see the drugs importer who supplied him wholesale. The phone call had come early this morning. Best respond quite quickly to an invitation from dear Barney Coss. Barney lived far away but he heard a lot. Barney saw betrayal everywhere. Barney protected himself. Barney acted affable and even humane, mostly. Barney sometimes wasn't either.

Maud, one of Barney's live-ins, had come on the extension phone: 'What we hear is you're doing some fucking backroom deal with London, you slimy sod, Ember.'

Barney had said: 'Well, yes, there is an uneasiness or two about the situation at your end, Ralph.'

Lately, Ember had started carrying a gun again. This he saw as indelicate for someone with decent community status and a splendid family, but you paid attention to the climate or where were you? The climate was potentially rough, and he had a pistol aboard today for this visit. Likewise, he would have it aboard next month for the business conference with Manse Shale and Ivis. Ember had bought a .38 short-barrelled Smith and Wesson Model 49 Bodyguard revolver from careful dealers, Amy and Leyton Harbinger, nothing too bulky. The Harbingers did a lot of East Europe stuff now the Wall was down and tried to sell Ember a Russian 9mm Stechkin blowback automatic. He would not listen, said S. and

W. For something he knew, Ember was ready to pay more, and it would have seemed disrespectful to contemplate shooting a lad as local as Manse or even Alf Ivis with a Cold War relic.

Beau Derek was with Ember on today's trip to Hampshire. This was the thing about Barney – he always phrased the invitations for 'you and your confrère, Ralph', which for the present meant Beau Derek, although Beau added up to just above nothing in Ember's firm, a baggage man. The baggage man refused to carry a gun.

'I think it's a lack in you, Beau – this allergy,' Ember said as they crossed Marlborough Downs. 'Oh, in some ways creditable, humane, yes, but, well . . . self-indulgent the word? Afraid so.' Ember drove, a new Saab.

'Firearms are not *me*, Ralph.'

That's how Beau could talk now and then, as if he had some kind of cherishable identity, like Job or Mandela. Beau lived with a woman named Melanie, who might turn out cherishable, but Beau, hardly.

'Guns are not *me* either, unless forced,' Ember said. 'My God, Beau, I write signed letters to the press on civic matters. Pistols are not how I'm perceived at all.'

Beau held up both gross hands briefly, a fleeting surrender. 'Yes, but Ralph, you know about gun-play from way back. All sorts of fabulous jobs. Me, I've always had this funny block. Sorry.'

'Is it selfish, Beau? Look, have you thought I might be shooting – I mean, *having* to shoot – I mean, today or next month with Manse – I might be shooting to save not just myself but you.'

I do know it, Ralph, and I'm aware of being a what – a possible liability? Safes I can deal with, not shooters.'

Beau had his red-cabbage face skin pulled together now to announce stubborn strength, and Ember let the subject sink. You could not bully such a good-hearted piece of wreckage. If it ever did come to a battle Ember would certainly try to save Beau, because this was often Ralph's style. Many would confirm that. Without reserve, Ralph believed in loyalty and in protecting team mates – especially nobodies – unless things went seriously bad. Clearly, if one of his full, true panics came, he might not be able to do anything except make a dash, supposing his legs held up. They said transcendental meditation was good for panics, and he had recently made inquiries about a course.

Beau said: 'Don't understand why you're anxious, Ralph. This is a sound arrangement with Barney. A sound arrangement with Manse as well. They're bound to see that. Would they destroy it?'

'Not *anxious*. Prepared. There's a lot of shit flying, Beau. Why I've been asked down here, I should think.'

Ember stayed quiet for a while. They approached the select riverside enclave where Barney lived, not far from Southampton and the Isle of Wight. The countryside looked good.

'Oh, I love these trips,' Beau said.

Of course Beau loved these trips. They made him feel substantial, not what he was, an extra. Barney had his property in a development called the Wharf. This was boating country, rich boating country: plump houses overlooking the water and a collection of moored yachts, most of them worth around a million at least, flying personal pennants and ready to compete with royalty at Cowes, or sail off to the Caribbean or Nice for international commingling with the loaded. Ralph Ember considered himself pretty well placed financially, but when he saw this sort of display he grew damned disturbed and wondered how they passed him. When had he slept? In his selfless style, had he given too much time to family and girlfriends?

Barney owned at least one of the yachts, though the importing was done in something less glamorous, of course, and not via distinguished river haunts. Yachts were pleasure and status only. 'So make it lunch time, Ralphy,' Barney had said, and around lunch time it would be. 'Both of you, of course, Ralphy.' Ralph always found it absurd and humiliating that at the Wharf Beau was regarded as his equal. Beau had definite plus elements, but he could be a full-scale embarrassment. He said too much, trusted too much, sometimes even believed that what people said was what they meant. Beau was juvenile, an almost bald juvenile of thirty-six with a flair for dealing with razor wire and balance sheets as well as the safes. Although, really, none of these skills rated in the drug trade, Beau had once done useful favours, so Ralph made a place for him. *Made a place for him*, squeezed him in – not offered a chieftain role, for God's sake.

It was hot but Ralph kept his jacket on, to cover the

loaded shoulder holster. That was not something you wanted noted from police patrol cars.

Beau said: 'I've never seen Barney with a—'

'Barney despises guns, probably,' Ember replied. 'He's above all that now. But do we know who else is in the house?'

'Those two hell-hole women.'

'Them and who besides?' Ember replied.

'But what's it about, Ralph? Why would he? Jesus, suddenly you suspect everyone.'

'Just alert.'

Beau had been around at all kinds of levels for a long time, but who'd credit it? Ember drove through the open gates of Barney's grounds and parked in front of the house. There were a couple of Volvos and a new Range Rover there, plus a worn-out-looking Mini. Barney might use that most. He did interludes of lowliness. One of his yachts was called *Modesty*. If he had another it might be *Shrinking Violet*. He came out to greet them as Ember parked, aglow with goodwill, his smile all happy reassurance.

'Christ, no, I don't like this,' Ember muttered to Beau.

Barney had on navy shorts, a football shirt and floppy white sunhat. He looked nimble and hale, like someone who did not touch the stuff he dealt in or fuck strangers. You could imagine him clipped to a life line in great waters and belting out shanties never mind the storm.

'Here you are lads, here you are,' he called joyfully, walking towards them. He spoke through the car's open window. 'Ralphy, such a treat to see you. Beau, such a treat to see you.'

It was like man management, keeping this mad parity.

Ember said: 'Always a tonic to come into these parts, Barney. You're looking fitter than ever. And how are Maud and Camilla.' Ignore that phone shit from Maud for now.

'Lusting for another sight of your Charlton Heston profile, Ralph,' Barney replied.

At least the bugger could not equal that one out, because Beau's profile was a tramp's boot. Folk called him Beau as a laugh, and because of Bo Derek.

'Oh, all that Chuck Heston rubbish,' Ember replied. 'An embarrassment, really. Can't see it myself.'

'Ralph gets *very* embarrassed by the resemblance,' Beau said.

'*Alleged* resemblance,' Ember replied. This mariner, Barney, was not the only one who could do the humble.

'Well, I won't keep on about it,' Barney said, 'though the similarity is quite wonderful.'

They climbed out of the car. Maud and Camilla in yester-year dresses, bare-legged and wearing white plastic sandals, came from the house and joined Barney.

Maud said: 'So you look at your supposed business buddy's prospects – I mean Mansel Shale – and you think to your wise and shifty self that this friend is suddenly yesterday's friend, don't you, Ember, because Shale's side of the trade was deep into the Eton? But the Eton is all at once blighted, a dud, dead – penetrated by this girl cop, Anstruther, and people killed there. Wise old, enduring old Ralphy gazes around in that brisk fashion of his for a different ally. And what does he see with those survivor's eyes? He sees

Everton Eva's Osprey and the Rt. Hon. up in London and panting to expand, doesn't he? Doesn't he, Ember?'

Beau said: 'Oh, this is *so* hasty Maud.'

'Rumour – you might well retort "Rumour only", Ralph,' Camilla said, 'and we are certainly open to such a . . . well . . . such an explanation from you. Oh, I hope so. Irrational otherwise? Yes. Unease, however. I feel you will appreciate that we might experience unease, if not more, upon hearing such . . . well, yes, admittedly unauthenticated reports. Yet alarming.'

The five of them were still standing near Ember's Saab. He felt the beginnings of a panic – that appalling flash flood of sweat and the deep, almost throttling ache in his throat and across the shoulders. He raised a hand to check whether the ancient scar along his jawline had opened up and was shedding something rotten and copious onto his collar. It never did open up, but in one of his full panics he would suffer bewildering messages from there, messages about unstaunchable decay and trailing nerve ends. Yet even as this spasm took strength, he could keep his brain going. And those survivors' eyes that this ancient plague Maud had mentioned – he could keep *them* going too, though with a bit of triple vision through stress. He glanced from window to window, searching for signs of Barney's staff thugs on call inside. His yacht crews might do heavy duties for him between voyages.

'Jeremy Littlebann,' Maud said. 'Prop. of the Eton Boating Song.'

'Yes?' Ember replied.

'Just a name,' Beau said.

'Enigmatic,' Camilla cried. 'Maud is. Yes, so enigmatic. She has this little way – just mentioning someone, no context, no . . . well, background, depth . . . just a name and expecting everyone to deduce the . . . the sort of significance. It can be . . . well, disquieting.'

'This bastard Ember can deduce all right,' Maud replied.

'Oh, Littlebann,' Ember said. 'Jeremy's someone rather given to falling into panics, I'm afraid. He'd say anything.'

Ember thought his voice came out almost all right, no fright squeal or huskiness from internal sweat. The word 'panic', which was one he hated speaking, had sounded fine. He continued to survey the windows and twitched his chest gently to get the comforting feel of the holster harness tightening across him. Even with his vision gone haywire through pressure, he believed he would be able to make out any sly movement behind the curtains. Recently, he had heard of a state called 'blindsight': some people with very defective eyes could still as it were 'see' certain objects they would not normally be expected to see. Ember reckoned he had blindsight. No matter how impaired his senses might become through terror, he was still always brilliantly conscious of anything near that menaced him, and which should be run away from. Blindsight had helped bring him his country house, Low Pastures, and the ownership of his club, the Monty, plus some useful capital.

Maud said: 'Littlebann is convinced you've been—'

'And so to luncheon,' Barney said. 'Come, do.'

They all began to walk towards the house. He put a welcoming hand on Ember's shoulder, feeling for the holster straps, probably. Ralph found he had no trouble walking.

'Reliability? Credibility?' Camilla asked. 'Ralph is entitled to question whether Littlebann has these. An interested party, clearly. Might he spread falsities? Imponderables, very much so. We receive this information about Littlebann at . . . well, at what might certainly be called a remove. Garbled? This is . . . not to put too fine a point on it . . . this is dubious ground, Maud.'

'I know what and who is dubious, and it's not the sodding ground,' Maud replied. 'Have you considered, Ember, that Littlebann might have spoken to Shale and Alf Ivis? Doesn't this trouble you? One of your get-togethers soon, isn't there? Are you going to be safe?'

'Those meeting are always very pleasant, constructive affairs,' Beau replied. 'I'm sure the next one will be too.'

'Yes?' Maud replied.

Jesus, but they always knew too much down here. Maud was right about next month's conference with Shale, of course. It might turn out grave. Ember could not yet tell exactly *how* grave. From very early in their neat business alliance, he and Shale had held these formal meetings every now and then over dinner somewhere to look at recent per-formance and talk prospects. This time, the kind of rumour Maud mentioned and responsibility for that disaster at the Eton would be on the menu. Usually there were four of them present at the dinners: Ember and Beau, Shale and Ivis. Alfie knew handguns, and Manse could probably make a show too.

'Oh, it's always a lovely meal, but dull, dull trade talk at these sessions with Manse,' Ember said.

'Yes?' Maud replied.

As they approached the house, Barney was on Ember's left, Beau close to his right. Ember felt Beau grip the sleeve of his jacket and give a small tug. When Ember glanced at him Beau twitched his head, signalling that they should not go in but get back urgently to the car. Although he had done his slice of blandness just now, anyone could see he was terrified. So like small-timers. Scruples stopped Beau carrying a gun, but now he wanted Ember to get him out of hazard. What Ralph would have forecast. Ember kept going towards the property. Could he stop, anyway, with Barney holding him? Looking at Beau, Ember began to feel strong. He had to protect this sad package. And he had to do what he generally managed to do and bring some positives from what might be an edgy situation. He pulled his sleeve from Beau's grasp and did not look his way again.

They went through the enormous, high hall, which was in the same sort of scruffy state as always. A couple of old-style, very rusted tin baths stood against one wall. There was a handsome glass-fronted rosewood china cabinet, empty except for two petrol cans on the central shelves. Above this hung a heavily framed oil painting of rural lanes. An incomplete exhaust system of a car was laid out on copies of *The Economist* and *News of the World*. To Ember, Barney always seemed bored by wealth. Ralph had come across a word on his mature-student Religious Knowledge course at university – *accidie*, meaning apathy, indifference. Barney was into *accidie.* He had the boat or maybe boats and the cars and the house, but he could not be bothered to do anything with the property: not decorate it properly, nor get enough decent furniture. And look at these two ragtaggle old pieces he presumably slept with, although he could have brought in so much better, bought in so much better.

Barney led to a magnificent octagonal conservatory at the rear, full of more junk, including a ruined trampoline, two mouldering kennels and an historic sewing machine worked by pedal. A table was laid there with some kind of buffet meal. But, no, Ember realized that would not do – not just *some kind of* buffet meal. When he looked properly he saw a very imaginative lunch, with what could be caviare, or at least lumpfish roe, smoked trout, smoked salmon, a haunch of cold pork and a range of salads. Generally when he came here, Maud and Camilla put together a clapped-out health-food snack and they drank weak squash. Today at the end of the table he saw bottles of red and white Hermitage, the white that magnificent Chante-Alouette. He could not make out the years, but these would probably be wines of a price he would buy at the Monty only for the most special celebration parties, say confirmations or a street-war slaying by one of the member gangs. Two waitresses in uniform stood waiting for them to the left of the bigger sagging kennel, and smiled a welcome. Barney must have hired caterers. There was real china crockery and good glass on show. Three ice buckets shone.

The waitresses helped them to food and poured. Camilla lifted a corner of the trampoline and pulled out some folded deck chairs. They sat in these and began their meal. The girls served more helpings and refilled the glasses. Ember would have preferred to eat at a table. He felt exposed in a deck chair, sort of laid out, an inert target, and the frame seemed to hamper his gun arm. In any case, managing the plate and a fork meant that both his hands were occupied. People could come at you from all round, here – from behind if they entered the conservatory via the house, or from ahead if they were in the grounds and shot through all this glass. He tried to finish the food fast so he would at least have his arms free. His panic seemed in abatement. That often happened when Ember occupied himself assessing the detail of a peril. It was when the thing suddenly ballooned and looked overwhelming that he might suffer deep collapse.

Beau said: 'Many consult Ralph, oh, yes.'

He was like that. He could not let a situation use its own pace. He had to try to guide and get control. That conversation about contact with Everton Osprey and the Rt. Hon. had disappeared, but now Beau was bringing it back.

'Who consults him?' Maud asked.

'Many,' Beau said.

'What type of many?' Maud asked.

'All sorts of types,' Beau replied.

'Consult about what?' Maud asked.

'This would be a range,' Beau said. 'Business matters.'

'Where from?' Maud asked.

'What?' Beau replied.

'Where are they from, these many types?' Maud asked.

'Many areas,' Beau said. He looked oppressed. 'Maud,

Ralph's the sort who will take a lot of foul-mouthing and won't answer back or turn savage, especially when it's a woman.'

Barney told the waitresses they could leave and pushed each a ten. Ember did not much like that. When they had gone, Maud said: 'Are they from London?'

'London, possibly,' Beau said. 'But from all over.'

Ember finished his main course and put the plate down. He tried to rearrange himself in the deck chair so he could bring off a quick cross-body draw. God, how many years since he'd needed to think like this? It thrilled him, appalled him.

'Reputation,' Camilla said. 'Nobody would deny Ralph has that aplenty. This would attract all sorts, naturally, for . . . well, consultation, constructive discussion.'

There was a noise from somewhere in the house, a footstep perhaps, or a door closing.

'Who else is here?' Beau asked.

'That will be the waitresses changing out of their uniforms,' Barney said.

Ember thought of standing so he could be mobile, not stretched out here hopeless, half dreaming he was youthful.

'I thought those girls went out through the garden,' Beau replied.

'They'd have to go in at the front of the house to get their clothes,' Barney said.

'Whose are all the cars?' Beau asked. He aimed for a prosecuting lawyer's rasp but still sounded Beauish and rubbery.

'They brought the eats and drinks in a Volvo,' Barney replied. 'Plenty of room in the boot.'

Maud said: 'So, these discussions he has – the discussion fans come from here, there and everywhere to enjoy with him – some of these discussions are with London admirers, yes?'

'London, Hull, Toledo, you name it, Maud,' Beau replied.

It was as though Ember were not present. He let them talk on, though. He could concentrate on safety.

Camilla got up from her chair in a series of awkward surges. Always it severely pained Ember to think Barney might be giving it to these two. Probably Camilla was pretty once. She had a delicate face except for her nose – a bit underclass, wrong for her voice. But Barney did not need to make do with the past. She brought around desserts and sweeter wines, Barsac and Sauterne, with clean glasses, everything so right today. Ember refused this course and stood up, as if wanting to return his plate to the table. He remained standing there, watching the garden and the door from the house.

Barney said: 'To us, Shale always looked so good, a worthy associate for you, Ralph. But then this incredible mess up at the Eton. Well, perhaps an arranged scenario involving the girl cop, Anstruther, but wholly mishandled.'

'Adjustment, adaptability, Ralph, qualities for which you are renowned,' Camilla said. She had sat down again. 'I don't believe I'm exaggerating when I say renowned. In other words, it would be within our, as it were, profile of expectations for you, Ralph, that you would regard Mansel Shale as . . . well, as finished. Perhaps, as Littlebann suggests, I think . . . perhaps you deliberately compromised the planned pre-Eton interception so Shale would be left nowhere. And, obviously, you will sort that out with him yourself, either at this impending meeting or when and where you will. But our concern, our indeed rage . . . yes, I'm afraid rage – our rage would be provoked if you were to turn as part of this response to . . . well, to turn to people whom we would regard quite specifically as enemies. One refers, of course, to Everton Evas Osprey and Basil Cope, the Rt. Hon., as he pathetically likes to be dubbed.'

'Nor acceptable, Ralph,' Barney said.

'Are you confederating with those two shits, Ralph?' Maud asked.

Beau said: 'Ralph is someone whose—'

'I think this bugger Ember's armed,' Maud said.

'Of course he's armed,' Barney replied. 'Wouldn't you be, coming into a spot like this in present circs?'

'Tailoring, svelteness – no reflection on yours at all, Ralph,' Camilla stated. 'The jacket – a credit to you, as ever. But is there a jacket anywhere that can conceal even a short-barrelled revolver plus holster? Say a .38? So, do we go into the Armani stockist and say, *Kindly show me your disguised-firepower range*? Facetious – do I strike you so?'

Ember went and sat down in his deck chair again. Suddenly, listening to Camilla boom and loop and watching Barney and countering Maud, he had come to realize that they were afraid of him, all of them. Maud's snarls were fright. Barney looked shaky. Camilla was, as almost always, placatory, but more than normal. They feared not just the .38. Barney could have easily brought in people to outmatch that. He probably hadn't, and Ember thought the noises about the house really did come from the waitresses leaving. He saw that these three fretted over the relationship he might have built with Everton Evas Osprey and the Rt. Hon. They longed to bracket Ember with Beau, reduce him, negate him, and pretended they could. But in fact they knew Ralph was a different breed – someone courted by a ferocious eminence like Everton. This showed Ralph's rank and towering quality, his unparalleled reputation. Barney and the women were afraid they might lose Ember and his operation and his influence and his power back home. Of course. Wasn't Ralph a main customer? And didn't he somehow bring weight and credibility to any enterprise he entered? Please don't ask him how he did it – simply a flair that flowed, as natural as speech or love. No wonder people craved to be associated with him.

Ralph stood again and helped himself to a good plateful of strawberries and ice cream. Previously, he had been nervy and rushed his meal to get a gun hand ready. Now, he felt relaxed, confident, hardly thought about the revolver, was almost ashamed of having packed it for this visit. He lowered himself into the deck chair once more and ate appreciatively, occasionally sipping Barsac.

'Who was it said the pleasure of ice cream was so great it should be a sin?' he asked. 'Well, ice cream plus strawberries would have to be mortal sin.' This he gave a bit of a chuckle and some wholesome nods. He ate a few more spoonfuls. 'I turned them down,' he said.

'Everton? Basil Cope?' Maud asked.

'They made an approach,' Ember replied. 'After the Eton they saw the town was much more hazardous territory than they'd supposed. They wanted a partner who would also be a local guide and hand-holder – help them parley with the Sioux.'

'You say you refused, Ralph?' Barney asked.

Ember ate for a while, letting them see the strawberries had his total mind. In due course he said: 'I refused.'

'Is this true, you scheming sod, Ember?' Maud asked.

Ember ignored the unseemliness. Yes, it revealed only nerves and even dread. But what had always irritated him badly about both these ropy women in their galloping fifties was that neither ever showed any sexual interest in him. Nothing. Barney satisfied them so brilliantly? Obviously, Ralph would not have fucked either even as a bet, but it hurt him that they could so flagrantly ignore his pull. Barney had mentioned their excitement about Ember's looks, and his profile particularly, but Ralph never saw any confirmation of this. Yet many women forced themselves on Ralph, cooed promisingly over the Heston resemblance, competed to fondle his scar and/or zip. With these two, though, nothing apart from business. Occasionally, Maud could be slightly less evil than she was today, yet he had never detected in either of them anything more heated than business civility.

Barney said: 'The Eton being dead, Ralph, we would like to propose an alternative, an alternative only you could make possible.' He tried to give it the sound of generosity.

Ember strawberried on.

'Opportunity, Ralph,' Camilla remarked. 'I don't think this is to misrepresent it.'

Ember stood again to get more dessert. God, he felt powerful, of the moment. This smug trio had learned to rate Ralph Ember – had learned at last. Glancing towards Beau, crouched forward in his deck chair, Ember saw he was as frightened as before, perhaps more so now, as if appalled by Ralph's casualness and contemplating a cry of warning. While refilling his plate, Ember observed the two waitresses in ordinary clothes and carrying holdalls cross the lawn on their way to the drive. Soon afterwards he heard a car start and drive away. So Beau's worries about noises in the house had definitely been absurd. Timorous. Pathetic.

'Tell us how the approach was made, Ralph,' Maud said.

He thought the bullying note had gone from her words. She was asking for information, not organizing an attack.

'From Everton and the Rt. Hon?' he asked.

'Of course.'

'Oh, a phone call initially,' Ember said. This would be enough on that topic. He turned to Barney: 'What was the alternative scheme you wanted to suggest?'

'Out of the blue?' Maud asked.

'The phone call?' Ember replied. 'Out of the *dark*. In two senses. One, it was late at night. Two, these are shadowy people. But, yes, a surprise. I don't know them. Didn't.'

Ember saw he had to play things right. He must not make the contact with Everton Osprey and the Rt. Hon. sound insignificant, because Barney and the two women feared this relationship. As they would see it, Ember might have

acquired some mighty and ruthless friends. The Osprey connection said prestige and influence, and Barney would not
want sweet *Modesty* scuttled one night for him, or a fire
bomb through a window of the house while he Maud and
Camilla interwove together in bed, combined ages up
towards two hundred. On the other hand, Ember had to
avoid looking treacherous. That could anger so many people
into frenzy, not simply Barney and the women. He must keep
his account of the connection and the rendezvous with
Osprey's firm to a formality, that only.

'They asked for a face-to-face, did they, Ember?' Maud
said.

'Interrogation, Ralph – that's what you're being put
through,' Camilla said. 'I don't think "interrogation" is too
strong a word. Maud reads a lot of Le Carré.'

'It came in the first instance merely as a general inquiry
about conditions post-Eton,' Ember replied.

'Who spoke to you on the phone?' Maud asked.

'Oh, Everton himself,' Ember replied.

'He came through to you direct – no assistant inter-
vening?'

'Direct,' Ember said. There had been two assistants, then
the Rt. Hon., before Everton Osprey personally took the
receiver.

'He wanted a heart-to-heart – like the hot line between
Kennedy and Kruschev?'

Again Ember turned away from her. 'I might be interested
in this alternative you mentioned, Barney. What Camilla
called an opportunity.'

'How did he address you?' Maud asked.

'Address me?' Ember replied, once more looking back to her and smiling, mouth half full. 'Lord, do I remember?' He considered. 'Mr Ember, I think, in the opening exchanges. I mean, Maud, he would know me only by report. How else would he speak to me? He's very decorous. And, naturally, I would call him Mr Osprey to begin with.'

'And later?'

'Persistence,' Camilla said. 'Do you see what I mean about interrogation, Ralph? Yes, that super-agent George Smiley in Le Carré. Trivial – seemingly trivial, merely social, questions, yet of eventual import.'

'Eventually, "Ralph" and "Everton"?' Maud asked.

'I expect so,' Ember replied.

'You know so, you suave sod,' Maud replied. 'Even "Ralphy"?'

'My name is Ralph,' Ralph said.

'I expect he's heard you called Ralphy,' Maud replied.

'I told you, he's very civil,' Ember replied.

'Ralph can't tolerate being called Ralphy,' Beau said. 'Would Prince Philip put up with "Philly" or General de Gaulle with "Charlie"?'

Maud said: 'This is Osprey phoning you to say, Well done, Ralphy, the Eton's finished, Shale's finished, so we'll make a future together, you and I, a new room for two room. Let the Eton and Shale dwindle together.'

'Oh, really, nothing so rough-edged, Maud,' Ember replied. 'Nothing so cut and dried.'

'But in that area?'

'He rang to propose further discussions,' Ember replied. 'I think that's the best way to put it.'

'And you agreed,' Maud asked.

'He said he would be passing through, could he see me? There was a brief meeting. I didn't wish to seem churlish,' Ember replied.

Opposite him, still sitting on the edge of the deck chair, his hands finger-laced worriedly in front of him, Beau seemed even more tense than when Ralph had glanced his way last time. Beau was listening, but listening for sounds in the house, not to this examination by Maud. Ember could hear nothing from outside the conservatory, and, of course, there should be nothing – the waitresses had left. Perhaps Beau had exceptional ears, used to detecting tumblers on the move in a combination safe. More likely he could hear his own nerves fluttering.

Maud said: 'Where? In your club?'

Ember forgot about listening to the house. She had angered him. Did she really believe he would hold a conference with offal like Osprey and the Rt. Hon. in the Monty? He was fighting to restore the club to its one-time respectability, even celebrity. For Ember, the Monty was holy, more or less. Letting Everton Osprey and the Rt. Hon. onto the premises would not aid the journey towards cachet.

'Is Littlebann saying I met them at the Monty?' Ralph asked.

'Does it matter who's saying it?' Maud replied.

'Littlebann would tell you anything, he's so desperate,' Ember said.

And then he did hear sounds from somewhere in the main house, sounds that persisted for quite a few seconds: possibly someone walking on a section of floor not covered by carpet, perhaps on bare boards or linoleum. There would be a lot of floor like that. He recalled talking with Barney on a previous visit in what was called the Games Room, where there were next to no games – an old, ruinously gouged dartboard, that was all – a Games Room where emaciated lino covered parts only of the floor. Beau heard the sounds too. Ember had resumed his place on the deck chair and was finishing his second plate of dessert. He put it down now hurriedly, still with some strawberries and ice cream left. Barney watched him, observed the failure to finish, perhaps read the move by Ember into readiness.

'We're not sure whether you invited them to the Monty. But we do know there was a meeting – perhaps a further meeting – at a private hotel in Bath,' Maud said. 'The Edmund. Osprey hired a small conference room in the mame of Bidgood, his butler.'

'Bath?' Beau shouted with a laugh. 'Why Bath?'

Ember saw he had spoken only to get Ralph to look at him again. With his eyes, Beau signalled growing peril.

'Neutral ground,' Maud said.

'It would be a damned long way to go for neutral ground,' Ember replied. Oh, Jesus, they had it documented. They knew he had taken real trouble, had travelled miles, to see Osprey and the Rt. Hon. 'A long way for him and me.' A long way to go to refuse outright. He *had* refused, though perhaps not exactly outright. Who knew when you might need allies? Ember had never favoured the outright.

'Osprey likes Bath. He's into architecture,' Maud said. 'He buys antiques.'

'Taste,' Camilla said. 'A quality that lights on the most improbable.'

Ember, trying to listen to the house and to Maud whenever she began again, could feel the swift restart of panic. All the symptoms – the sweat, the paralysing ache, the sense of sudden dissolution of his scar – all these, but also a disgusted wonderment at the complacency he had felt not long ago, that strawberry arrogance. *Who was it said the pleasure of ice cream was so great it should be a sin?* Oh, God, the de-luxe prickishness. And his belief that they feared him: insane. Him! They had him nailed. And there were people in the house to complete that nailing. Yes, these three were right to rate him with Beau, if that. Beau at least had enough brain to know they were in an ambush.

Maud said: 'So, the detail, Ralph. You have the phone call which is general chat, you tell us. Then possibly the Monty, despite what you say. Now tell us what was decided at Bath.'

'Bath's a mystery to me,' Ember replied. He had denied Bath because Bath was enthusiasm and effort, and had to stick with that now.

'Oh, don't piss us about, there's a dear,' Barney said.

Maud said: 'You were there too, weren't you, Beau? You're another whose class soul is wowed by Regency terraces?'

'In a hotel in Bath?' Beau replied. His voice was almost nothing, a guilty child's, part from horror at finding how well they were briefed and part from the dread of what could come through the door or the fucking acres of conservatory window. 'Can't help on that.' It was brave.

'This will be to finalize the business plan: you, Osprey and the one they call Noisy Graham setting up a distribution centre to replace the Eton in Noisy's restaurant, Seconds, yes?' Maud asked. 'Littlebann's finished, long live Noisy. What it looks like to me, to us, is betrayal, Ember.'

'No, no,' Beau gasped. 'Only if Ralph accepted. Surely only if Ralph accepted – you've got to admit that, Maud. And he didn't, I can swear.'

'You *were* there then, were you, Beau?' Barney asked.

'Beau is part of all major decision-taking,' Ember replied.

'I thought you'd understand that, Barney. All right, we *were* at Bath, but I'd given my word to Osprey that this would be secret, whichever way the decision went.'

'And the decision was against,' Beau said. 'Rejection.'

Maud said: 'Our information is that—'

The door from the house into the conservatory opened suddenly. Ember had heard no further footsteps, and perhaps Beau hadn't either – too busy trying to talk himself and Ralph out of disaster. Ember wanted to stand again, but did not know whether his legs would take it. He did not even know whether he could move his hand for an across-chest grab at the .38. Crazily, it seemed a greater priority to get his fingers to the jaw scar and feel it for ooze. Yes, crazily. He dismissed that need and had his right hand going fastish towards the gun when Barney stood suddenly from his deck chair, took a step and held Ember's right forearm in an inflexible, jolly tar's grip, stopping the progress towards the revolver, or at least delaying it. Ember did try to break out, but most of his strength was going in sweat.

'Now, here's Rosemary, my accountant, Ralph,' Barney cried rapturously. 'She can put to you better than myself – even better than Maud or Camilla – put to you expertly the potential of this alternative scheme we mentioned.'

Ember saw a red-haired woman in her mid-twenties wearing a blue-silk suit. She smiled hearteningly and was carrying a transparent plastic envelope of papers. Beau turned to stare, also. Rosemary came towards them, still smiling, an elegant, happy stride, full of purpose and hormones, and Ember saw that Barney might have cleverly moved on from Maud and Camilla for some needs after all.

Rosemary held out a hand amiably to Ember, and he was damned glad to see she knew whom to greet first of him and Beau. He responded. She said: 'Oh, Lord, Mr Ember – Ralph, may I, but *may* I? – oh, Lord, I'd been told about the Chuck Heston resemblance, naturally, but this is quite unbelievable. Chuck when young, I mean, of course.' She was still holding his hand. 'Sorry, though, I expect you're hopelessly bored by hearing folk react like this, women especially.'

Camilla said: 'Instinct, Ralph. Entirely forgivable, indeed understandable, instinct, Ralph, in your resolute, smooth reaching for the gun.'

Ember was still seated. Rosemary did now let go of his hand and turned to greet Beau. Ralph was glad to see the contact here was briefer, not much more than nominal. This was a girl who knew how to dress and walk and smile and

generally radiate possibilities and, at the same time, appreciated the league difference between someone like Ralph and a
tip-top hanger-on like Beau, but a hanger-on. Ember thought
that in the accountancy field this girl's breasts would not be
easily bettered, nothing flamboyant but cheery.

Maud said: 'Rosemary's got a nice scheme, Ralph, which
would utilize existing facilities. Incredibly simple, really. Brilliantly simple. Difficulties with Shale would result, certainly,
but who's Shale now?'

Rosemary said: 'To muck up that dockside interception
the way you did, Ralph, so that all the shooting took place
aboard the Eton – brilliant. You knew it could never survive
such a fracas. That means virtually unlimited opportunity for
you and, Barney hopes, for us.'

Ember gave a tiny nod, but meaningful and gracious.

'Rosemary's scheme? Well, it involves the taking of an
existing asset and maximizing,' Camilla said. 'But perhaps
this is to put it *too* simply. Yes, I think so. Are there not *three*
assets? Oh, indeed. First, of course, there is Ralph himself.'

'Kind,' Ember muttered.

'*In situ*, established, respected, all of these,' Camilla said.
'I don't think I exaggerate.'

'Thank you,' Ember replied.

'Then Beau,' Camilla said.

Of course, this rambling bitch would have to undo everything she had just said. 'Certainly,' Ember replied.

'Absolutely,' Barney said.

'Beau is essential,' Rosemary said.

Tits aren't everything, you sprightly piece. How about

some sense of proportion? 'Beau always goes the distance,' Ember replied.

Beau held up a chunky, greasy hand to show acknowledgement, a gesture he favoured, either with one hand or both. You would never think someone with cosh fingers like that could be smart with safes.

'The Monty,' Camilla said.

'What?' Ember asked.

'The Monty,' she said. 'Our third existing asset.'

'My club?' Ember replied. 'How the hell does the Monty figure in—'

'Rosemary looked at things for us, Ralph – looked at things post-Eton and saw at once what was dead and what had promise,' Barney said. 'The Eton being patently dead, the Monty is the future.'

'I don't think I understand this,' Ember replied.

Rosemary said: 'Osprey, the Rt. Hon., threshing about, trying to set up a new drugs shop in Noisy Graham's place – pathetic, really. What kind of reliability in Noisy? None. Why that nickname? Because he talks. Seconds itself is utterly unsuitable.'

'Rosemary made a trip and did a survey,' Barney said.

'Too small. Everything would be obvious,' Rosemary replied. 'If you ask me, they're right off balance, Everton and the Rt. Hon. The Anstruther episode at the Eton, and then the intrusion of this girl Esmé and her death – it's made them frantic, made them think they've become losers. They *are*. I'm damned surprised they dared ask someone of your standing to be part of it, Ralph. When Barney told me

Everton was setting up those meetings and inviting you, I thought to myself and actually said to Barney, "This is Osprey gone frantic. Ralph will refuse any amalgamation.'"

'Meeting, not meetings,' Ember replied.

Rosemary said: 'Yes, one wondered why would Everton imagine Ralph Ember might join something so palpably doomed? Ralph Ember, one of the most far-seeing business folk ever. And the only answer I could find was that Everton and the Rt. Hon. have been unhinged by events.'

'This is true, and why I refused,' Ember told them.

'I think we do more or less accept this, Ralph,' Barney replied.

Maud said: 'You say so, Barney, but—'

'The Monty. How does that come in?' Ember replied.

Rosemary was sitting on the edge of the wrecked trampoline. Beau had helped her to some strawberries and ice cream but she was not eating. Her legs were fine too. It astonished Ember that Maud and Camilla would put up with an assembly like this close to Barney.

Rosemary said: 'Ralph, we recognize – of course we do – we recognize that one of the central ambitions of your business life is to bring the Monty to a position where it might stand comparison with some of the famous London clubs – the Garrick, Boodles.'

'It's a slow job, though, Ralph,' Barney said.

Maud said: 'If the jail terms of your membership were laid end to end they'd reach back to Moses.'

Ember said: 'My club will soon—'

'Discreet, high-quality dealing at the Monty would help

transform its standing, Ralph,' Rosemary replied with a great, very personal smile and some symbolic lip-rounding. 'Think how it would be if you brought over the clientele Littlebann had at the Eton. Many of these were influential people, full of prestige and money. This kind of crew would not object to the present racy image of the Monty, so skilfully created by you. That excites them, excites them almost as much as the prospect of picking up their commodity, as long as raciness doesn't slip into massacre. Littlebann had professors, judges, priests, nuns and, naturally, MPs and top-line pimps, among his regulars.'

'Accountants too, Rosemary,' Barney said, grinning.

'Accountants, media execs, porno magnates, solicitors, football managers, video shop owners, high sheriffs, of course,' she replied.

'*The Monty* would be transformed, Ralphy,' Maud said, 'more or less overnight.'

'Basic change of nature,' Camilla said. 'Nobody would deny, I think, that this is what is proposed. Sentimental objections – these are natural from you, Ralph. Indeed, perhaps it is wrong to term them sentimental. That might sound . . . well, dismissive. There are . . . yes, *moral* aspects. I do not think this is too pi a term, moral. You have been struggling for the soul of the Monty, Ralph, just as, for instance, Billy Graham would struggle for the souls of his congregation. It is . . . well, yes, it is a noble purpose. Possibly you feel that a drugs commissariat at the Monty would imply, yes, a kind of degeneration, even if the trade were carried out with supreme discretion. I think we may say that all of us do appreciate this, Ralph – Barney, Maud, Rosemary and myself, oh, indeed, yes, but—'

'Fucking sink or swim, Ralph,' Maud said.

15

Naomi Anstruther began to concentrate on being careful. Harpur wanted to give her a proper, continuous official guard. She refused. It would have more or less imprisoned her, and she had private things to do. There was a debt to Esmé, wasn't there? Naomi could not be sure she had the . . . had the what? The guts . . . the madness . . . the devilment to deal with that debt? But she would not even have the chance to deal with it if Harpur festooned her with nannies.

Of course, Naomi knew Harpur might have put twenty-four-hour watchers on anyway. How would it look for him, and for the force and for the chief, if a girl officer who had just survived one murderous gun battle was left unprotected afterwards and slaughtered? The media noticed such mistakes. But, although she was not trained in surveillance and counter-surveillance, she thought she would spot any attendants. After all, Erogenous Jones, the only real genius at eyeing unobserved, was dead. So, she tried to pick out loiterers charged with her safety, and loiterers charged with something else. And she tried for comfort by repeating to herself that if the people who killed Esmé had wanted to do her as well, they could have, at the same time. Yes, she tried.

Just the same, she stayed vigilant, whether in the flat or outside. She followed a drill, part common sense, part basic trade tips she had absorbed at work. She already had bolts on the front door and now screwed down the windows. She opened the door to nobody without asking identity. Before going out, she would spend a bit of time concealed at the window and survey the street. Naturally, you looked for people who appeared to be idling, but you should do more than that: important to keep vigil long enough to see whether someone who strode past purposefully strode back again purposefully a little later, and then strode just as purposefully past once, twice, twenty times more, seeming to look absolutely nowhere but ahead, and looking absolutely everywhere.

There was a rear-lane entrance to the flats and she used that off and on, though without liking it very much. As tricks went it seemed elementary and obvious, and the lane was very solitary and unlit at night. In the middle of the town, she took to entering one or two of the big stores and standing just inside to scrutinize who followed. Then she would leave, cross the road and turn to watch who came out. If who came out matched who went in after her she would know she had a tail. But, unless she recognized him/her, that would not tell Naomi whether it was a benign tail or a threat. She had not settled yet how she would decide, nor what she would do about it. Run to Harpur or Iles and ask them to sort it out? So far, she had not needed to decide because she had detected nobody. Would a hunter, hunters, give her time to run to Harpur or Iles anyway? Perhaps David and Lee had been told, and really told, not to fuck up this time – to leave no awkward bits, no crazed and therefore dangerous would-be avengers. Oh, Christ, Esmé, how did you ever slip that violent buzz into my mind? But Naomi knew. Her mind was open and changing and available, wasn't it? Rockmain had explained this and gloried in it at Hilston. All that flexibility was a boon then. Rockmain would most likely have told others about his findings too: probably another reason Harpur wanted her continuously in sight. Now, at the window and watching for David or Lee or both before risking a sortie, she realized she was not just untrained, she was an untrained fool. Would Osprey and the Rt. Hon. send the same identifiable men, for God's sake? Anyone out there would suit, either sex. She would really fucking object to being killed by women.

16

Iles said: 'When I survey the situation post-Eton, whose name do you think is the first that bustles into my consciousness? Well, Ralph, obviously, Ralph W. Ember's. I've mentioned this to Harpur, haven't I, Col?'

'Just a general visit, Ralph,' Harpur replied. 'Club licensing formalities, that sort of thing.'

'I'll get some drinks,' Ember said.

'And to the chief – yes, I mentioned you to the chief himself, Ralph,' Iles said. 'I told Mr Lane that you would be a sort of touchstone in the uncertainties after the Eton incident.'

'Port and lemon for you?' Ember replied. 'And yours gin and cider, Mr Harpur, half-pint mug.'

Ember poured Kressmann Armagnac for himself. They took a table at the end of the Monty bar. Harpur longed for the clean, sharp smack of the mixed drink, and the burn in the balls it almost always brought. There was what sounded to Harpur like old-style jazz playing quietly on the Muzak system – one of those Bessie Smith social-conditions numbers, *Woke up this morning and bed bugs had ate my man*.

'Since the Eton Everton Evas Osprey and the Rt. Hon. will know this realm is uniquely difficult to colonize,' Iles said. Here be, as it were, dragons and cannibals. Everton will want

Bill James

to find a local adviser to pilot his missionaries in at least the early moments. What better adviser than Ralph W. Ember? They've approached you? I can *feel* they have. Tell me their fucking plan, Ralphy. I have to put it to you direct because, although Harpur certainly has data-rich insights from one of his crooked whisperers, he naturally doesn't disclose such information, do you, Col, you internalizing wank?'

'The club's looking splendid, Ralph,' Harpur replied. 'Brasswork beautifully cared for and the rubber plants so plump.'

'Thank you,' Ember replied. 'One must offer a decent setting to patrons, that's how I see it.'

Iles said: 'When I suggested to the chief you and Osprey might be in talks, Mr Lane laughed – I'm afraid so, Ralphy. Ever seen the chief when he laughs: the rude vividness of his gums and those unmistakably low-born, unmerry eyes? He asked whether Ralph Ember was really of a crook status to deal with Everton Evas Osprey and the Rt. Hon. Rest assured I told the chief that there was a good deal more to Ralphy Ember than jibbering cowardice, though admittedly there *was* jibbering cowardice, often bordering on incontinence and/or paralysis. Hence, possibly, the failure to intercept at the Eton – though I do see this might have been long-term strategy also. I mentioned to the chief as the positives your Heston looks, your scar, your family, the women, and those accumulations of villainous wealth, naturally.'

'Harpur still shagging your wife on an intermittent basis, Mr Iles?' Ember replied. 'I think it's large of you to bring up that child of hers, what with the possibilities.'

'Some new venue, Ralphy?' Iles asked. 'That what they're looking for? And you'll lead them to one? Have you considered that Jeremy Littlebann will hate you for Pied-Pipering his few last distinguished customers away? Could Littlebann of the Eton turn murderous, do you think, Col, if stricken by frenzy?'

'Is your university course still in suspension, Ralph?' Harpur replied.

'And then there's Mansel and Alf Ivis, your seeming established associates,' Iles said. 'Don't they mind if you ditch them and cuddle up to Everton – that's besides making them botch the Eton interception?'

'So much work with the club lately, Mr Harpur, that I had to ask for a year out,' Ember replied. 'The university was very reasonable.'

'Luckily, Ralph Ember knows about self-defence,' Iles said. 'Oh, Ralphy panics, yes. But Ralphy also knows the front of a pistol from the back when it's *his* skin perilled.'

'So they *should* make all efforts to help mature students, Ralph,' Harpur replied. 'They have all kinds of problems beyond the academic.'

'Of course, you're into students now, aren't you, Mr Harpur?' Ember said. 'I think I saw her around the common room occasionally. Very young and vulnerable but above consent age, definitely, or how could she be an undergraduate?'

'Manse Shale would never act hastily, Ralph,' Iles said. 'This will be a boardroom matter and he'd want a proper assessment of the scene before ordering anything brutal against you. Or your lovely family. Well, one of your daughters is pretty safe anyway, isn't she, at that finishing school lock-up in France? What's the airport for Poitiers? I don't see Manse sending hit people out there, though, for heaven's sake, do you? Your house, on the other hand – Low Pastures – perhaps a bit exposed, set in all that gorgeous open ground and woodland? Put up wire and the whole ducal ambience is spoiled, I agree. Who wants to live behind a Berlin Wall? Not your wife. Margaret, is it? Oh, things will probably be all right. Manse likes due process. And I don't believe Ivis would do anything wild, uncommissioned by Shale, though Alfie did have a lovely flair with handguns once, didn't he, Col? Remind me – was it Alfie we thought did Big Paul Legge?'

'I envy you your courage in taking on new intellectual challenges at the college, Ralph,' Harpur replied.

'This is a girl with a perfect chest, yes, Mr Harpur?' Ember asked. 'I suppose it would be. Denise something?'

'Yes, Legge,' Iles replied. 'Back in the 1980s? Of course, Littlebann might turn out less self-controlled than Manse, Ralph. Jeremy's a man very likely obsessed by grievance. I expect you carry something. Been to see Amy and Leyton Harbinger?'

Harpur and Iles were on an evening visit to Ember's club. Harpur swallowed half his drink. Ralph always managed the right proportions, one-third, two-thirds gin to cider. Gazing around at the mahogany panels and rich-coloured hardwood floor, Harpur could nearly imagine the club back to its former role as meeting place for professional and genuine businessmen. The Monty remained influential, but in a changed style: probably some of the most celebrated recent local crimes germinated here, and even jobs more far-flung. Iles loved to visit. He would stride in, staring around, alight with that terrorizing grin of his, noting former targets and targets to be. He could bring thirty or forty seconds' silence when he appeared in the doorway of the Monty's bar, jolly as the Last Trump. He adored this effect. It was the ACC who had proposed a call on Ember tonight.

Iles took a long pull at the port and lemon, held some of it in his mouth for a while, savouring, swallowed rapturously and said: 'Ralph W. Ember is someone whose loyalties are above all else local. He would not sincerely want to bring in London traders who've already done deaths on our terrain. All right, he might *appear* to have fallen into an agreement with them, but this is no enduring relationship. A compromise Ralph has been forced into temporarily. Yes, pressure. I reminded Harpur that pressure was something Ralph Ember tended to give way to rather than resist, owing to his poltroon core, but I also pointed out that Ralph Ember was capable of second thoughts, some sturdy. Ralph would wish to help us stop this hellish incursion, I remarked to Col fondly.'

Ember smiled a little, so that his jaw scar stretched and grew beautifully luminous. 'Pressure? Yes, I do get correspondence from various pressure groups with London headquarters, it's true, Mr Iles. These would be organizations who've spotted my letters on mainly environmental matters in the press and wish to offer or, indeed, ask for help. Such interest in my small efforts are very gratifying.'

'So where are they fucking going, Ralphy?' Iles replied.

'Who?' Ember asked.

'Everton.' Iles became reflective. 'Or then there's the Monty itself. People coming into the city, looking for a distribution point – isn't the Monty just made for it?'

He waved a hand to indicate the club's rich scope and suitability. Their table was near the famous framed, enlarged photograph of Monty members leaving on an excursion to Paris around 1990, a joyous picture, with Caspar Nottage and Bespoke Vincent prominent and looking very *entente cordiale* at this early stage. During the trip these two kidnapped a tart for something over thirty-six hours and broke the arms of at least one pimp who came searching for her. Caspar was badly clawed by the girl and still carried the marks on his neck. Bespoke had his nose smashed in a fight during the attempted rescue, disfiguring him permanently too. He had a happy nature, though, and could joke about his present ugliness and breathing difficulties.

'I should have thought before of the Monty,' Iles remarked. 'Heard anything along those lines, Harpur?'

'Here's Beau now,' Harpur replied.

'Beau!' the ACC cried, delighted. He stood with his arms open, offering a welcome. 'Suave as damned ever. Don't part with that bomber jacket. It's emblematic. We were just saying what a brilliant trading spot the Monty would make – a brilliant *quality* trading spot, a spot with lineage. This been mooted in your presence at all, Beau? Clearly, they'd have to consult Beau.'

'Trading? Are you by any chance referring to drugs, Mr

Iles?' Beau replied. 'I hope not. The integrity of the club is central to Ralph's thinking. In my view, nobody would have the gall or crudity to put such a proposal to him.'

'Ah, so someone *has*?' Iles said. 'This is Everton or other nice, thoughtful folk?'

17

'And the Lord said to the man sick of the palsy, "Take up thy bed and walk."'

'Allelujah.'

'Praise the Lord.'

'He had been changed, that man sick of the palsy – in an instant.'

'Amen, amen.'

'He could be changed like that by the Lord's word, and anyone here tonight who is sick in spirit and helpless, he or she, can be changed, in an instant.'

'Praise the Lord.'

Naomi Anstruther loved these meetings. The minister's name was Anstruther too. That coincidence delighted her almost as much as the services. It was worth the risk to get here. Always she came and went by taxi. That meant some walking to find a cab rank or reach a street where they cruised. Obviously, she never phoned to be picked up. That much at least she had learned from Harpur and Iles in the safe-house days. The walking and hanging about were the worst part of things, but she tried to keep an eye everywhere and did one of those long surveys from the flat window before leaving, telling herself it might be David or Lee or both or neither. She would try to get out when there was nobody in the street at all, or nobody she could see. Then she went fast towards the taxis. And more or less the same drill when the meetings ended. They wouldn't kill someone on the way home from church, would they? No?

At the gospel hall services she could bask in this message of change and newness. The Rev. Anstruther taught that a person's 'self' could suddenly become a different self. There were times when she needed to be assured this was OK and better than OK. Now and then it terrified her that she could shift so easily in and out of various identities, various versions of N. Anstruther.

The minister told his congregation: 'And this man sick of the palsy, he had been changed even before the strength came back to his legs. Yes, the Lord had already said to him, "Son, thy sins be forgiven thee." Suddenly all that load of sin is gone. Gone!'

'Amen!'

At Hilston Manor, Andrew Rockmain had used the term 'protean' about Naomi's ego, meaning it took any number of forms, like the sea god in classical myth, Proteus. Wow. On some days she was still a standard-issue cop, with a standard-issue respect for properly regulated behaviour. And then, abruptly, she would slump into that obsession with violent, lawless private vengeance, first suggested by Esmé. Slump? Maybe it was a *climb*, a soaring of the best of her.

When such doubts tore at her lately she would try to get to one of these services at the Church of the Free Gospel, with its long, plain benches and plain, small pulpit. It had terse texts painted on plain white walls, between big plain glass windows, protected outside by heavy mesh. Everything was solid and simple, except the beliefs. Central to the faith of people here was a certainty that the self could diametrically switch. *Ye must be born again*, was one painted text. To the congregation here, this kind of transformation was not simply credible but crucial. *Ye MUST be born again*. One or more of them would always mention the persecutor of Christians, Saul, who in a flash turned himself into St Paul on the road to Damscus. What did that say about the consistency of someone's being? It said it did not exist. Naomi was not looking for conversion, but she was looking for happy illustrations, that what anybody seemed to be one day need not be what she had to be non-stop.

The minister continued: 'And such wondrous change and newness – newness inside, not just his legs – that newness through the Lord is available to each and every one of us now, today.'

'Allelujah.'

The variability in her selfhood scared Naomi. Rockmain had been thrilled by the 'flexibility of your psyche', as he called it in one of his more intelligible slabs of bullshit. And he had quoted several of the biggest operators – Jung and Holub were names that stuck – quoted these to prove that everyone had some of this flexibility, and that it was a positive, a desirable plus. Jung had declared he did not fancy being forever Jung, Jung and more Jung, apparently, even though by then the name Jung was obviously a goer.

To Naomi this inconstancy sometimes sounded like madness, felt like a slide into jumble, chaos. Iles seemed to think so, too. She often recalled a scene from a Woody Allen comedy, *Broadway Danny Rose*, where some cracked American-Sicilian screams from a balcony, 'Vendetta! Vendetta! Vendetta!' after love trouble. Had the deaths of three people close to Naomi pushed her into spells of craziness? Had spells of craziness become normal to her fluctuating personality? Personalities.

The Rev. Bart Anstruther announced in his lavishly refined accent: 'I'm going to ask one of our number, Graham Goff, to come up here and tell how the Lord changed his life and gloriously made him whole, within and without.'

'Hallelujah.'

Naomi knew Graham Goff. When he was a small-time drugs pusher doing mainly cannabis but some heroin he was called Untidy Graham, in part to distinguish him from Noisy Graham, who ran Seconds restaurant, and in part because Untidy and the dump where he lived were so damned soiled. She had been on raids at his unbelievably grubby rooms. Untidy was inclined to get born again, then slip back to work for a while, and subsequently get born again again and so on. During these Godly stretches, he would street-preach and carry a banner. Tonight, he had on a quite spruce cord jacket and a clean collarless shirt. He began to talk enthusiastically about his progress from hash and smack trader to satisfied soldier of the cross. Naomi enthused too. Untidy showed what could be done with an adaptable soul.

After the service he came down the aisle to talk with her, beaming like the returned Prodigal's father.

'I'm really glad you're out of street trading, Gray,' Naomi said.

'With the Lord's help.'

'Pity there aren't more like you.'

'Ah, true. I fear, though, the empire of the devil grows, not shrinks. I pray to the Lord that he will turn back these evil forces, but – Well, not yet, it seems, but in the Lord's good time. Probably you know about Panicking and these London people.'

The organ was playing 'Will There Be Any Stars in My Crown?' as people left. She wasn't sure she heard him properly.

'You mean Everton Osprey? The Rt. Hon?' Naomi asked.

'With Panicking and that other Graham, the one they call Noisy.'

The minister approached. He was beautifully dressed in a dark double-breasted suit and radiant dog collar. 'Ah,' he cried, 'a lady I once knew as Angela Rivers, yes? But then I learn from others and from pictures in the newspapers and on TV that she is actually a police officer called Naomi Anstruther – yes, Anstruther! – but was working undercover and needed an alias. Does it matter? I don't think so. The Lord can see who we are.'

'When I first came it was to suss out this other Anstruther I'd read of on campaign billboards,' she replied. I was curious. Yes, that was pre the Eton fracas. I was someone else then. But not.'

'Perhaps you thought I might be family.' He laughed. 'But the Rev. Bart Anstruther is Jamaican and black. Naomi Anstruther who was Angela Rivers is English-born and white. To the Lord, though—'

'None of it matters,' Naomi said. 'I love all the variety, the vagaries of names, nothing, but nothing, fixed.'

Untidy said: 'Absolutely. Two Grahams, two Anstruthers, Angela Rivers who was *not* Angela Rivers.'

Bart Anstruther said: 'And you, Naomi, are you now like Graham, one of the Lord's? There is room in His father's house for both police and ex-pushers.'

'Tell me more about Panicking and these London biggies, Graham,' Naomi replied.

'Unholy people,' he said. 'Panicking is what we would call an off-white sepulchre, isn't that right, Bart?'

'Whited sepulchre.'

'The pure exterior – these letters to the paper on civic matters, daughters in private education, many a gymkhana,' Untidy said, 'and underneath always the corruption, the greed, the beautiful knack of getting away with it.'

'Oh, you're interested in all that commercial scheming by the drug combos, are you, Naomi?' Anstruther said. He sat down on one of the benches alongside them and carefully settled a trousers crease. 'The Eton sinks, as it were, and somewhere else is urgently needed to replace its dirty trade. Evil does not sleep, Naomi – not until the Lord returns, and then it will sleep for ever, the sleep of the dead.'

'And do Osprey and the Rt. Hon. come into the town now, to plan, Gray?' Naomi asked.

'They meet with Panicking and Beau,' Untidy said. 'Maybe in the town. Or I heard Bath. An hotel? Could be a place called the Edmund. Sometimes with Noisy, I suppose. Why do you ask, Naomi? I think you wish to carry to them the words of salvation, yea, even to such seemingly lost ones.' Untidy's long, knobbly face grew encouraging.

'Or for some other purpose, Naomi?' the Rev. Anstruther asked, eyes worldly all at once and sharp. 'These crooks have offended you, given you grief? They are very heavy people, very hard. Take it easy, kid. Remember, "Vengeance is mine, saith the Lord. I will repay." *His. He* will repay, not you. Will you be all right going home? These are not kindly streets. They don't just pass by on the other side, they run across and bop you. And your pal's funeral. Esmé. I've read about her in the press. Mind you look out if you go. I hear from one of the clubs – the Chiffon, was it? – that she's a friend of yours. People tell the Rev. Bart things, you know. This is a community. You'll be a right target there. Considered that? There are coroner's delays? Think about not going. Please. What did the Lord say: "Let the dead bury their dead"? He could be a hard one, you know, not all "Blessed are the meek." '

Untidy said: 'Having eternity on tap, He was able to visualize far ahead to such situations as Esmé's funeral.'

18

Mansel Shale did not mind London too much. He liked Regent Street – that curve at one end and shops selling Scotch blankets to tourists. He hated streets that were too straight. Where was the fucking style in streets like that, just onward and onward? Right back in the old days, some smart burgess type must of seen the plans and asked for a slight but important change: 'Give that street a bit of a curl to it, would you?'

Shale said: 'We need a procedure in case there's more than the two of them, Alf. They come with personnel, we leave right away. No need to pull weapons – unless they do, naturally – but one of us keeps facing them the whole time we're getting to the door. You. If it's locked we'll know complications and we're into shooting. You do the Rt. Hon., me Everton. I won't enjoy this. Gunfire in someone's accommodation – uncivilized. If I go down, inform Lowri. I promised her she'd be first told when I'm destroyed. She been close to me for weeks at a time, that one. The other girls will pick it up from TV and that, but keep them away from the funeral – women fighting over a body in the crematorium, it's crude.'

'I think things will go fine here, Manse,' Ivis replied. 'If I may say, you've achieved a true diplomatic stroke. By agreeing to meet on their ground and after earlier enmities you've put them under an obligation.'

Of course, originally this conversational bugger Alfie had said Shale should not come at all, too perilous. Shale trampled that, and Alfie knew how to make the best of whatever Shale decided. Alfie took orders, this was his personal flair.

'I hope I know about reasonableness in business,' Shale replied.

'Your essence, Manse.'

'So what the fuck else could I do but come? They want a peace meeting. They say "Get here." Choice? Some ways London's a fucking pain – taxis all over that Pall Mall supposed to be going somewhere vital – I mean, what ponce would call a street Pall Mall? – but if I don't show, they go on with Panicking and cut me out, meaning worse than cut me out. And you.'

'With respect, Manse, we do not know, I mean really *know* they've talked to Ralph Ember. This is Littlebann's word only. My own feeling is that Osprey and the Rt. Hon. have looked around post-Eton for the most effective means of access to our realm and they inevitably came up with the name of Mansel Shale. We, perhaps, don't disclose we know they may have spoken to Ember.'

'Where'd he get a name like Everton Evas Osprey? You telling me that's genuine, even for a black? Evas – what's that? Some Peruvian hair gel?'

'They want it up here for security, Manse. Everton wouldn't like to be spotted in our domain at this stage. He mustn't hint his intentions to other traders or the police. Nor to Panicking, obviously, in case he has to be, well, sidelined – especially if they've had earlier talks with him.'

'So, when they met Panicking did they drag him to London, did they shit? A hotel with character in Bath. I bet wide old washbasins.'

'It's only Littlebann's word says Ralph's gone over, Manse.'

'I would of preferred this meeting in a club, something like that, Alf,' Shale replied. 'Expensive West End flats – soundproofed, unfavourable. But what London club would let Everton in?'

He and Ivis were making their way on foot up Piccadilly. It was a mild, high-skied summer's day and he watched people doing that special London style of walk – strong legs, jackets open and flapping, full of destination. Like the taxis. There could not be that many places to fucking go to.

'They're auditioning, that's what, Alf. They see Panicking first and ask him do a turn, show his range. Now me, us. Not to boast, but I'm used to being top banana, like a matter of course. *We'll be in touch. Possibly.* Pissing me about, Alfred. Us.'

'My view, for what it's worth, Manse, is they'd possibly suck all the information they could from Panicking – and it can't be denied that Panicking would have some of that – then they discard him and move on to the real choice. That means Mansel Shale, Manse.'

'Take him out?'

'Everton is known for thoroughness,' Ivis replied. They

walked past some big art gallery in Piccadilly, with a crowd queueing, mad for paintings. It was David Hockney, those blue swimming pools in California with several bits of light to them. Shale still preferred the Pre-Raphaelites. Swimming pools were fine but they only went so far.

'Well, Everton's going to look at us, Alfred, and think here's the outfit what got itself penetrated by some kid girl cop – Anstruther. Think of Panicking putting in the venom with them re that. Panicking got words, you know, a slab of education. Yes, perhaps he been alive too long.'

There was a drill for getting into the flats that Shale did not like, first a voice box, and then another door with a porter to take you up in the lift. To Shale this porter looked damned nimble and eye-bright for a porter, and too much respect, no uniform. Porters should be old with a limp and couldn't care less. This looked like it could be a hazardous spot and Shale did not feel sure they could cope. For someone with such a nice accent, Alfie used to be very quick and on the spot with a gun, but this was a long time ago – nothing since Big Paul Legge, probably, nothing except duck, and rat broods in his lighthouse.

Everton Evas Osprey said: 'Tell me now, Mr Mansel Shale, please, what did you expect to see on meeting Everton Evas Osprey today, friend? I'd really like you to be frank about this, you know, because I believe a man is made up not just of what he sort of *is* but also, you know, of others' impressions of him, feelings about him, even if those impressions and feelings come prior to the person in question actually being met. As I see it, we are all accumulations.

This is a word you'll often hear me use, Mr Shale, and not to do with commercial gain, which might be your first thought, naturally, but to do with magic layers of the personality in every damned one of us. This is something I read a lot about. Everton Evas Osprey! Here's a charming mouthful, yes? Don't tell me you came here expecting someone white and considerate – looking like ex-Bishop David Shepherd of Liverpool or Mr John Selwyn Gummer, once Minister of Agriculture.'

'This is Alf Ivis,' Shale replied. 'He takes care of some of my accounts. Luckily, he got contact with all sorts at many levels.'

Osprey said: 'The Rt. Hon. here, he wanted to place this meeting in the RAF Club just up the road, you know, the Rt. Hon. having been quite a flight-lieutenant or more in his earlier days, before investing the final gratuity in look-ahead business. His Royal Air Force flying career had some episodes of distinction, almost a gong. But me, I preferred the privacy here for our get-together, feeling that you would too.'

'This so-called fucking porter,' Shale replied. 'He one of your roughies?'

'Danielle?' Everton replied. 'Comes with the flats. Danielle's a lovely asset to our lives here, useful when the butler's off. Mr Shale, Danielle moves with such deftness you would not believe between genders, and when I say Danielle I do so, you know, because that is the present preference as I understand, rather than Frederick. These aspects of a personality accumulate, and they separate too.'

The Rt. Hon. said: 'Everton mentions the RAF. One thing

among many one learned there is never allow the loss of men in action to deflect policy. That way stagnation. Yes, we took casualties at the Eton. Hired hands, sure, but I'm hardly one to think of front-line people as fodder. This is not the damned First War, I hope. We note the casualties, regret them, naturally, but we find lessons in that hard incident. We do not abandon our project in your area.'

Ivis said: 'Mansel's exactly the sort to understand resilience, doggedness, for these are qualities he has in abundance.'

This flat had some good furniture, genuine wood on all sides, and Shale took a long gaze at it while he worked out angles of fire. The Rt. Hon. had stayed on his feet. He wore a purple-and-black-striped soccer shirt, grey waistcoat with pockets and jeans. The waistcoat pockets looked deep and one of them had something more than a letter from his mother in it. The Rt. Hon. paced about now and then, like he was used to patrolling the heavens in his valour days and still needed movement. If it came to anything he could be down behind one of those big cream settees very fast and sweetly placed to bang off at Shale and Alfie in the big cream armchairs. This was fine fat furniture and the settee would stop anything up to cruise missiles. The fat arms of the fat chairs would put frames around Shale and Alfie for him – just to fire anywhere between would do damage, and this was without Everton himself opening up, plus that fucking Danielle coming in from one of three doors with weaponry as soon as she had the signal. Or Frederick. Shale did not mind cream as a colour for furniture. It showed there was money around and not too much worry about stains, it could all be replaced. Yes.

Everton said: 'Things change, you know, things change. Accumulations. Not just accumulations of impressions about folk, but I mean new conditions coming from all over. I suppose we were like enemies. There was Mansel Shale and Alfred Ivis against us, Everton Evas Osprey and the Rt. Hon., because we were interested in your territory. And Ralph W. Ember is maybe an enemy too. Did he drop us in that situation at the Eton Boating Song? Ralph's a matter of difficulty. But change. The Rt. Hon. and Everton Evas Osprey look towards that territory now, today, and we see people there who are familiar with that territory and maybe can help us. And you, Mansel Shale and Alfred Ivis, perhaps you look *our* way and see people who can give you some dimension in that region, extra dimension, you know. Here we have a new situation, built by these accumulations, so you are willing to come to London and right into our fastness here, and we are happy to welcome you. I see all the currents coming together for a time, forming for the present one steady, serene yet powerful relationship.'

Ivis said: 'Manse dotes on serenity.'

'Look here, Shale, at this point we'd like to bring in a third participant on our side of the meeting,' the Rt. Hon. said. 'Not something we would do from the outset or without your permission, since a superiority in numbers might trouble you.'

'This is that Danielle?' Shale grunted. He sat up straighter in the fat chair, glanced about more.

'Danielle is but Danielle,' the Rt. Hon. replied, 'or Frederick. No. Would you object to Lincoln W. Lincoln joining us? This is the lad known in your region as Lovely Mover, I believe.'

'He got away from the Eton?' Shale replied.

'Him,' the Rt. Hon. said. 'Clever boy.'

'On the run,' Shale said.

'He's a trained warrior. He keeps in touch,' the Rt. Hon. replied. 'Lincoln knows your domain well, having lived there. He'll have a contribution to make in talks.'

'Where is he?' Shale asked. 'In the flat already?'

'Not at all,' the Rt. Hon. replied. 'That would be extremely improper and potentially threatening from your point of view. We can phone Linc, if you agree, and he'll be here in five minutes. Alfred can, of course, frisk him.'

'Can *we* frisk *you?*' Shale said.

'Or we you?' the Rt. Hon. replied. 'Two to two. Balance of power, as the strategists call it.'

Shale saw Alfie staring at him, trying to read him. Then Alfie said: 'This is a new aspect, someone extra. We need a spell to consider it.'

'Of course. As I said, it would take five minutes,' the Rt. Hon. replied.

'Well, five minutes,' Alfred said with a hurt gasp.

Shale said: 'I get brought into this territory, and then I get asked if I'd like to meet someone who came into *my* territory and tried to kill one of my people. Quaint?'

'Not actually one of your people, was it, Manse?' the Rt. Hon. replied. 'This was the officer, Anstruther, a plant.'

156

'It *could* of been one of my people. This Lovely Mover and the others would of still tried to kill her. On your fucking orders.'

'Ah, this is what I mean when I say accumulations,' Everton replied. 'Changes – they accumulate. There are shifts, there are new tones. People like Mansel Shale and Everton Evas Osprey know how to adjust.'

'Lovely Mover?' Shale said. 'A short-time visitor to us, that's all. What'll he tell me about my area I don't know already? But bring the fucker in if you want to. Am I scared of some slippery corporal?'

Ivis said: 'Manse, I wonder if you've thought that—'

'Yes, send for him,' Shale said.

'The accessory aspect,' Ivis said. 'This is someone sought for murder, two men down. If you are subsequently found to have known his whereabouts and to have been in discussions with him—'

'Yes, send for the bugger,' Shale replied. 'I suppose he's waiting in Danielle's cubbyhole.'

'Danielle's very fussy about whom she admits to her cubbyhole,' Everton said. 'Frederick less fussy, you know.' He phoned somewhere for Lovely Mover.

The furniture in this flat looked a mixture to Shale. There were the big settees and fat armchairs and then straight, narrow white and black wooden chairs with very tall slatted backs, like they were made in case of a sudden flood, so you could locate people sitting underneath the water. The walls were white. The lampshades looked like nesting boxes.

The Rt. Hon. saw Shale staring about and said: 'Basically, Rennie Mackintosh in style, with some additions, of course.'

'I love her,' Shale replied.

'Charles Rennie Mackintosh,' the Rt. Hon. said.

'I love him too,' Shale replied, 'and Danielle and Frederick.' If you saw Osprey and the Rt. Hon. outside this top-grade flat and away from the top-grade hotch-potch furniture, you would not of thought they had power. They were both small, no shoulders or weight. You might of thought they were a couple of assistants in a quality shop selling ornaments or Chinese fans, something delicate like that.

'Ah, here's dear Lincoln now,' Everton said. 'I'd like you to let Mr Alfred Ivis examine you for armament, Lincoln.'

Lovely Mover cried 'Oh,' and swiftly put a hand over his dick region, like a girl hearing a suggestion from someone old or with boils.

'It doesn't matter,' Shale said. 'Would you offer it if he was carrying?'

Lovely Mover said in that London slob voice: 'Yes, when I was down your area I did a little survey, of course, which it works out you and Panicking take about six hundred grand a year from trading, before costs.'

Alf had a not bad giggle. 'This sounds like a figure someone dreamed for you, I'm afraid,' he said.

'We don't consider six hundred K negligible, Shale, nor anywhere near negligible, but nor do we consider it anywhere near optimum,' the Rt. Hon. said. 'We see potential and are sure we can help you towards it.'

Lovely Mover said: 'Costs like cooperation money to

Jeremy Littlebann at the Eton. Fifty grand p.a., plus payments to some police, and which were about thirty, thirty-five, but not top police, just Drugs Squad low-life.'

Ivis said in friendly style: 'More make-believe, I fear.'

'These are high overheads,' the Rt. Hon. replied.

'Littlebann's finished,' Shale said. 'Not a charge now.'

'Of course Littlebann's finished,' the Rt. Hon. replied. 'That's where the new needs start, don't they? But there'll be canvassing for another distribution point. Trade has to continue. And that franchise figure will be known and regarded down there as standard. Don't be offended, but we doubt whether locals like you and Panicking could reduce this, as it most certainly should be reduced. You're associated with prevailing values there. This will be the beauty of coming in from outside – no precedents, and some uneasinesses about how Everton might react if there were resistance to tighter terms, like fifteen, twenty grand. Everton has that kind of image.'

You could see why the Rt Hon. might of been a top pilot, if all that RAF shit was true. He had a little, very round head that would fit so sweetly into a flying helmet, nothing knobbly. His face was round too, but not boyish – more like a school-size old white football that had lost some air and went in a bit on one side, the right today. But maybe it would be the left on some days, or both.

Lovely Mover said: 'You and Panicking struggling all the time for a fix-up with the big police there, which is Harpur and Iles and maybe the chief, but this never even gets off the ground, and you're putting cash to like just sergeants and DCs, which leaves a lot of gaps and you're missing out bad.'

'Listen, you prick with your prickish walk, if I'm missing out, how come I'm asked here so urgent?' Shale replied. 'Everton wants to join up with someone who's missing out? Some fuck-up you and your friends done at the Eton. What else you going to fuck up? Christ, you really think you could do a proper survey of my business?' Shale disliked these figures getting put around in front of Alfred. Alf did some of his books, but not the main books, obviously, and hearing of amounts like this could give him a reaction. Shale said: 'What goes on between me and top police is not something to be discovered by a kid with a fucking name like Lincoln W. Lincoln.'

'I know you have been wondering why we don't offer you refreshment after all this journeying,' Everton Osprey replied. 'We did not want to seem to be softening you up for a deal, or clouding your gun eye in case of a little outbreak here. But now we've had a few exchanges, some quite stern, you know, I feel drinks and a canapé or two might be useful, don't you, Mr Shale? Bring in the trolley from the other room please, Lincoln.'

This might of looked pretty good to some – Lovely Mover in his fucking flash jacket treated like the butler – but Shale did not like it.

'Me,' he replied. 'I'll bring the trolley.'

'Ah,' Osprey said. 'You suspect that if Lincoln had been searched you would find no gun, but now he can go out of sight and pick one up. A plot. All the same, I would prefer it, you know, if you allowed Lincoln to bring the trolley,' Osprey said. 'Call it a whim?'

Ivis said: 'Nobody admires whims more than Mansel, but—'

'Oh, let the bugger fetch it,' Shale said. Always he wearied of safety routines. They could seem so damned impolite.

Lovely Mover went into an adjoining room, stepping with that famous springy ease, like he knew he would win. He had the sort of face that could act harmlessness from Adam's apple to hairline. He did not seem to have any scars, though he must have pissed off many heavy folk with his ways. Alf crouched forward in the fat armchair. He still kept his hand off the gun butt under his jacket, but looked very ready. The wooden trolley came through ahead of Lovely Mover. It did not look like a trolley. For a second, Shale was not sure *what* it looked like, and then he saw that Lovely Mover, pushing it, was different. He had put a blue yachting cap on the back of his head and held a short pipe unlit between his teeth, like Popeye. The idea was he was a sailor suddenly, and the trolley had been turned into a boat. They had fixed wooden struts to its front joining into a point, and tacked bits of plywood to these to make the bows. Black circles had been drawn on the wood, meaning portholes. Also a name for this vessel was printed here, FRIEND-SHIP, what you could call a joke. In the front of the top of the trolley stuck into some sort of weight there was a mast made most probably from half a broom handle, and this had a piece of white material tied to it, maybe a piece of tablecloth, and the other end fastened to the back of the trolley. On this sail was written in the same kind of black letters, WELCOME TO M. SHALE. Lovely Mover was not really walking but skipping, maybe supposed to be a hornpipe. Some fucking farce. The name FRIEND-SHIP was also written on his hat band.

Osprey said: 'I thought a little gesture, you know, to show appreciation for you coming here from your wonderful sea-girt town. And then Panicking. His supplier is into yachts. We have to keep up.'

'This is certainly appreciated,' Shale replied, and he gave quite a smile as well as a nod. 'Touching.'

'If there's one thing Manse is in sympathy with it's the whole maritime ambience,' Ivis said.

Osprey poured drinks. There were some bits of things to eat.

The Rt. Hon. said: 'You'll know, of course, that we talked to Ralph Ember.'

Osprey said: 'People like Mr Shale are never short of information.'

'Originally, we thought that a good agreement might be arrived at between us on the one side and you and Ember on the other,' the Rt. Hon. said.

'So you talk to him separate and in secret in a fucking nine-star Bath hotel,' Shale replied.

'Information!' Osprey cried, and had a guffaw. 'Bath I adore, as you've probably heard too. Was there ever a period for style like Regency?' His face went really content.

Osprey could been liked by many, except for the way his moustache sat there so sick, like a roadside refugee in the war. He had on a short-sleeved pullover in a paisley pattern which did not seem right for someone doing smack, crack and everything else super-wholesale. It might be to show he had no armament aboard, but his trousers were loose lightweight, and would take a pistol in a side pocket.

'The talks with Ralph were a stage, that's all,' the Rt. Hon. said. 'Everton likes to follow protocol, accommodate all parties. It was always our intention to bring you in.'

Osprey said: 'Look, now, Lincoln has been joshing you about the level of your police contacts, Mansel – all right, to call you Mansel at this stage?'

Ivis said: 'Manse hates formality.'

'But, you know, Mansel, Lincoln appreciates and we all appreciate that you may be working towards a charming agreement with substantial officers. Well, to name names, Detective Chief Superintendent Colin Harpur, Assistant Chief Desmond Iles, and even the chief himself, Mr Mark Lane. We know that such negotiations take much deftness and much time.'

'We would be prepared to invest on a mega scale in any firm that secured such an arrangement,' the Rt. Hon. said.

'So you do your best to fuck it up,' Shale replied. 'Senior officers get edgy when a gang shoot at their girl detective and then kill one of that girl detective's friends, plus defacement.'

Osprey said: 'I had to ask myself what should be done when a girl comes into our trading area and aims very improper questions. Now, I expect you thought it would be a constructive idea for you to knock over the people who did that girl in Cardiff, so putting you very right with Anstruther, who would talk to upper ranks on your account. We understand that, Mansel. Perhaps you planned doing it at the funeral. But this excellent meeting today has really moved many of those considerations into the past. I see now it's not wise to target the girl, Anstruther, despite the brutal intentions she had with the other one, Esmé. Yes, if we expect you to produce an agreement with high police, it's counterproductive to damage subordinate police.'

There was real comradeship in Osprey's big sigh and in his eyes. This was a sod you had to watch non-stop.

Osprey said: 'Here's what happened. We've decided, after consideration, and after further information, that we must forget Panicking Ralph Ember. Oh, I know he's been your associate, but he's unreliable, Mansel. This is someone getting considerable pressure, we believe, from his supplier in Hampshire. Ralph is not the kind who can withstand that kind of pressure, regrettably.'

'He'll set up an operation, backed by Barney Coss, in his club, the Monty,' the Rt. Hon. said.

'So you come to me,' Shale replied.

'You're lucky,' Lovely Mover said.

'You exclusively, Mansel,' Osprey said.

'This is all the finance and know-how and protection you're ever going to need,' Lovely Mover said.

'Manse is short of none of these,' Ivis replied. 'But, of course, I cannot pre-judge his response to your offer.'

'We know that response will be positive,' the Rt. Hon. said.

'What happens to Ember?' Shale asked. 'Look, don't tell me to get rid of Ralphy.'

'I'm certain you don't speak out of fear,' the Rt. Hon. replied.

Of course, in slimy London lingo this meant he wasn't a bit certain.

'He's too local,' Shale said.

'You've had to take out local folk before, I expect,' the Rt. Hon. replied.

Shale said: 'But Ralphy is big local, like really part of things. It would seem ... oh, seem *disgusting* for me to do him.'

'The *feel* of the situation,' Ivis explained. 'Manse is always so hot on that. Decorum.'

'You heard of the Leaning Tower of Pisa – a landmark that's more important than the town,' Shale said. 'Ralph is like that in our realm. He's our trembling tower. He's a feature.'

'Oh, don't worry about Ralph,' the Rt. Hon. replied. 'Everton is always very thorough.'

'Yes, I know,' Shale replied, 'but how will—'

'Really thorough,' the Rt. Hon. said.

In the Jaguar on the way home, Ivis said: 'I don't think triumph is too strong a word to describe your achievements there, Manse. This was people paying homage. That sailing boat and Lovely Mover's cap – brilliant but deserved tributes to you. And their policy change.'

'Which?' Shale asked.

'Well two, really. First, they'll drop Panicking. Second, they'll leave Anstruther unharmed.'

'Did you hear him? Accumulations,' Shale replied. 'Accumulations! Jesus, Osprey's mad?'

Denzil was driving, pretending not to hear – that fashion he had. There should of been a partition for private talks in the back, but Shale would not have one. It would seem high and mighty to block out the chauffeur, even a fucking chauffeur like Denzil.

'We won't need to get to that funeral in Cardiff now,' Alfred said.

He would think this was a true blessing.

Shale said: 'Yes, we'll go. Maybe I'll mock up a little attack and, like, save her from it. Then, afterwards, we can do some talking to her again, but some *real* talking – get her to work on Harpur for us like we planned, from gratitude, and even Iles and Lane.'

Alf said: 'Well, Manse, I don't really think that's—'

Alfie was not always too good at seeing all the aspects. He was hardly ever good at seeing all the aspects.

Shale said: 'Everton and the Rt. Hon. expect us to give them a nice arrangement with the police. If not, the deal is no deal. And also if not,' they start thinking of us the way they suddenly started thinking of panicking – a nuisance to be got rid of. These are very changeable people, Alf. Osprey believes in a police arrangement. This girl's important. A funeral is a happy place for constructive talks.'

Denzil said over his shoulder: 'Yes, but don't expect me to lay on some fucking imitation attack. You're not going to bang away at me, Manse, aiming to miss, sure, but who knows? Get some proper stuntmen in bulletproofs, right?'

'Just drive, will you?' Shale replied.

19

The chief called an afternoon meeting. Again it would be in his suite. The days of informality seemed forever gone. Harpur still feared it meant a weakening in Lane. Events and Iles – Iles particularly – had torn at the chief's confidence, and perhaps he continually needed to proclaim leadership through locale. On a wall in the suite was a chain-of-command diagram with Chief Constable represented at the top by an aggressive purple rectangle, and the letters CC centred in heavy type. Perhaps this bucked him up. Harpur dearly wished Lane would retire or make it to the Inspectorate of Constabulary while his mind remained more or less workable. Not long ago he had gone under to one breakdown. It was terrible to watch a decent man dwindle.

In the morning, just before lunch, Iles looked in on Harpur. The ACC arranged himself as he often did in Harpur's room with his legs over the arm of an easy chair. Also as he often did, Iles gazed for a while at his slim legs in the trousers of a navy pinstripe suit. Iles idolized his legs, and probably thought pretty well of his slim black lace-ups. 'Shale,' he said.

'We're talking to all sorts, sir, following the Eton. Francis Garland is handling it.'

'Some massive alliance shifts taking place, Col.'

'They're all off balance. Aftermath.'

'Oh, God, labels.' Iles had on a fiercely white shirt, dark-blue-motifed tie and the ruthlessly tapered suit trousers. He looked spruce and intemperate. He continued to let his grey hair grow longish these days after a period of harsh severity. He could have been someone halfway up the management structure in Gas or Home Improvements. 'I get a little word from a chum in the Metropolitan force, one-to-one basis. Luckily, I'm not like you, Col – dishonourably hoarding bits of information that should be disclosed to colleagues. Myself, I'm a sharing person, Harpur. At Staff College I was known as "Distributive Des". Earlier, my mother used to call me "Selfless". I'm going to let you in on what I've heard.'

'Thank you, sir,' Harpur replied.

Iles waited, though. Then he said: 'You're pretty close to the Holy Twitch these days.' Iles signalled upwards with a fine thumb towards Lane's rooms. 'So why the crisis call for this afternoon? He's going to resign, the sweet threadbare functionary? Haven't I always maintained, Col, that no man deserves so many disabilities?'

Iles liked answers to his questions. 'Are you saying Mansel shale is doing something with London now?' Harpur replied.

Iles removed his lace-ups and socks, stood and took a pair of scissors from Harpur's desk. He sat down again and began ferociously to cut his toenails, as though pruning sins. Fragments flew and crackled against the breaking-and-entering graph, still rising. 'What is it between you and Lane?' he asked. 'He's agreed to blind-eye your closeness to the student? What's her name again – Denise? But you're a widower now. Aren't you entitled to go where you like, even if she *is* not much more than a busty child?'

'Yes, Shale's probably off balance after the Eton,' Harpur replied.

'You might get trouble from her parents,' Iles said. 'Some mothers and fathers wouldn't take well to a lumpy old sleep-around like you moving in on their undergrad daughter. If I can help with a character testimonial do call on me, Col, no matter how late at night.'

'Thank you, sir.'

Iles began to yell. 'After all, I could avow that you are not someone sickly obsessed only by juvenile flesh, Harpur, and will bang mature women such as my wife also.'

'And whether Mansel and Panicking will maintain their partnership now – that's another uncertainty,' Harpur replied. 'There must be grievances, suspicions.'

'The Met. keep themselves informed on Everton.' Iles returned gradually to normal speech and wiped some shining spit flecks from his lips and chin with a current rota sheet he took from Harpur's in tray. The ACC began to put his shoes and socks back on, appreciatively fingering his arches. 'They must have a voice in Everton's West End flat block. My Met. chum gender-bends rather obviously or he/she would be Commissioner by now – such damn prejudice! – and this voice is probably one of his/her playmates. Mansel and Alfie were there this week. Things appear to have been genial. No shouting or gunfire.'

'We have identifications?' Harpur replied. 'Everton

wouldn't tell some porter or doorman who his business visitors are. Is this descriptions only?'

'There *are* descriptions. They fit Manse and Ivis. But this voice gave my Met. contact a ring while the two were still inside, and he/she sent over a tail. Manse and Alfie eventually went back to the Jaguar parked in a multi. The computer coughed Mansel's name and address as owner. Or would my contact have phoned here?'

'They've dropped Panicking?'

'Perhaps Panicking wants to do something on his own account. He can be headstrong when not pulped by fright. The Monty might be turned into a nice socially OK trading centre. All its mahogany and brass and history.'

'Ember would never let the Monty sink like that.'

'Ember might have to,' Iles replied. 'Possibly other big folk are nudging him. Our domain's a prize, you know.'

'He's in peril then.'

'From all round,' Iles said. 'We've told him so. I'd hate to see Ralphy dead or even paralysed. He's part of the greasy fabric here. We might need to protect him, Col. And we *must* protect Naomi Anstruther.'

'She won't have it.'

'Bollocks. Protect her. Armed people, obviously.'

Harpur said: 'I don't think they'd want to hurt her now. If Everton's putting all his bets on Manse, it's because Shale looks able to provide an accommodation with us, his eternal quest. Killing cops would be at variance.'

The ACC stood and paced a little, trying out the new feel now his nails were disciplined. He adored his own nimbleness. He groaned, but not about his feet. 'Nobody would ever persuade me you are a total fool, Harpur, but—'

'Thank you, sir.'

'Think: if Naomi finds out Osprey and the Rt. Hon. are moving into the domain, she might go looking for them here in her vengeance mood, supposing Rockmain's got it right. And Rockmain's the kind of subfusc jerk who does get things right. She might have found out already that Everton and the Rt. Hon. will be around. After all, she *is* a detective. Then, no need to go hunting in unfamiliar, hostile London like the other girl. Of course, she'll make a mess of revenge. I'm having her gun trained because she's obviously at hazard, but even so she'll make a mess of it. However, if Everton and the Rt. Hon. get scared and try to defend themselves our protection people can shoot back. Likewise with Panicking.'

'Your famed bait tactics, sir.'

'No London crew will be allowed to establish their filthy business here,' Iles replied.

'Shale and Panicking established a filthy business here.'

'Shale and Panicking are gentry, local gentry, Col. They know about decorum. Anstruther will probably go to the funeral of that Cardiff kid. I'd like people with her.'

'It's not our ground, sir.'

'Put people with her, Harpur. Perhaps go yourself.'

The chief said: 'With, one hopes, all due tentativeness, I'd like to give you my view of how the drugs business stands in our realm following the Eton incident.'

'This will be invaluable, sir,' Iles cried.

Lane flourished a hand to repel accolades. He seemed almost ebullient, almost in charge. In his eyes, Harpur saw something like resolve, though only something like. Wearing uniform after a lunch function, the chief had undone the top two buttons of his tunic and partly rolled up one sleeve. Always he showed true flair for the slatternly.

'Please, I know that I sit here, far from the nitty-gritty. You lads, and especially Colin, are deep into that nitty-gritty. And yet perhaps an overview is possible from this position.'

'Overviews are what we crave, sir,' Iles replied. 'I speak for Colin. But not any old overview. Your personal overviews are prized, Chief, throughout this police force. I have the feeling that, were one of those association tests tried on almost any officer, the word that would instantly come to his or her mind on hearing your name is "overview". Isn't that so, Col? One of the words.'

Harpur said: 'I hear the Eton may well have to shut.'

'I think so,' Lane replied. 'My wife and I dined there last night. It's why I called this meeting.'

Iles yelled again, but this time joyously, wonderingly: 'You took Mrs Lane, sir? Bravo! You speak of being far from the nitty-gritty. But does not this visit gainsay that, sir? This is nitty-grittying indeed, a credit to you both, if I may say.'

'Occasionally one has the wish to see at first hand,' Lane replied.

'And is there anyone better qualified?' Iles said. 'Can you think of anyone, Col?'

'I take it custom at the Eton was down, sir?' Harpur asked.

'Dismally down,' the chief replied. 'In ordinary circumstances, we would have been quite depressed to sit in that
huge as it were ship's state room with only two or three other
tables occupied. But, knowing the reason, we were quietly
jubilant.'

Iles clapped his hands noisily three time. 'Excellent, sir, if I
may say. Quiet jubilation is a mood that would sit well on
Mrs Lane. Raucous jubilation less.'

'The proprietor, Littlebann, did appear briefly,' Lane said.
'To both of us he looked – he looked defeated. Even routed.
Sally came up with that word, routed, and I had to agree. Oh,
naturally, she does not know the full tale behind the Eton
gun battle. Much of that has to be confidential even from
her.'

'Indeed yes, sir,' Iles replied.

'But she reads the papers, of course,' Lane said.

'The incident reports?' Iles asked.

'The press, obviously,' Lane replied.

'Ah,' Iles said.

'She is able to understand the outline, as would any
reasonably informed civilian,' the chief said.

'Right,' Iles replied.

They were in the conference area of Lane's suite, all in
easy chairs, the chief with his shoes off, despite the stately
surrounds. It was a feet day. Lane had a sheet of foolscap on
his lap, as if for prompts, but rarely glanced at it. Perhaps he
really was breaking back into poise. Harpur remembered
Lane when he was a fine detective on the neighbouring
ground. Iles often said the chief illustrated the maxim that

people were promoted disastrously to one point above the level of their competence. 'Think of St Peter or J. F. Kennedy,' he would urge. Think of Desmond Il(-)?

The chief said: 'Briefly then, my hunch is – and I hope a gifted hunch, an overview hunch – my hunch, for what it's worth, is that drugs business at the social level previously represented mainly by the Eton Boating Song is finished in our purlieus. This is an achievement, and I congratulate all concerned.'

'Thank you, sir,' Iles replied. 'Col is grateful.'

Lane said: 'I looked into the bar and at the notorious seat where a favoured franchised pusher used regularly to preside, I gather. This would be Eleri ap Vaughan, until she was murdered, and then Simon Pilgrim, also murdered. Dismaying, horrifying sequence. The seat, in fact, where Naomi Anstruther bravely, and almost fatally, performed so recently in her undercover role. It was empty. Gloriously empty.'

Iles said: 'I can see us out of work, Harpur, if the chief takes on these investigative tasks himself – with Mrs Lane as back-up, of course. Can't you envisage that, Col?'

Harpur said: 'These are good signs, yes, Chief, but we—'

'You might say that Littlebann would recognize me in the restaurant or even coming aboard and clear the trading area. This is a fair point, but I don't really believe it was the case, and neither did my wife.'

'This is the value of having someone like Mrs Lane to check and endorse your own impressions, Chief,' Iles said. 'Don't you agree, Col?'

Harpur said: 'Possibly there are other signs that we should—'

'And it's not just the matter of loss of the Eton as a venue,' the chief said. 'My feeling is that the people who dealt at that select level are terminally demoralized. We looked at Littlebann and both of us thought – quite independently of each other – each of us decided for herself, himself, that this was someone who would never come back. His fall had been too great, too traumatic. In the past, we have watched this disgusting business conducted at the heart of our patch and were unable to erase it because of the cleverness and caution exercised by the principals. I blame nobody for that.' Probably Lane lived with the conviction that Iles and possibly Harpur himself were on a syndicate's payroll. His voice had gone hollow. 'No, I certainly blame nobody.' He gazed down at his splayed hand on the desk.

'Thank you for withholding censure, sir,' Iles replied. 'This is generous, isn't it, Col, typically considerate of the chief.'

Harpur said: 'The London end of things could still—'

'Don't think I underestimate outside elements such as London dealers,' Lane said. 'Hardly. One knows the power of greed. But my analysis, based on drugs trade research I've seen from other provincial cities, is that outsiders cannot move into an area without the cooperation of solid local syndicates. The "hand-holders", as I believe they are known. I think we are entitled to feel post-Eton that the potential big-time hand-holders here are as severely hurt, even flattened, as Jeremy Littlebann. I mean Shale and Ralph Ember. The

Eton ambush must have been a devastating and enduring setback to them, and I repeat – congratulations to all who organized it and took part.'

'Thank you, sir,' Iles replied. 'Col was outstanding. This is the kind of simple heavy stuff he's made for. A whiff of cordite, a whiff of pussy, they turn him on absolutely equally. Well, look at his face.'

'I certainly don't say forget altogether about Shale and Ember, but we must reduce their target status, as they, personally, have been reduced,' Lane stated. 'My own reading of things at present – and this, too, is a view shared by my . . . My own reading of things at present suggests that the London magnates – people like Osprey and Basil Cope – I damned well refuse to call him the Rt. Hon. – pollution of a fine title – I accept that these will not give up their attempts to invade here. But they will be asking dealers with much smaller operations than Shale's or Ralph Ember's to assist their entry, because Shale and Ember are more or less commercially dead. When Osprey and Cope cry out, "Hold my hand", it is going to be to ordinary street pushers, people undamaged by the Eton occurrence. Locals like Bright Eddy, Luke Malthouse, Rufus Maitland. Consequently, I think we must move to a drive specifically against *them*. I mean both direct and undercover. Having closed off Osprey's major points of intrusion, we should now shut down the rest. Let us complete the fine work already done and secure our domain against drugs.' His voice climbed. His eyes still had near-resolve in them.

Harpur said: 'Sir, the ACC has information that—'

'The ACC has?' Lane snarled. Eternally the chief waited for his special schemes to be flippantly vandalized by Iles. Lane's pale jumpy jaw tightened. 'What kind of information?'

'Osprey and Shale might be in touch with each other,' Harpur replied.

'What status does this *information* have?' Lane asked.

'From some kind of flunkey in Osprey's West End flat block,' Iles replied.

'Saying what?' the chief asked.

'That Shale and Ivis visited,' Iles replied. 'Were summoned.'

'But not about the purpose?' Lane said.

'This is a porter or liftperson, something like that, sir,' Iles said. 'Not a party to the discussions.'

'Exactly,' Lane replied.

Now and then the chief would cling indomitably to an idea that he or he and his wife had hatched, because his soul and status were radically implicated. Today, the suite and its hierarchy sketch were not enough to prop him. He could not back off from his plan, and certainly not when it was Iles who menaced it. Mrs Lane would have warned him to expect derision from the ACC, and to fight it, fight it – to guard his essence.

The chief asked gently, uncompromisingly: 'Can we really believe there is an alliance between firms which only weeks ago were trying to wipe each other out?' He shook his head slowly and with conviction. Then he said, though: 'But, all right, let us suppose that they are indeed mooting an agreement. Is there any reason to think they mean to come here?

Wouldn't Shale be looking for new ground, after the Eton catastrophe? A little while ago you were telling me it was *Ember* who might join with Osprey and Basil Cope. I fell sceptical about that, and I am sceptical about this more recent theorizing. I'm sorry, Desmond, Colin, but I must prefer to believe what I observe for myself. Perhaps this is what one means by the term "overview".'

'Poor thing, poor, poor thing,' Iles said as he and Harpur went down in the lift. 'I've seen people like this before.'

'What happened to them, sir?' Harpur asked.

'Oh, they went into the priesthood, or joined flamenco evening classes.'

20

Naomi said: 'I had to see you. So, I drove here on the off chance. You understand my . . . well, my *self*, don't you? I need someone like that now. I've had some counselling, but no use. Too positive. Too negative. She talks to me as though I'm entitled to be traumatized, and will be for a decade. They've put me on gun training, for my own protection, but you – I need *you*, the psychological stuff.'

'That's me, all right.'

'Listen, *only* that,' Naomi replied.

'Do your bosses know you're here – Harpur, Iles, the chief?'

'I want them to. Why I've come. You've got to tell them I'm ready to go back to work, undercover work. My salvation.'

'*Are* you ready?'

'You've been in touch with them about me, haven't you? I mean, recently.'

'I was a bit worried. If you're here, it shows you're worried too. Long trip. I might not even have been around.'

'I'm terrified,' she said.

'That's an advance. Shows you can see the dangers. Yes, together, Naomi, we can probably work on them.'

She hated the way he dropped her name in there. Suddenly, it sounded like juicy comradeship, his lips ripe. 'Listen, only psychology,' she replied. 'No other kind of relationship in view.'

'Other? What other? We've decided I'm a psychologist.'

'Fine.'

'Terrified of what?' Rockmain asked.

'Oh, of what I might do. Not *do* – try. Of what I might become. That slipperiness of self you liked in me – good for undercover work. Get me back there. Please. I can use it then as a decent, legal skill. Outside my job, it's perilous.'

'Yes, I know.'

'You told Lane and the others that, did you?'

'I had to warn them.'

'This vengeance madness,' she said.

'Yes.'

'I wouldn't know how. I'll get myself killed, even with gun training. A friend of mine was killed.'

'I heard about that.' He stretched his arms high and gazed interestedly at his hands, as if they were geese flying south for the winter. He yawned. She reckoned these were preparations for changing tone. This bugger wasn't the only one who knew psychology. 'It could be argued that such losses of people very close to you make vengeance seem almost logical, not mad,' Rockmain said. He brought his eyes back down to watch her.

'I'm a police officer, for God's sake.'

'But if other police officers fail to get the killers, doesn't it seem—'

'Are you leading me on? You're a police officer yourself.'

'Some think that veering the way you do between

extremes – police officer to maverick, for example – is good – the route to wisdom. They said that about the supposed excesses of R. D. Laing. Divided self and all that.'

'Save us.'

'Tell me about the funeral,' Rockmain replied.

'How do you know I went?'

'You're the kind who would.'

'The kind? I thought I didn't stop still long enough to be any kind.'

'Right. But whatever kind you might be at any one time, you'd still be the kind who goes to the funeral of a friend.'

'They came for me there,' she said.

'Who?'

'The people who killed her. People sent by Osprey and the Rt. Hon., probably. Maybe by Panicking Ralph Ember too. I'm told he's negotiating with them. Panicking's a big local. Or Shale.'

'Yes, I've heard of them. What do you mean, "came for me there"?'

'In the church.'

Rockmain wrote something on his skeletal wrist in biro. What? *Church? Lies? Make-believe?* They were seated opposite each other on a pair of low-backed beige sofas in a big, otherwise bare white-walled room at Hilston Manor. It was here that Rockmain had assessed her suitability for undercover work months ago, and declared her ideal. All Britain's police forces used Hilston as a test centre, and Rockmain, with his meagre physique and disarming get-up, was its principal psychologist, the star of this elegant theatre.

'They think I'm a peril – their enemy,' Naomi said. 'Vendetta.'

'Aren't you?'

'I'm a police officer.'

'Now. Today,' Rockmain replied.

'Get me back undercover and I'm that permanently. The changes become part of the job then, and are inside a framework.'

'You want to hunt them?' Rockmain asked.

'Not now. I don't feel that now, today. Revenge sounds ridiculous, like the Middle Ages.'

'But sometimes you do? That's the person you become then?'

'I don't know how to hunt,' she said.

'But sometimes you want to hunt them?'

'They've killed three people I liked. One I used to love.'

'Yes – what I said,' Rockmain replied. 'I'm surprised they give you gun training.'

'Iles insisted. But I'll get *myself* killed,' she replied. 'What *I* said.'

'You didn't get yourself killed at Esmé's funeral.'

'People looked after me.'

'Which people?'

'Some heavies.'

'Criminals?'

'The people I infiltrated before the Eton.'

'Shale?'

'Shale and Ivis.'

'Why would they look after you? Why were they at the funeral?'

'Shale's like that. He believes in making a show.'

'Of what?'

'Grief, local solidarity. Look, are we still talking psychology?'

'Probably not. I need the picture,' Rockmain replied.

Are we still talking psychology? His eyes were sometimes upwards, like in donnish thought, but for a slice of the time they fluttered on her jeans junction. *I need the picture.* He had told her last time she was here he did a lot of fantasizing. With looks like his, he'd probably need to, or starve. All right, as long as he knew things were not going beyond that. *Are we still talking psychology?*

'A proper church funeral,' she said, 'the vicar in full garb, reading the service, getting the responses from us. I'm sitting near the front, just behind the family. The place is packed. Harpur's there, plus some of our people. Harpur has to do a lot of funerals these days. This was Esmé's, but it was the boy called Lyndon's not long ago.

'Shale and Ivis made sure I knew they'd come. They waited at the back until I arrived, gave me sad smiles, and then moved into a spot about three rows behind, Shale with a black bowler hat. Towards the end of the service there's a din outside the church, and soon a din inside. First, the sound of a car driven fast and braking hard. Then someone tugs at the church door, closed for the funeral. Yelling starts. It's Shale: "Don't be frightened, Naomi," he calls, "leave these bastards to us." Next, I hear movement and when I turn

Shale and Ivis are pushing their way out of the pew and running down the aisle towards the door, Shale first, without the bowler. Harpur moves too, and comes from his place and stands in the aisle alongside me, facing back towards the door. Jane Bish, a detective sergeant, joins him. I find after-wards they're both armed. Shale unfastens the door and he and Ivis charge out. The vicar stops the service, is bent forward, horrified, over Esmé's coffin. Everyone has turned to look towards the door. Shale and Ivis disappear. More shouting – unintelligible – and then what could be a shot. The car roars again and screams away. In a while, Shale and Ivis come back in. Shale waves to the clergyman, a kind permission to proceed. Also, Shale waves to Harpur, like telling him the trouble's been sorted. The service resumes. Harpur and Jane go back to their own places. At the end, Shale and Ivis loiter outside, Shale under the bowler, Alf in a homburg. Harpur is with me. Close.'

'How close?' Rockmain asked.

'Shielding me.'

'From?'

'Any more gunfire, obviously.'

'Oh, that,' Rockmain said.

'Then Shale tells him: "We saw them off, Mr Harpur. Had a tip. She'll be all right. She can go to the cemetery, follow her dear chum to the conclusion. We'll be there. Don't worry."

' "There was shooting?" Harpur asked.

' "Not from us," Shale said. "I mean, who'd bring wea-ponry to a funeral for God's sake? Decorum, please."'

Rockmain said: 'I read something about it in the press. And there were TV pictures – men in masks?'

'The cameras were waiting outside, yes. The funeral was news.'

'Nobody caught. Nobody identified. An abandoned stolen car. Was it all real? A Shale put-up job to impress Harpur? *Didn't I save your officer? What about some* quid pro quo, *partner?*'

'It felt real.'

'Not the same,' Rockmain replied. 'Now we're back to psychology.'

'No, we're back to likelihood. My friend and I were shadowed, menaced, by two men. Next, she's killed. Next, this at the funeral. A pretty sequence?'

'That's how Shale might want it read, yes,' Rockmain replied. 'I think your state of mind behind all this is still vengeance, private vengeance. Not much about you is stable, but, yes, this. You'll adjust facts to suit that illegal purpose.'

'Adjust? Harpur thought it was real, didn't he? He came to protect me.'

'But didn't actually pursue these mystery figures. He likes getting close, doesn't he?'

Naomi stared into the small egomaniac eyes. 'You won't let me go back undercover?' She felt like crying, but wouldn't. She felt like leaning across and touching him on his blousoned arm, or one of his goose hands, or even on that goldfish face – a plea for help – but wouldn't. His flinty, small-boy features flattened her. She would not let them humiliate her, though.

'Wait here,' he said, and stood suddenly. On those short, all-bone legs he hurried towards the heavy wooden double doors, a flash of high-style faded denim, his would-be statement on ranklessness. She noticed now that he had grown a pigtail and this bobbed and swung like an old sea dog's in a boarding party. He was one of the lads. He was a cop in commander rank at, what, thirty-six? He was an ace psychologist. If he had ever managed a shag with any woman for free Naomi would like to get a look at her. 'Yes. Perhaps,' he called over his shoulder and pigtail just before he went out. What sense did that make? *Yes* – yes, what? Undone by *Perhaps.* Perhaps, what? This bright piece of democracy might have her sanity and safety in those flying-geese hands.

In those flying-geese hands when he returned was a folded newspaper. He sat down opposite her again and produced from the wrapping a grey-blue automatic pistol, not a type she recognized. He handed it to her. 'Come to my room tonight,' he said.

'It's loaded,' she replied, weighing it on her open palm. 'Suppose someone looks in here now, a clerk or receptionist, with a message for you.'

'I'll say you're deranged and threatening me. We get lots of quaint ones here. *Of course* it's loaded. Come to my room tonight. Kill me, Naomi. Kill me now you know guns.'

She tried to return the automatic to him, but he pulled away primly, like a Mother Superior declining a fix. 'Come to my room. Kill me as I sleep,' he said. Lavish excitement juddered in his whispered words and he reached up and fingered his lower gum gingerly. Perhaps one of his teeth had been shaken loose in the gallop of blood. 'As if.'

'As if?' she replied. 'With a loaded pistol?'

'I'll risk it.' He gulped at the thrill. 'As if I were Everton Osprey or the Rt. Hon. These are your vengeance targets, yes? Come to my room, put the Luger to my head ... or better still into my sleeping, gaping, catastrophically vulnerable mouth, and make as if to kill me. Oh, yes. Oh! Oh!'

'This is one of your kinks, is it?' Naomi asked. 'Get many chances of running it?'

'Here could be the chance of quelling the whole vengeance absurdity in you. We confront, enact, expose, exhaust, purge.'

'Exorcize?'

'One loathes that sacerdotal word.'

'Exorcize?'

'Yes, exorcize.'

'Plus you get a stiffy and consummation in your lonely bed.'

'Most likely. But that's an incidental and very innocuous. Yes, incidental, innocuous. I put my sheets direct into the machine. It's you I'm thinking of – your fine yearning to return to undercover, yet this fine yearning menaced by another yearning, an illicit, ignoble yearning – yes, illicit, ignoble – this illicit, ignoble yearning to bring havoc, and easier now you're into handguns.'

'You're proposing a deal, are you?' she replied.

'We bring out the sub-personality in order to destroy – dispose of – that sub-personality.'

'Whose?'

'Come to my room tonight, you untiring spirit of vengeance. God, I quake . . . an agony of fright.'

She examined the gun. 'I don't know Lugers. Is there a safety catch?'

It was as though she had spat on him. He flinched massively. 'Damn, yes. But you won't engage it, will you? I mustn't suspect that. Mustn't. Mustn't. It would destroy the lovely moment -- fracture the authenticity. Swear now that you won't. Don't come naked, or anything like that.'

'What's it mean, "anything like that"?'

'This is a job, an assassination rendezvous. Come in due gear.'

'Dressed to kill.'

'I was afraid you'd say something corny along those lines – but I know I can't have everything.'

'Anything?' Naomi replied.

He gave her a room not far from the staff wing and she slept until 4 a.m. She might have slept right through. Her plan was to ring him on the internal at breakfast time, tell him to get his psychological marbles together and then leave. The trip had been ludicrous. She would put the Luger on her bedside table with a note, 'Do not disturb', and possibly stick another on his door with chewing gum, 'Do not disturb, he's disturbed enough.' She awoke, though, aware that someone not tall, not weighty, was standing by the bed, slightly crouched in plea.

'Please, Naomi, come now. It's such a waste.' He had on a kind of sarong or kaftan.

'Lovely gear.'

'What are *you* wearing?' he asked. 'You don't sleep bare, do you? I really don't want someone raw in my room, in the circumstances.'

'I'll dress for you, you victim.'

'Oh, exactly – victim,' he gasped. 'Thank you for that – victim, victim. Give one time to compose oneself, will you? As if asleep. As if a target. I will not leave my door ajar, though. You must force entry. I won't lock it.' Dejected feelings hummed: 'How totally you must hate me, if all you wish is my violent end. Yet you are perhaps justified.'

When he had gone, she put her clothes on, took the gun and went quietly down the corridor to the short flight of stairs leading to the staff wing. All the best psychologists were barmy, the way the best marriage guidance people slept around. At least five British police forces had their own investigative psychology units now, and it was worrying to think that some might have items like Rockmain aboard. This psychologist lay on his back, almost lost in the king-size double bed, like one marked day on the year-at-a-glance calendar. As he had promised, his little mouth was as wide as it would go, and he breathed with magnificently deep regularity, mocking up the happy sleep of a tycoon pusher. He kept his eyes shut, and his head was turned slightly towards the door, making things convenient for her. A night-light burned. She stood gazing down at him for a while. He would profit by the anticipation. Then she shoved the muzzle of the Luger jerkily between his teeth, hoping to chip one or two. 'Pow! pow! pow!' she said. 'Die, degenerate.'

A blissful tremor went fast across his features and his eyes stayed shut, probably for concentration on lower workings. She withdrew the gun and turned to leave.

'Oh, yes, degenerate, so true! – Pow! pow! pow!' he said. 'Come tomorrow night too. Do kill me again. There are still five rounds in the box. After that I'm sure you'll be on the certifiable mend.'

21

Ralph Ember knew he was at his most exposed driving home after locking up for the night at the Monty. Always he did the trip alone, and almost always the time was about the same: between 2 and 3 a.m. Once a fortnight he would hang about in the club for a while to vary this routine, but even then he generally reached his house by 3.30. Anyone waiting would wait a little longer, knowing Ralph was sure to show before dawn. Tonight, as a matter of fact, he was exceptionally late – after 4 a.m. There had been some fighting at the club. That did happen once in a while, usually about share-outs from a job take, or girls, of course. Ember had stayed to swab the floor and clean up fitments after it finished. But anyone waiting would wait a little longer still, just as sure Ralph must show before dawn. He carried two pistols with him these days, and nights. Tonight. He liked to show purpose.

His house, Low Pastures, was a lovely country place, well outside the city, and the last few miles of road were deserted and dark at this time. In the town, Ember could alternate routes away from the Monty, but there was only one final approach to the property. He neared it now. Occasionally he thought of paying someone to accompany him, either with another vehicle or riding shotgun in his. But it would have sickened him to admit he needed minding.

Instead, he had doubled his armament. In a waist holster

he carried the short-barrelled Smith and Wesson Model 49 revolver. Under the passenger seat he kept a 9mm Parabellum Bernadelli PO 18 automatic. Combined, these gave twenty-two rounds without reload. Such totting up was academic, Ralph knew that. This would not be the battle of Stalingrad. In an ambush, he might have time to get off one or two shots, and if they failed he would be dead, or turned liquid by fright. The second gun comforted him, though. He liked to feel surrounded by firepower, his own. The S. and W. was on his right hip, the Bernadelli to his left. And when he tried to visualize an attack, he thought of that in pairs too. It might be Osprey and the Rt. Hon. in person. Those two wanted him gone. He had read this in the bastards' geniality and encouragement at that jolly meeting in Bath. If it wasn't them, it could be Shale and Ivis, put up to it by Osprey and the Rt. Hon. or perhaps it would be the couple of louts gossip said had tracked the girl cop Anstruther and her friend, then slaughtered the friend, defaced the friend. Oh, God. Things were getting intolerable. Even the Monty, which contained so many of his roundest hopes, could sometimes agonizingly depress him. Tonight's fighting, for instance.

He and Julius had dealt with it on their own: for Monty barmen, a chief qualification beside cocktail skills was this flair for hitting hard enough with a baseball bat to contain folk, but without causing fractures or, say, blindness, especially to women. Somehow, Ember never panicked when dealing with club outbreaks. Clearing up alone after the carnage, he had wondered – wondered again – about permanent flight to a warm and possibly tranquil haven. He had enough stacked. Italy? Portugal? France, where one of his daughters was at school? Immediately, though, Ember quelled this escape notion. Surely, emigration was a terror thought and he must resist. It was probably weeks since he had suffered a genuine, heavyweight panic. Hadn't he grown out of that at last?

But now, as he turned into the straight, narrow side road leading to Low Pastures, he suddenly felt what might be the customary start of disabling alarm – copious back sweat and a ravaging ache across his shoulders. He could make out ahead in the darkness what looked like a big Toyota parked facing the open gate of a grazing field. As far as Ember could recall, Aspley, the farmer, had no Toyota, and why leave it in the field anyway? Ralph did not stop, but reached down and touched the butt of the Bernadelli. Yes, yes, his arm and hand would still work, by God. And his legs. He pushed down a little harder on the accelerator, but nothing obvious, nothing . . . nothing panicky. The Toyota rolled forward slowly, though fast enough, and blocked the way. It showed no lights. If Ralph had not been so appalled, he knew he would have felt huge rage. Disgusting to witness this sort of tactic with a foreign car on the decent English rural road leading to his own residence and grounds.

He pulled up, about forty yards from the Toyota. There seemed to be only the driver aboard, but you had to wonder who was flat in the back, or who was behind the hedge. Ember brought the automatic from beneath the seat and put it into his jacket pocket. He took the revolver from its holster and kept it in his right hand. His arms and hands were still fine, but his vision began to cloud, and sweat formed a cold circle around his body, where it had run down his stomach and back to the waistband of his trousers. Instinctively his left hand went up to check his scar. Always it stayed dry, of course. Always the instinct ruled him, though, even when he might need that reserve hand for the Bernadelli. He wondered about sitting tight. He wondered about getting out and perhaps making a run. There were woods at the edge of his land and he might get cover there. But it would mean crossing two open fields, and he was not sure of his legs. When he fell to this state the power would sometimes drain from them completely. Or they would seem all right at the beginning of a dash and then fail. That could be worse – to start and then collapse in view. Farce, perilous farce, and not Ember-like – at least, not as Ember mostly thought of Ember. He sat where he was and locked the doors. There was the car phone, yes, and someone else driving home at 4 a.m. and confronted by a road block might have dialled the police. Ember could not do that. Call Beau? It would take Beau half an hour to get out from against Melanie and drive here, and Beau would be useless anyway. Beau did not do guns.

Ember kept his headlights on main beam. Forty yards was a long way to shoot with a pistol but he would try it if he had to, and the lights might dazzle the opposition. He rested his Smith and Wesson on top of the steering wheel and aimed at the Toyota driver with a two-handed grip. Ralph's eyes were still not good, but he stared ahead and also tried for some edge vision in case people rushed him from the sides. 'Abroad, here I definitely come,' he muttered. 'If possible.'

The driver's door of the Toyota opened and a man stepped out, closed it quietly behind him and began to come towards Ember's car in an easy, even beautiful, striding walk. He seemed to have no weapon. Both hands were in view, swinging as he approached. Ember wanted to yell at him to stop and to get his hands above his head, but for that to carry he would have to open the side window and he did not want to loosen his hold on the revolver. Also, he felt that to stay safe he must not break the glass seal on himself – pathetically illogical, but logic had left him. He screamed the orders anyway. The man did not hear, or ignored them. He was in his twenties, middle height, wide neck, bulky shoulders. The fresh-looking face was unknown to Ember. The man's features looked screwed up a bit in the glare, but Ember thought it might also be because he was smiling. It was the kind of pitying smirk some of those London sods could put on, even someone low rank like this lad would surely be. Ember touched the scar again. Suddenly unsupported by the other, his gun hand began to shake and slide across the top of the steering wheel, moist with sweat. He grabbed his right wrist with his left hand again to try to steady himself. Leaning forward, he put the muzzle of his pistol against the windscreen, so the lout could see it. He had to be told this was not some easy picking, this was Ralph Ember. But, of course, the fucking highwayman would see nothing behind these headlights.

So, why not fire, why not fire, why not fire? The distance was fifteen yards only now . . . twelve, ten, eight, three. He could not have missed, could he? Yes, he could, in this quivering condition, his mind half on his scar, the muzzle of the pistol skidding now on the windscreen with a squeak, as it had slid across the top of the wheel. If he pulled the trigger and did not hit him, would it bring retaliation – possibly not just from this man but from all round. Yet Ember knew his hesitation was not really about possible retaliation. This thug acted as though Ember would not shoot. And so Ember did not. His will was in pieces. That happened in panic. Circumstances would stipulate his role, and he could not counter them.

This gangster was past the headlights now and would be able to see him, stuck here in a capsule, waiting for it. He stood against the driver's door and bent down to look in. Yes, he was smiling. Ember managed to swing the pistol around and this kid in a pink jacket smiled some more. He did not try the door or knock the window, just smiled and smiled. Then he spoke. Ember part heard it, part lip-read it: 'Mr Ralph Ember, I presume.'

A joker with it. He frowned at the pistol still pointed his way, but not a severe frown, not one that stopped his smile. 'I wonder if a little talk that could be of mutual interest. True not an ideal setting nor the best of hours.' He straightened and stood waiting for a response, superbly relaxed. If Ember had fired it would have taken him in the balls. He let down the window.

'You've come from Everton Osprey?' he asked.

'Well, in a way you could say that.' Yes, cockney right through.

'Which way?'

'Or perhaps we could get off the road into your house. It's, like, obvious here. Shepherds up at dawn from their mangers and that. The country's such a solace. You're lucky, Mr Ember. But also you've earned it, I heard. My view is these talks should be tonight – this morning. There's a touch of urgency. Well, which you can see – the crudity of the interception. Sorry.'

'Pull back into the field,' Ember said. 'Then follow me.'

'What I thought.'

'Are you alone?'

He did not bother to answer that, though, and began a another magnificent bit of strolling, this time back to the Toyota. Ember put his S. and W. on the passenger seat and drove behind. He could have run him down, but this lad clearly thought Ember would not, so Ember did not. The Toyota was moved out of the way and Ralph led to Low Pastures. Once in a while he did let work acquaintances into the property. Was there a choice now? Of course there was a choice. Ember had the guns, didn't he? But what choice did they give if you couldn't use them? The revolver was back in its holster and he pocketed the automatic.

'Beams, exposed beams, I love all that,' the visitor said. He kept his voice low, considerate for those asleep in the house. He gazed about the hall and reached out and touched stonework in a wall. 'It's like feeling the pedigree, the genuineness. I should think a house like this got a paddock as well, not to mention cellars.'

'Yes,' Ember said. 'Paddocks.'

'This is a place that says achievement. Not gaudy, but

interesting. This is a place that says something which continues.'

'Why not?'

'Exactly. You got every right.' In the same helpful, warm voice he said: 'You're on your fucking own, you know, Ralphy. You need backing.'

Ember took him into the drawing room and poured a couple of Armagnacs. 'Are you the one they call Lovely Mover?' It was a flash, a stab.

'Lincoln W. Lincoln,' he replied. 'You've got the W. mid-initial too, yes? Like blood brothers.'

'I've heard of you, obviously,' Ember replied.

'Ditto. Lucky the police haven't give my pic to the media. They worry these days, in case the lawyer says it biased the jury. That is, if they can find me.'

'But I thought I read about a tan or gold jacket.'

'I changed – for disguise.'

Ember asked: 'Couldn't you have picked something—'

'What, duller? Don't like dullness.' Looking at the round rosewood table, the Regency sideboard and Wellington cabinet, Lincoln said: 'This is a room likewise with period. A room such as this needs someone who can really appreciate it, which would be namely, clearly, you, Ralphy.'

'What backing?' Ember asked.

'You're looking so formidable,' Lincoln replied, nodding towards the holster bulge and the pocket bulge. 'Well, it's a jungle area, I expect.' He smiled some more, as though, being a Londoner, he could conquer the whole county in six or seven minutes. 'Do I come *from* Everton and the Rt. Hon? Yes, I come *from* them. Very from.'

'You've got a message?'

Lincoln sat down in an easy chair. He would. Ember took a straight-backed one at the round rosewood table. Lincoln said: 'Yes, I got a message.'

'I met them at Bath, you know. They want to confirm a partnership? That your message?'

'This message is from me. It's what I meant when I said I had come *from* them. Like really *from*.'

'What, you've broken away?'

'Absolutely. But no announcement, clearly. They don't know and won't for a while.'

'What message?'

'A message what says it should be you and me, Ralphy.'

'I'm Ralph. Ralphy's someone's vegetable-state cousin.'

'It should be you and me, Ralph. I want to see you and yours live out a grand life in this grand spot with paddocks. I appreciate your style.' He nodded again towards the two gun bulges.

Ember said: 'Well, I—'

'You reply I'm a fucking liability, being on the run since that Eton rumpus. Which is some truth. Why I had to accost you this rough way in the dark and on a B road.'

'I'm thinking of retiring abroad,' Ember replied.

'What, Poitiers direction, where your little girl is?' Lincoln said. 'Not so little.'

'How?' Ember replied.

'How what?'

'How you and me?'

'You're asking what I got to put in as against what you'd put in, which is fair, me being what the law calls "wanted", whereas you – you're local dignity. To which the answer is . . . well, like guidance, Ralph. The word that come first to my head was information, but no – it's guidance. That's a word with more, like, scope.'

He had a sort of kid face, and the pink coat made him look more kid. This was someone dodging all the police of Britain and the twat wears a pink coat. Great to get guidance such a genius.

'Look, they don't want me around, do they, Ralph?'

'Who?'

'Everton. The Rt. Hon. Do you know what I am? I'm a fucking fugitive. Which means I'm not employable, except in footman jobs, internal lark-abouts. And that won't go on. They've behaved all right to me so far. Well sort of all right – like I said, low-level work only – but they'll get tired of that and then . . . Well, the procedure. You know what they're like. You know what Everton can be like if he gets tired of someone. Everton's not a caring person, not in the way people usually mean. And I know too much about the Eton. You can forget Bath. Forget a partnership with them. But I should think you knew that already.'

'Maybe.'

'Why you said abroad.'

'Maybe. I haven't decided. What guidance?' Ember asked.

'I'm still working for them – as far as they know. This is what I mean – information, guidance. Like insights on what they're doing. They've turned us into a team, Ralph. I'm going to help you fight them. Did I come with armament tonight?' He flipped the pockets of the fucking pink jacket to show they had no weight, then opened it and there was no holster, waist or shoulder. 'Why do I come gunless? Because a man does not call on a team mate pointing armament. *You* had armament and still have, but that's all right, because you did not know then about the team. This was just someone coming at you out of the dark, and you're edgy. Bound to be, in view of things. This is someone looking after skin and home.'

'I'm sorry,' Ember said.

'I think this could be called guidance that I'm giving you now, tonight, Ralph, for instance. I'm telling you, Everton will get me out of the way and he'll get you out of the way. He got plenty of assistants – Brian Bernard Rayne and Gordon Lusse. Who did the girl in Cardiff, most probably. Yes, you knew it already, but this is confirmation. And I'll be able to let you know how they're going to do it to you. Guidance.'

'Unless they do it to you first,' Ember replied.

Lincoln tried for a grin, but it was obvious he did not like those words. Lincoln thought he had to be the one to run things, chat included. Ember had known a lot like that. Some were dead, some inside for more or less ever. Ember was not someone to just tag along. Ember could look at all the range of a situation and see the contours, especially when he was not right down into dread, and he had begun to come out of this panic now.

Lincoln said: 'Then don't I hear you might have pressures from somewhere else too? Which is the big supplier from way down south. The yachtsman. Ralph, I know you're not stupid, and you would never tell me you can handle all this by yourself. Then Beau Derek, what kind of help is that one, except for springing a safe, and this is not about safes? The yachtsman been looking at the Monty, yes? He knows some rough people too, and not just them two women. We have some repelling to do, you and I, Ralph, and some construction, naturally. This is where my guidance will come in big. No, you are not alone, Ralph. Perhaps we'll think for ourselves about the Monty, though I realize it goes against the grain most probably. Or some other venue. We won't be stampeded, Ralph. That's the last thing Ralph Ember would be is stampeded. I've heard a lot say that. Ah, this must be Mrs Ember. A privilege.' He stood up.

The door to the drawing room opened slowly and Margaret came in wearing Ember's heavy dressing gown. 'It's nearly five, Ralph,' she said. 'I woke up and—'

'Forgive me, do,' Lincoln said. 'A business matter, obviously. Ralph is so difficult to reach in ordinary office hours.'

'We had to postpone discussions, dear,' Ember said. 'Club trouble.'

'Disruptive of your household, regrettable,' Lincoln said. 'But Ralph wanted it immediate. You know how he is for hospitality and do-it-now.'

'I was worried,' Margaret replied. 'Some of the brutes at that club. But as long as you're all right, Ralph.'

'Brutes is right, I'm afraid,' Lincoln replied. 'They try to exploit Ralph's patience. They forget he got core, though. I expect this is one of the things you love him for, Mrs Ember, his core.'

Ralph offered Margaret a drink, but she would not take one and turned to go back to bed. It was clear that she did not expect to be told Lincoln's name, did not want to ask it. She sensed by now how some of Ember's business operated, and liked to keep the knowledge to its minimum.

'But I must go,' Lincoln said. 'I think Ralph and I have reached a good degree of understanding.'

'Oh?' Margaret replied.

'Yes,' Lincoln said. 'Wouldn't you agree, Ralph?'

'I'll come out and point you right,' Ember replied. 'The country looks wonderful in the dawn light. I really envy you the drive.'

The three of them stood in the hall and Lincoln refingered a section of stone wall, savouring lumpiness. 'Although old, this house seems to me a happy house, Mrs Ember. I decided that right away. That happiness, I'm sure, is very much your work. It might be difficult for you to contact me, Ralph. I'm here and there these days. Unpredictable. I fear this is how business is in our modern, demanding times, Mrs Ember – as you no doubt are aware. But I know now how to reach you, Ralph. We done a nice bit of foundation-laying tonight. I'm going to inform Ralph as soon as I've taken things further, Mrs Ember. There's a bond between us, isn't there, Ralphy?'

22

Harpur tried the door with his shoulder but could not shift it.

'This is the kind of street where folk tend their defences,' the Rev. Anstruther said. 'Especially folk like Untidy, as you call him. In the old days, before conversion, he would have had a lot of valuable commodity in there, and takings.'

'Which of his conversions?'

'Oh, there is only a single conversion when somebody accepts the Lord and becomes one of His saints. Lapses are possible, yes, but . . .'

'Yes.'

'But eternal life is eternal life – only one glorious, instant salvation. It's available for you too, you know.'

Harpur moved back and then gave the door a meatier dose of shoulder. He felt it wince. He rearranged himself.

'Shall I try?' the Rev. Anstruther asked. He might have been ten stone, but resolute-looking.

Harpur said: 'It would disturb your suit, Bart.' He hit the door again and it groaned and crackled, sagged and opened. There was an immediate unwelcoming odour from inside, which might be death or just Untidy's untidy haunt. An aged pair of torn beige trousers lay on the floor of the little hallway, possibly Untidy's second best. The place was always filthy. Harpur had been here before once or twice when Untidy's sainthood was in remission and he had reverted to drug trading. Perhaps there had been a smell then. Harpur tried to remember. He went into a lot of grubby spots. It was called policing. Normally, someone like Untidy would have been dealt with by the Drugs Squad only. But, because he had seemed ready now and then to give up pushing for ever, Harpur used to call and try to talk him back into the ways of righteousness, or at least legality, perhaps without a prosecution. Now, he said to Anstruther: 'Cleanliness is next to Godliness, but Untidy settled for Godliness.'

'Mr Harpur, are you—'

'Armed? We're in Britain, Rev.'

A middle-aged black woman in a vividly new red leather suit had come out onto the landing above during the din. She gazed down at them over the banister rail. Bart flashed his dog collar and skin and called up to her: 'This is for the best, sister, believe me. Even the breaking down of doors can be the Lord's work. This is Detective Chief Superintendent Harpur himself.'

'Really?' she replied. 'Who wouldn't know his face? So does that make things good or bad? What is it Conrad says?'

'Which Conrad?' Harpur asked. 'Conrad Royston Usher, the ladies' underwear thief? He lives in this block?'

'Is it in *The Secret Agent*?' she replied. ' "The mind and instincts of a burglar are of the same kind as the mind and the instincts of a police officer." ' She stared for a while longer and then went back into her flat, her outfit rustling like wind through a turnip field.

'Oh, I fear for Graham,' Bart whispered. He seemed reluctant to enter Untidy's place, not because he was scared of opposition but because he was scared he would find a saved life destroyed by something from its dirty past. All the same, Harpur stood back for him to go first. This, after all, was the minister's party. Anstruther did up the second button of his double-breasted jacket and adjusted his half-moon spectacles, both acts designed as if to hold himself together. He said, 'This kid, Graham – I tried to teach him some basic tact, you know, as well as the Gospel. The Lord's business has to be done, but done in a hostile land, and some delicacy is needed. The Lord is perfectly *au fait* with that. He wasn't born yesterday.'

'Delicacy is not a strong point with Graham,' Harpur replied. 'You've done all you can for him – are still doing all you can for him. That's what Hazel meant – the Good shepherd.'

Anstruther had turned up earlier this evening at Harpur's house wearing the splendid dark-grey suit and looking intolerably anxious. 'It's about Graham Goff,' he had said, that magnificent Oxbridge accent flaky now through stress. Pleaful.

'Which Graham's this, Dad?' Jill had asked.

'Untidy.'

'I like him,' Jill said.

'He's disappeared,' the Rev. Bart replied.

Jill said: 'The one who Bible-punches outside C&A's in those waistcoats – when he's not pushing?'

Apparently, the minister had tried at headquarters first, then come on to Arthur Street when told Harpur was not there. These days, Harpur took care to get home whenever he could. Since the death of his wife he liked to spend adequate time with his daughters: what upbringing manuals called 'quality time'. They hated it and went out more. Jill had dubbed him Earthmother. Occasionally he could corner them, though. This evening he and the two girls had been helping Denise with a university essay which asked whether Man Friday was the real hero of *Robinson Crusoe* when Hazel looked from the front window and said, 'The black Rev., Dad. I'd say he's got trouble.'

Jill had gone to bring the minister in, and the Rev. Bart blurted his worries.

Hazel had tried to console him: 'What you have to remember, Rev., is, someone like Untidy, they come and go. Flotsam on the dark tide of urban modern life.'

'Hazel's into phrases,' Jill stated.

'I wouldn't fret,' Hazel told Anstruther. 'Yet you're the Good Shepherd, I expect – ninety and nine safe in the fold, but you seek the hundredth.'

'Graham shoots his mouth off all over, Mr Harpur,' Bart said.

'Some people might want to silence him,' Anstruther said.

Denise said: 'You mean he talks about things that—'

'Graham, since he became the Lord's, is so set on showing folk their sin that now and then he'll say more of what he knows – knows, I mean, from his past and about old colleagues – well . . . say more than is necessary.'

'He hasn't simply gone back to trading, has he?' Harpur asked. 'That's happened before.'

'I've been around the dealing streets, inquired here and

there. People haven't seen Graham – *say* they haven't seen him. I've rung him and tried his flat five or six times.'

Harpur had telephoned the Drugs Squad office and spoke to Daphne Ann Calt. She looked at their collator reports: no sightings of Untidy lately.

'This could be bad,' Jill said. 'Yes, I've heard Untidy spouting in his sermons about people he knew in drugs, naming names. I knew most of them before, mind.'

'And about the future even,' the minister replied. 'Speculating on criminal intentions by some. This would be provocative.'

'Dad will come and look for him with you if you're bothered, won't you, Dad?' Hazel had asked. 'Denise won't mind – not for a little while. He's always ditching her here. We can help her with the Man Friday job.'

'I'd be upset if anything happened to Untidy,' Jill said. 'He could really show hell to the shoppers.'

'Yes, look after Denise for me,' Harpur said, and Anstruther had driven him to Untidy's apartment block in Stipend Road. Anstruther was moving ahead of him into the flat and Harpur touched his arm. 'There could be defacement,' he said. 'Be ready.' The Rev. Bart paused, perhaps about to let Harpur precede after all and see first whatever was here. But then the minister fiddled with his spectacles again and stayed in front, as though it were his duty.

In Untidy's living room they found one of the famed old waistcoats and other pieces of his clothing scattered among the takeaway cartons, used crockery and cutlery, dog mags, porno and computer mags, and packets of Born Again tracts.

Untidy himself was in the kitchen, naked and curved over the gas stove so that his stomach and chest were resting on three burners. His head and hands hung down one side like game in a shop, his wrists bound together with a rope, an end of which then passed underneath the stove and held his ankles. The burners were not lit now, but they had been while he was fixed there. Perhaps Harpur should have noticed a scorch element in the smell. One of Untidy's hugely soiled tea cloths had been rolled up and rammed into his mouth. Harpur could not tell how he had died. Pain would sometimes produce enough shock to do it. He could see no blood around the stove or on the burners. He looked at the back of Untidy's head and neck, in case a gun had been fired into his mouth and the cloth used to stop the flow, as well as the screaming before. The exit wound might have been visible, but Harpur could not spot it.

'Was there a need to torture him?' Anstruther asked. 'Did he know anything?'

'Not much new, I shouldn't think. But he talked too much, as you say.'

'Punitive?'

'Like that,' Harpur replied.

Bart said: 'I wish I could cover his arse with something. It looks so . . . oh, I don't know – so untragic. But perhaps your experts wouldn't like interference with the body.'

One of Untidy's street-preaching banners stood in a corner of the kitchen and Harpur brought it over. He stood the pole upright between Untidy's legs and then drew the blue square of cloth with its gold-lettered text over Untidy's lower back and buttocks. The banner read: *It is appointed to men once to die but after this the judgement*. Then he went through all the rooms of the flat doing a quick survey, and searched the clothes. On Untidy's phone he reported the death.

Anstruther had remained with the body. Harpur returned to the kitchen and they sat at the Formica-topped table. On it was the remains of another takeaway meal in its carton, and an open copy of *Night Life of a Dildo*, its illustrations a bit stained by food, probably. They were silent for a time.

Eventually Bart said: 'I don't believe in prayers for the dead, yet I yearn to pray for Graham.'

'Why?' Harpur asked gently. 'He's in a better place.'

'Yes, I know.' He looked urgently at Harpur. 'You – do *you* believe he's in a better place?'

'Most places are better than this.'

'Yes, but—'

'Here's the chief and Mr Iles,' Harpur said.

They must have been on their way to or from a ceremony of some sort when the call came and wore full dress blue uniforms. Harpur welcomed this formal show of order here. Untidy's place needed something of the kind, and especially the present stove scene. Lane and the ACC went forward and stood near the body. Iles took off his cap, bent low and put his face close to Untidy's, gazing at him with abounding matiness. 'I feel this has become a kind of sacred place,' he whispered.

'Indeed,' Anstruther said.

'He's known to you, Desmond?' Lane asked.

'This is one of those symbolic crimes you demand to visit in person, sir – rightly, if I may say,' Iles replied. 'Oh, yes, overtones. Why I suggested we come swiftly.'

The chief nodded towards the banner. 'But the placing of this text. Is it satirical? some religious war going on on our ground?' he asked.

Iles said: 'This lad was a piece of unmitigated nothingness, and yet he had a lovely way with women junkies, I hear, and with the Mothers' Meeting at your church, Rev.'

'They responded to his vulnerability,' Anstruther replied.

Iles fingered the roped wrists. 'Yes, he had enough of that.' The ACC half stood and moved around to the stove's front, where he could examine the burning. Harpur had seen him do a kind of vivid obeisance to murder victims before. In the uniform he looked brilliantly high gloss and hangdog.

Harpur heard vehicles outside as the murder crew and Scene of Crime people arrived. The ACC looked suddenly enraged. He fiddled with the banner, getting it to lie more symmetrically. 'I thought we could have lifted him down from here before this mob turned up,' he said.

'They know about it. I said what was what in my call,' Harpur told him.

'Fucking cop photographs of him in such a pose – all that. I don't want it,' Iles replied.

Anstruther said: 'Surely evidence should not be disturbed in this kind of case.'

'Certainly not,' the chief replied. 'Mr Iles was speaking a wish, not a real possibility, obviously.'

'What do you mean, "this kind of case", you dreamy nonconformist ponce?' Iles asked Anstruther. 'You think there are special regulations laid down for a corpse stuck on a stove like toast?' He went to the window, wiped a gap in the grime and looked down to the road. 'Yes, them,' he snarled. 'I won't have the details of this tableau spread, Harpur – the cookery. And you, Rev., keep that gift-of-tongues gob shut about it, yes?' He turned to the chief and sweetened his tone. 'I know Mrs Lane is the last person you would think of describing something like this to, sir, in your evening talks, and may I say I'm grateful.' He indicated Untidy with his thumb. 'An account of this would suggest to many that evil is in control. It *is* in control, but we don't issue bulletins.'

'No, no, it is *not* in control,' the chief cried. '*Not, not.*' His voice fluted and hammered but was easily absorbed by the muck strata on Untidy's walls and produced no confirming echo. The ferocity in Lane's denial was typical: he dreaded signs of disorder's wholesale and final triumph on his ground. It was this fear, plus, of course, Iles, which had driven him into clinical breakdown not long ago. Lane was dogged by a terror that wrong might finally conquer in his domain and spread from here to the rest of the world, and then the cosmos. The ACC said this anxiety was so vivid that Lane constantly reread the Book of Revelation, searching for some prophecy of a marshmallow chief constable starting the Apocalypse.

'As I mentioned, we don't tell even Mrs Lane, sir,' Iles said.

'Oh, evil can never win, though it might *appear* to win,' Anstruther said briskly from where he sat with Harpur at the kitchen table. 'To speak of such a dark victory would be unscriptural.'

'It would be a heresy,' Lane said.

For a second, Harpur thought Iles might savage Anstruther or the chief, or both, and stood, ready to get between the ACC and them. Iles did not mind contradiction but loathed theology. Then, though, the assistant chief looked back to the stove and brushed Untidy's shoulder briefly, lovingly, with the first three fingers of the hand holding his cap. 'I do want you to be right, Barty. I know you have a line to put, a vocation to square. I don't believe it, sadly – this inevitable defeat of evil. If you were *right* I could rest from time to time. I might trust others to do some of the fighting.' He glanced towards Lane but frowned minutely and plainly dismissed him as a contender. 'Perhaps Col could handle it. Yes, it *is* possible, I insist, despite how he looks. If you were right, Bart, and there were a possibility of a victory for good, and if – a much larger if – *if* Col could only enter a spell when he wasn't dick-led – a spell just long enough for him to get his head up and view the general crime and retribution scene from somewhere other than pussy – in that case, he might be able to do something.'

'Thank you, sir,' Harpur replied.

Francis Garland and the Scene of Crime people were entering the flat, and Garland came through to the kitchen. Iles turned and stared at him as Garland stared at Untidy. 'I was just instructing Col, Garland, that some humane editing of this incident is necessary. News management. You are used to confidentiality, I think. And so, of course, is Harpur.'

Abruptly, the ACC was going into one of his yelling periods. It sounded out of harmony with the tasteful shade and cool cut of the uniform.

Lane muttered: 'Please, Desmond, not in these sad surrounding.'

Iles bellowed: 'When you two were having my wife, Garland, Harpur – I don't say contemporaneously, Chief – no, no, not at all – the matter fell into a decent sequence, certainly – yes, when you were having Sarah, the two of you, I think you were each able to keep matters reasonably secret, at least for the moment, yes? You are both experts at discretion.'

Alec Chase, a Scene of Crime sergeant, had been about to enter the kitchen with his gear, but, observing that the ACC was into one of his wife fits, withdrew.

Garland said: 'Is this death down to Everton?'

'Of course it's down to fucking Everton,' Iles replied. 'I've told the chief, it's a symbolic death, a signal. They're coming. This says, Keep out of my way and don't broadcast. Do we want to add tickertape to his coup? Do we wish it proclaimed that heavies can come onto our ground cook some harmless slob in his own disgusting nest and get away with it?'

They haven't got away with it, sir,' Garland replied. 'We'll find them.'

'Oh, exactly,' Lane said.

'Yes?' Iles replied. 'How long since this was done? Where are they by now?' He grew fairly quiet again and Chase reappeared and began procedures for sealing the room. Iles came over to the table, put a glove on one hand and picked up

Night Life of a Dildo. Glancing at it, he said: 'Oh, Untidy, Untidy, lad. You were a bit adrift even before this suffering.'

Bart drove Harpur home. Garland could get the inquiries under way. It was late, but Hazel came to the door to greet him. She was in pyjamas and a raincoat as dressing gown. 'The other Anstruther's here now,' she said. 'Don't worry. We've been taking care of things.'

God. When Harpur went into the sitting room he found Naomi and Andrew Rockmain talking to Denise and Jill. He thought Naomi looked much more settled than when he had spoken to her last. She, Rockmain and Denise were drinking whisky. Jill and Hazel had cider. Harpur mixed himself a gin and cider and sat down with them.

'Is he all right?' Jill asked. 'The Rev. getting steamed up for nothing?' She was in pyjamas too, and one of Harpur's sweaters, ankle-length on her.

'You should be in bed,' he replied.

'What, he's not all right?' Jill asked. 'Don't keep this secret from us, the way you did with Esmé's death.'

'I'll talk to you about it tomorrow.'

'He's dead too, is he?' Hazel asked.

'I'll talk to you about it tomorrow,' Harpur said.

'Dead how?' Jill asked.

'Does this like . . . betoken something?' Hazel asked.

'Does what?' Harpur replied.

'What's betoken?' Jill said.

'Does the death?' Hazel asked.

'Is this town all evil – if they'd kill someone like Untidy, Dad?' Jill asked. She turned to Rockmain: 'He's just some chickenfeed crook and God-botherer. Really half-soaked and nice.'

'This could be elements from outside,' Hazel replied.

'Go to bed,' Harpur said.

'Something like this will really upset the Rev. Bart,' Jill said. 'Untidy was what's known as a trophy of grace.'

'Thanks very much for looking after my guests for me while I was tied up,' Harpur replied.

'We told Commander Rockmain and Naomi that things were really coming apart in this area, and that you had to be very hands-on,' Hazel said. 'What I meant by "betoken". Does such a death as this show that all decent standards and restraints have gone?'

'Mrs Lane will do her nut,' Jill said. 'Poor Chiefy. Was Iles there?'

'Where?' Harpur asked.

'The death scene,' Jill replied. 'I would of thought he would of come back with you, adrenalin all up after this incident, to see Hazel.'

'Shove it, leper,' Hazel replied.

'He *was* there, was he?' Jill asked. 'It's serious, is it?'

'Somebody's dead, you dropping,' Hazel replied.

'And Mr Lane?' Jill asked. 'I'm just trying to work out the importance, that's all. The "betoken" element.'

Harpur stood, went to the door, opened it and waited there.

'My own feeling is this was a death in terrible circum-stances,' Jill said. 'Like a warning death.' Her voice trembled a little.

'Have you lot let the whole bag of tricks get out of control?' Hazel asked.

'Which lot?' Harpur asked.

'Oh, *which* lot?' Hazel replied, sneering.

'Out,' he said.

The children came towards him. Hazel did not go in for kissing any longer but said, 'Good night, Dad. You look ghastly.'

He bent down to Jill. She held Harpur around the neck and gave him a couple of kisses on the temple. There was a long gap between, while she hugged him madly and whispered in his ear: 'It's all right. I mentioned to Denise when we were alone getting glasses from the kitchen that you definitely do not fancy this Naomi, and I told her the two of them were nearly equal on breasts, that being a taste of yours. Denise was feeling a bit hurt, you know. You inconsiderate, do you think, Dad? Anyway, Naomi's got this creepo with her, but don't tell me she's hooked on that.'

After they had gone upstairs, Harpur took his seat again. 'And *have* we lot let this whole bag of tricks get out of control, sir?' Naomi asked.

Rockmain said: 'Look, Harpur, I wonder if we could talk for a moment. This is police business.'

Denise said: 'I think I'm going back to my flat,' and stood up, holding an envelope file.

'No,' Harpur said, 'no need for that.'

'Yes.' She did sound hurt.

Harpur got up and put an arm around her. 'Please,' he said.

'We won't be long,' Rockmain said.

'Then you can discuss the essay,' Naomi said.

'Please,' Harpur said. 'Wait upstairs.' He turned to Rockmain. 'Five minutes?'

'I certainly don't want to come between you,' Rockmain replied.

'Are you sure about that, Commander?' Naomi asked.

Denise laughed suddenly. 'All right, Col,' she said, and followed Hazel and Jill.

'Lovely girl,' Rockmain said. 'Established?'

'What is it?' Harpur replied. 'Why are you here?'

'I wanted an informal approach, in the first instance,' Rockmain said. His little features beamed closeness.

'Hilston Manor thinks I'm now almost ready to resume my undercover role, Mr Harpur,' Naomi said.

'Yes, more or less,' Rockmain said.

'I didn't know you were still seeing Naomi,' Harpur replied.

'Follow-up. We believe in follow-up at Hilston,' Rockmain said. 'Naomi thought an unofficial contact with you first, then, naturally, a proper recommendation in due course from me through prescribed channels and supported by you.'

'It's crucial for me, sir,' Naomi said. 'I need an anchorage.'

'The vengeance thing,' Rockmain said. 'She might run wild.'

'Do you mean I'm the one to save her sanity?' Harpur asked.

'I thought that was *your* job.'

'Oh, he's mad himself,' Naomi replied. 'You remember that TV cop psychologist, Cracker? This one is crackers.'

'Probably you'll ask, how can she go undercover when her cover's blown?' Rockmain said.

'Yes.'

'That's obviously an operational decision – nothing to do with me,' Rockmain said. 'But perhaps the fact that she suffered trauma in the Eton incident is relevant. People could be led to believe it had meant a disaffection from police work, and from the police cause. This would be quite a credible outcome, in the psychological sense. Such disaffection might mean she would really, as it were, sink into the life she learned something of when infiltrating previously. There have been similar cases.' He nodded and grinned. 'Here, then, is her new cover.'

'I suppose you'll have to see her again now and then, will you?' Harpur asked. 'More follow-up.'

'This is a possibility,' Rockmain replied. 'Her needs are quite complex.'

'How about yours?' Harpur replied.

'Oh, yes,' Rockmain said. 'I love mutuality.' For this trip away from his own fortress, he was not in denim but a suit – a green-cord suit, though.

'I'll think about it,' Harpur replied.

'Thanks, sir,' Naomi said. She got up. 'Now, we mustn't keep you.'

'Can I be sure that if I put her back to work she still won't turn private avenger?' Harpur asked.

'Psychology *is* a science, but not one that deals in certainties,' Rockmain replied. 'However, I do believe that as long as—'

'Great,' Harpur said.

In bed, Denise asked: 'Did I seem like a jealous, foot-stamping kid when I said I'd go back to the flat?'

'Of course.'

'I'd have been desolate if you'd let me.'

'I know that,' Harpur replied.

'What are you, then, some sort of tame psychologist, like him?'

'Not like him, but I do study you,' he said.

'What do you come up with?'

'A lovely profile,' he replied.

'Left or right?'

'A soul profile,' he said.

'Are you into souls?'

'I'm into all sorts.'

'Your kids think I'm just jealous or pissed off when you sneak away to work like that, or have dealings with these pushy people.'

'Which?'

'You know which.'

'Naomi? Is she pushy?'

'But actually I'm scared more or less speechless for you, that's all, Col. Look, am I too young for such worries? I get them every time you go out on some jaunt, every time I see you getting shanghaied into more dirty plots.'

'I realize that,' he replied.

'Oh, don't be so fucking know-all.'

23

Ember had the two pistols aboard again, and maybe he *looked* as though he had two pistols aboard. Ivis especially would spot that. If it came to anything, Ember must put all his first fire into Alfie. And tonight at this traditional partners' dinner it *could* come to something. Shale might turn savage about that failed interception at the Eton. Shale might have intructions from Everton and the Rt. Hon. to remove Ember.

Mansel himself was not bad with weaponry, but Alf had been a star. Alf had killed Big Paul Legge. Christ, Paul Legge. All right, that was the 1980s, but Alfie could probably still do it. Otherwise, would Manse keep him as a staffer? Polished marksmen like Alfred could drop into accuracy no matter how much they'd drunk: reflex. If Everton and the Rt. Hon. had suggested seeing off Ember, the orders would obviously go by protocol to Shale as commandant, but for delegation to Alfie. In the car on the way here Ember had warned Beau to stay unboozed enough to spot if guns were imminent. Then Beau might be able to get to the floor in time, possibly underneath the big banqueting table. But once Beau started drinking he had to fill himself, and he had started before anyone else. He might not be able to find the floor.

At the bar, Shale said: 'As a matter of fact, Ralph, I look over our scene and despite all events and so on I wonder whether anything major, I mean *really* major, has *really* changed since the Eton. I don't say there been absolutely no shifts. After all, Littlebann's finished, probably. And then these deaths. Unkempt. But do any of it affect the . . . affect the . . . call it the *centrality* of things? For instance, we still enjoy this comfortable get-together. We meet as four cooperating businessmen, and I think I can also say four friends, no question. We come together as ever to discuss past and future, and although, yes, there are some anxieties about this or that possible development – yes, although all this, we are still operating within a grand and stable framework like we always did, and I wonder whether anything at all could really shake that framework, it's so good and solid and . . . and needed.'

Beau pounced in his floundering style, waving one fat hand around to signal through-and-through agreement: '*Needed.* The *mot*, Manse. The crux. This continuing demand we meet is an eternal passport.'

Alfie said: 'There *is* a sense in which these various events – the Eton and peripheral incidents like the unforgivable deaths of the girl Esmé Carpenter-Mace and Graham Goff – a sense in which these are merely small waves lapping vainly against the solid strength of our firms.'

Ember had guessed how it would go, the plump comradely wordage, the lulling. He wished he could keep his drinking modest in this aperitif session, but they would be watching for that. Shale and Ivis seemed to be putting gin and peps away at the usual festive rate, and of course Beau was happying fast on rums – why he had only one hand to wave with. Gunless, Beau did not matter much – a dead-weight liability drunk or not, talking or not. In fact, for nearly a week he had tried to persuade Ralph they should dodge out of tonight's meeting: the way he cracked at Barney's. As late as this morning, when apologizing again for his twitch about guns, Beau said: 'Normally, Ralph, yes, a convivial occasion with Manse and Alf. But now, these uncertainties. Maybe Everton's told them to knock you over. Thought of that at all?'

Yes, you could say so. All the same, it had upset Ralph to hear this tame twat get graphic. 'Beau, would I let someone like Manse Shale terrorize me out of a customary social gathering?'

'You're so damned unshakeable, Ralph. I can see it would be an image matter.'

'I don't think in terms of image. More a matter of self-hood,' he had replied. 'Certain compulsions confront us all.'

Now, relaxed in a loose-covered armchair showing tri-angular-faced minstrels and rampaging boars, Shale said: 'Business is down, of course it's down. Lose a spot like the Eton and there'll be a gap for a while. But only for a while. Alf estimates a 15 per cent turnover fall lately, mostly charlie, of course, because charlie was the Eton vogue. That match your thinking, Ralph?'

'Thereabouts,' Ember said. 'Right, Beau? Beau nurses the books.'

Beau said: 'Probably less than 15. Ralph's outlets were not on the Eton. Lucky. Naturally, there's been a general dip through police intensity afterwards, but I'd say only a 12 or 12.5 per cent slump, and grass mainly for us, not coke. It's all picking up again now, as street people come back out of retreat. These are bonny folk who can't be long suppressed. Untidy and the cooker? Well, OK, that did cause another scare, but only a blip, say 2 per cent down for a couple of days, then normalizing. Yes, need is our mainstay.'

'That gas stove upset many, and Manse deeply,' Ivis said. 'Violence via kitchen equipment Manse hates – feels it undermines all household and family should stand for.'

'Texting his arse like that,' Beau said. 'We couldn't decide, mockery or respect.'

'I know Iles wanted to censor publicity details,' Ivis said.

'Iles got some sweet decencies to him whatever they say about the strutting, grey-quiffed ponce bastard,' Shale replied. 'Untidy's family wouldn't want the foul intricacies of that death discussed widespread. Iles sought decorum by concealing the vilenesses. It's personal to him. Don't tell me they got decorum classes at police academy.'

'But the chief's wife goes to the same hairdresser as mine,' Ivis said.

The girl came out and told them their meal was ready. Beau walked into the dining room as well as could be expected, Ember would admit that. They wore dinner jackets and black bows for these levees, and although Beau was never going to look human in that kind of gear, he did not seem to realize this and got a thrill from the formality. Ralph thought nothing would happen while the waitress, barman and chef were still around. Alfie Ivis had fixed for these meetings to take place here every few months on a night when the restaurant would usually be shut, generally a Monday. It was an imitation castle that did medieval-type banquets. Card-board halberds and longbows hung around the walls and suits of plastic armour stood guard. There was a gallery and a huge fireplace for doing deer. Shit, the whole thing, but Ember went along. He and Shale paid for the evening in turn. At least the waitress did not dress up in one of those tit and bum wench costumes or chant lewd ditties with a lyre. The main thing about the place was a car park right off the road and plenty of trees and shadow. Best that Shale's vehicle was not seen standing alongside one of Ember's for hours, making an announcement.

The banqueting room had a long dining table for all the night-out barons and squires and their women to roister at six nights a week, thirty pounds each not including drink. Ember and Ivis sat on one side, Shale and Beau on the other. The girl had been told to lay no places at the head or the foot. This gathering must look democratic regardless. They ate goose fresh from a local farm and drank champagne. The staff would leave when the meal had been served, trusting Alfie to lock up. Ember thought things might get vicious then. It was a possibility he accepted. He could have dodged out of this meeting, as Beau wanted. He could have done more than that. He might have fled everything and escaped for keeps to Spain or Portugal or France. *Abroad, here I come.*

Ember had not gone, though. He had thought about it, and then thought about it some more. But he had also thought about what he would sacrifice if he ran. He would leave behind a fine club, a fine property and grounds, a select, worked-for civic reputation – and leave behind too the certainty that whoever first called him Panicking had been inspired. Ember realized how people would react if they heard he had ejected. He could visualize the giggling, imagine the unsurprised nods and shrugs for *dear old yellow Ralphy*: people like Iles, even Lane... heavies in the Hobart... his own Monty members... O God, God, possibly one or two of his best women. What would he do in fucking France, play fucking boules? He had resolved to hang on. Couldn't he cope with pressure – Barney pressure, Lovely Mover pressure, Everton pressure, Shale pressure, Harpur and Iles pressure? Perhaps it sounded worse and more than it was. Didn't it? In the past he had seen off enemies bigger than any of these, Iles included, hadn't he? Hadn't he? He possessed the cleverness, the judgement, the durable selfish tact. Although his colouring was not altogether right, Ember could visualize himself now and then as a mighty Viking type. Didn't he recall from reading tales as a child that there had been an audacious Norse warrior called Ralph?

So he stayed and he attended the dinner. Over the goose the four talked trade figures for a while more, not brilliant figures, but good figures when you thought about the recent setbacks. Shale was right on that: the partnership had a magnificently constant, untroubled base. Yes, it had been right to come.

Then, all all at once, with the gravy boat in his hand, Manse said: 'What about this fucker Lovely Mover?'

'The one who got away from the Eton?' Ember replied.

'He's been seen in this area again,' Ivis said. 'Manse regards him as wild, unanchored, a threat. In a Toyota?'

'This will be a lad who might be looking for friends,' Shale said. 'He's treated like rubbish by Everton and the Rt. Hon.'

'Rubbish?' Ember asked.

'Given down-grade work. For now. They won't keep him. He's a weakness.'

Beau said: 'This a real identification? Wouldn't he be crazy to show here?'

'What else he got?' Shale asked.

'Manse wondered if he'd been in touch, Ralph,' Ivis said. 'We'd greatly hope no dealings with someone like that, but we did wonder.'

How long did the East End slob stay in this area, driving that big showy crate and in the jacket? He could make Ember look like a traitor, if Shale had him tailed. That would be put alongside the Eton failure. You could not keep much quiet in this trade. Barney knew everything, Shale knew everything. Ember felt the full sweat coming. His eyes saw an infinity of blurred longbows, like a history film in some art house. He compelled himself to keep his hands from the holstered Smith and Wesson and from his jaw scar. He tried to get a glance into one of the fucking medieval mirrors also spread around the walls to see if he looked like disintegration. But either his eyes would not focus or the mirrors had joke glass in them, the way mirrors probably did in those merry old days, and Ralph could see only a huge pair of uncoordinated eyes and two stone of chin.

There was quite a troublesome silence and then Ivis said again: 'A Toyota.'

Beau said: 'What, contacting Ralph? That at all likely?'

'As Manse sees it, Everton's going to get rid of Lovely Mover, so Lovely Mover wants a new business basis, a new ally. Where does he look? Which ground is familiar to him? He knows someone else Everton's got a down on – Ralph Ember. Wouldn't it make sense to seek him out? Allies in joint adversity. This is Mansel's reading, and Mansel's readings generally prove spot on, if I may say, Manse.'

In that rummed-up, brilliantly correct, blundering fashion of his, Beau said: 'Manse, you mean Lovely Mover knows Everton hasn't got what you call a *down* on you and Alfie, *only* on Ralph, so he comes to make a pact between him and Ralph to fight you and Everton? This would make Lovely Mover your enemy and then Ralph your enemy. Is this what you're stating now – at what would otherwise be a genial outing? Is this the talk of a colleague? Are you saying Ralph would get a furtive agreement going with Lovely Mover?'

'You been negotiating with Lincoln, Ralph?' Shale replied.

Yes, just like that harsh confrontation with Barney and Maud.

Beau said: 'Manse, you haven't answered this point I—'

'Beau, some decent fucking silence, if you would,' Shale replied. 'A Toyota, come your direction at all, Ralph?'

Ember's brain had stayed sharp in the general break-up and told him these questions contained their own answer. Shale might know somehow that Lovely Mover and the

Toyota had been night-visiting at Low Pastures. Yes, somehow. Which somehow?

Beau said: 'Personally, I object to the tone of these questions, Manse – their suggestion of betrayal. This is hurtful to Ralph, I'm sure.' It was how Beau could be when he had swallowed a drop – defenceless and cocky, weak and loud, inept and loyal.

'As a matter of fact, yes, I've had a word or two with Lincoln W. Lincoln,' Ember said. 'He introduced himself.'

'More than the one meeting at your place, Ralph?' Ivis asked.

'What meeting?' Beau replied.

'A one-off,' Ember said.

'Some agreement?' Ivis asked. 'Some promises?'

'Oh, no more than a very general survey of the scene,' Ember replied. 'Background.'

'At 4.30 a.m.!' Ivis said. 'I'd have thought a pressing item, a specific item.'

'Christ, have you been damn well snooping on Ralph?' Beau cried.

They had reached the coffee and Tia Marias. The barman handed the keys to Alfie and put a notepad on the table for listing further drinks. The bill would come later to Ralph, but he tipped them a twenty each now. A useful move. If there was no panic paralysis and he could bend his arm and grip his wallet, he knew he would probably be able to handle one of the pistols all right too. Ivis poured some more drinks and entered them. Ember thought about bringing the revolver out then, while Alf was occupied: maybe not fire, but lay it on the table, to show he had that perfect control of at least his upper limbs and probably more, and to show he could smell how the atmosphere had turned malevolent, soured into suspicion. But Ember's head held that memory of wagging the gun, guns, at Lovely Mover, and Lovely Mover unworriedly offering the big ignoral. There had been humiliation in that. Show a gun only when you would use it.

'Did he mention Manse?' Ivis asked.

Ember said: 'A general survey. Background. Could there be a general survey or background without mentioning Mansel Shale Inc. and Manse in person?'

'Hardly!' Beau cried.

Shale said: 'What's a mystery is how this fucker knew he could come and talk to you, Ralph, and get no difficulty. I mean, this is a lad you might of thought was real peril after the Eton.'

'Can Ralph read his mind?' Beau said.

'What are you asking, Manse – had I been in contact with him on the quiet before, smoothing things?' Ember asked.

Beau said: 'This is what I mean – the snooping, the insulting tone.'

'You want to break from me, Ralph?' Shale replied.

'That's crazy,' Beau replied.

'Ralph?' Shale said.

'Never,' Ember said.

Ivis said: 'I'll go and check on the curtains and doors. We don't want a patrol car nosing, wondering why there are lights on a Monday.'

'Curtains where?' Beau asked.

Ivis went out of the dining room. There was another door behind Ember. He moved in his chair so he could still watch Shale opposite but also had this door just in vision. More hellish echoes of Barney's place. Was every meal with colleagues, partners, associates going to be a threat from now on?

'And inviting him on to your property, the sacred Pastures,' Shale said. 'I wonder whether you'd ever invite me, Ralphy. Arm's-length for a partner, a full-out welcome for *him*. In this I got to detect a statement. I got to read exclusion in all respects, business and individual.'

Beau said: 'Listen, Manse, if fucking Ivis comes back in here everything blazing, we're ready for him. Aren't we, Ralph?'

It was Beau's way of alerting Ember, in case he had not spotted the hazard. Beau always feared he was so clever that others could not keep up. Jesus, what would he look like in one of the mad mirrors wearing that suit?

'Well, you truly are a fierce one, Beau, boy,' Shale replied. 'I've heard reports about you when your back's to the wall.'

'My back's not to the fucking wall,' Beau shouted. His voice bounced around the wide room and came back hard off the phoney rafters. 'You'd really know it if my back was to the wall. I'm here in a business capacity, that's all. I thought I was among confederates.'

'Here's Alf now,' Shale replied. 'Nothing blazing. Alf's not a blazing kind of person.'

Ivis came back through the same door as he had used to leave. He was pushing a stainless-steel display stand fitted with castors, and placed it in front of the fireplace near the head of the table. 'The manager said I could borrow this. They have company seminars and so on here. But the flip chart is our own. I've just brought it in from the Jaguar boot. No security risk, I assure you.' The display stand had a low shelf, and Ivis bent and picked up the chart book and hung it on the stand, its cover still down.

'This we burn in the ancestral fucking hearth before we leave, obviously,' Shale said. 'We got some interesting pictures here on the later pages but not for general show.'

'Well, no, I don't think so, Manse,' Ivis replied.

'But, like Beau just said before you come in, Alf,' Shale went on, 'this is a gathering of confederates, which brings complete confidentiality, I know.' The snub face under a stack of dark hair looked the way it always looked, damned sure it had things right. The bugger did not need Alfie to keep telling him that.

Ivis stood alongside the display stand. The clothes made him seem masterful. He said: 'Manse wanted to consider our new position in a proper business fashion and asked me to prepare a presentation, which I've been very happy to do.' He drew the flip-chart cover up and let it hang over the back. At the top of the first page in heavy black crayon was written:

RALPH EMBER AND ASSOCIATES

Goodwill and other unquantifiable assets:

1. Locally established business with solid history and unwavering trust of street dealers.

2. R.E.'s growing legitimate civic status based on family,

genuine interest in environmental matters and on proprietorship of an esteemed club.

3. Possible backing from London interests: Everton Osprey and the Rt. Hon., following Bath meeting.

Negative factors:

Nil.

Ivis moved to page 2.

MANSEL SHALE INC.

Goodwill and other unquantifiable assets:

1. Locally established business with solid history and unwavering trust of street dealers.

2. Likelihood of unofficial police support, possibly enhanced by funeral intervention at Cardiff on behalf of N. Anstruther, an officer.

3. Possible backing from London interests: Everton Osprey and the Rt. Hon., following Bath meeting.

Negative factors:

Nil.

'Now, let's do the same kind of appraisal on London,' Ivis said. He exposed the third page:

EVERTON OSPREY AND THE RT. HON.

Goodwill and other unquantifiable assets:

1. Possible alliance with Mansel Shale Inc. and/or Ralph Ember and Associates (see pages 1 and 2).

Negative factors:

1. Lack of local contact.

2. Unfortunate violence record: the Eton Boating Song incident with fatalities; the deaths of Esmé Carpenter-Mace and Graham Goff. The attempt on N. Anstruther (see para 2, page 2).

3. Absence of police influence and probable police hostility. (see para 2, page 2).

4. Possible objects of vengeance (see para 2, above).

Shale said: 'Thank you, Alfred. I hope I would never prejudge a decision, Ralph, but when I look at a beautifully set-out assessment like that, I got to think there's only one answer to it. This being that Mansel Shale Inc. and Ralph Ember and Associates got nearly all the pluses in their pocket already, so what the fuck do they need someone from outside for, and especially when the someone from outside got so much going against them? In fact, when their only true asset is us.'

'Manse is going to speak really frankly, Ralph. This has my absolute concurrence,' Ivis said.

Shale stood and walked to join Alf at the display stand. Ivis put a welcome onto his slabby face. Shale pointed to paragraph 1 on the Everton page and read it aloud: ' "Possible alliance with Mansel Shale Inc. and/or Ralph Ember and Associates." I got to say, Ralph, that this is not quite accurate. That's not Alfie's fault – I told him to include it. But there's not no possible alliance by this London crew with Ralph Ember and Associates. They've wrote you off, Ralph.'

'I did tell you Manse would speak frankly,' Ivis said. 'I feel it's necessary, in the context of what he wishes to propose.'

'Probably you knew already that they would cut you adrift, Ralph,' Shale said.

'Of course he did,' Beau replied. 'Are we infants?'

Shale tightened up his square short body in the dinner jacket. 'Lovely Mover must of told you, yes. And it goes on. They wanted us to—'

'To wipe us fucking out,' Beau said. 'Tonight.'

'Beau's got it,' Shale replied. 'Yes, you knew that too, Ralph, which is why you arrive full of excellent cannon at this meal.'

'I know I speak for Manse when I say we find the pistols altogether understandable, Ralph,' Ivis stated.

Suddenly, Ember began to feel strong and exuberant again. That kind of wonderful return to optimism would often transform him. It had happened for a while at Barney's. This was not an execution. Yes, thank God he had come, had shown grand fortitude. These people, Shale and Ivis, had discovered they could not do without him. He offered hugely more than Everton Osprey and the Rt. Hon. Ember had always known that, of course. Now, the revelation had reached Shale. The flip chart was a plea – *Love me, Ralph, stay with me, Ralph*. They would forget about the sabotaged interception before the Eton. They would overlook the possibility of a link with Lovely Mover – or he had convinced them it did not exist.

Ember said: 'I feel that the first duty of someone in my position is to ensure his own safety. Others depend on me. So, yes, I am adequately armed. I would not step naked into the conference chamber.'

'Ah, your politics studies,' Ivis remarked. 'You quote Aneurin Bevan?'

Shale said: 'I don't mind a fucking quote here and there between friends. For instance, my mother always used to say, *A word is enough to the wise*, which is from Latin or President Eisenhower. So, all this London end don't come into it, do it really, Ralph? We heard you done the Bath meeting, and likewise ours in London. But what do they mean? Nothing.'

'Manse feels Everton and the Rt. Hon. have absolutely no role here, except a role as would-be plunderers of our achievements via a supposed "alliance", to be discarded by them as soon as they were established,' Ivis said. 'Mansel's view – so simple and yet so penetrating, if I may say, Manse – Mansel's view is that this present partnership – Mansel Shale Inc. and Ralph Ember and Associates – has everything required, and, indeed, rather more. Asset upon asset, in fact. Manse is confident that your supplier, Barney Coss, will certainly see the beauty of this revitalized compact between you and Manse, Ralph, and will be eager for association with it, dropping his own recent demands, inappropriate in the new circumstances. Hence, from now on one of the partnership's main functions, besides, clearly, the day-to-day efficient conduct of trade – one of its other main functions is to use the combined power which already exists to repel these would-be London marauders. Manse is convinced that you will accept this, Ralph.'

Ember said: 'Naturally.' This was not abject gratitude, or relief at probably getting out of here alive, just agreement among equals.

'You heard of the Vikings at all, Ralph?' Shale asked. 'Oh, forgive, of course you fucking have – you getting them lectures down the coll and that. Vikings used to sail in on other people and take, take, take. Fire raids. How I see Osprey and the Rt. Hon. Well, they won't do it here, Ralph.'

'Some of the Vikings were marvellous figures,' Ember replied. 'As a matter of fact, I believe there was one called—'

'And I mean *all* London bandits,' Shale said.

Ivis folded back page 3 of the flip chart. Two colour photographs of Lovely Mover's Toyota had been stuck on page 4. The windscreen and driver's side windows were shattered, as if by gunfire.

Ivis said: 'Manse knows you'll forgive us, Ralph, for talking previously tonight as if Lovely Mover were still a reckonable and, indeed, insidious force.'

'I had to be sure where you stood, Ralph,' Shale said. 'I'm satisfied.'

'Absolutely,' Ivis said. 'Manse's belief in you never faltered, Ralph, believe me. Just a formal check.'

On pages 5 and 6 of the flip chart were more photographs, more colour, these of Lovely Mover. He lay on his side beneath the steering wheel of the car, eyes open, blood congealed from a wound just under his right eye and on the left lapel of his pink jacket.

'God, who did that?' Beau said.

'This lad had become surplus to so many people,' Shale replied, and shrugged to show what a puzzle it all was.

Beau said: 'Christ, yes, Shale, you've been talking at Ralph like Lovely Mover was still alive and around. You've been playing with him, us. This is so damned insolent. I've never been in another meeting with so much damned insolence.'

'Formality,' Ivis said again. 'Of no import, believe me.'

Ember did not like it. This had been an exam. He seemed to have passed, but who had the right to examine him, some rich lout like Shale and his flunkey? And had Ember really passed this test? Were they watching him to see if he twit-ched or even wept when suddenly shown Lovely Mover dead? At least half Ember's exuberance left and his eyes started to blur again.

There was a genuine metal spit in the fireplace and Ivis speared the flip chart lengthwise on it. They made a good fire underneath with a couple of *Daily Star*s found behind the bar and some mock copies of old volumes, supposed to be the Domesday Book, Magna Carta and parish registers, which filled shelves near one of the joke mirrors. The shelves were pine and these burned all right too. Ivis turned the spit slowly and soon the flip chart began to smoulder, then caught alight. Ember watched a portion of page 5 or 6, with half of Lovely Mover's dead face on it, float down and curl into ash. Ember thought there was something sad about this, but not much.

'Who *did* kill him?' Beau asked.

'You know, you remind me a lot of myself, Beau,' Shale replied. 'Always first-class questions.'

'Yes?' Beau said.

'Oh, yes, indeed,' Ivis said. 'Manse is famed for that.'

'Yes?' Beau replied.

'Oh, yes,' Shale said.

'Well?' Beau asked.

'Oh, yes,' Shale replied.

The fireplace was only a piece of period nonsense and had no real chimney. Smoke filled the banqueting hall. Just the same, they waited coughing until all the pages of the chart were burned, then doused the remains of the fire with bottled beer.

Shale said: 'One of my mother's other quotations was, *Leave a place as you would expect to find it*, but fuck that, we pay enough.'

24

Again the chief called a meeting in the conference area of his suite. Once Harpur and Iles were seated, Lane returned to his desk area, where Harpur had noticed a metal display stand. Lane pushed this towards them on its castors. He set the stand to the right of his chain-of-command diagram. 'I've prepared some visual aids, personally,' he said. 'These may help us towards that "overview" of the situation we spoke of last time.' A flip chart lay on a low shelf of the display stand and the chief bent now, picked this up and hung it at shoulder height, the cover of the chart still down. 'I found that the complexities of recent happenings were beginning to slide into a . . . well, yes, into a kind of chaos. I felt we all needed – oh, myself included – I felt we all needed some graphic means to make things coherent, or as coherent as they can be made.' Modesty and resolve jostled in Lane and made the left side of his neck throb.

Iles's features grew almost manic with gratitude. He looked as if he might leap to his feet, perhaps wave his arms and shout, as people did for goals at a football match. 'Remarkable! Remarkable!' he declared. 'This exactly chimes with what Harpur was asking me about only yesterday. Col's words were, "In the midst of such a rush of appalling incident upon appalling incident, I yearn for someone to lead us through this infinitely baffling, even defeating, jungle." Am I giving your words fairly, Col, with a slight tidy-up for literacy's sake?'

'My mother always said one picture was worth a hundred words,' Harpur replied.

'She'd have got on so well with the chief.'

Lane lifted the cover of the flip chart. A large colour photograph of Untidy Graham over the gas stove and with the banner in place was stuck on page 1. Harpur had seen this picture or others in the group too often to be shocked, but he resented the theatrical way Lane pulled back the cover to reveal it. 'This terrible image vindicates, I think, my forecast that the main drive by London drug kings into this area would from now on be via comparatively small operators,' the chief said. 'Graham Goff was certainly that – when he was operating at all. We can assume that in some way he offended one of the London factions, and suffered for it.' The chief spoke with unusual confidence. Harpur felt pleased for him, and intolerably anxious for him. Lane must have decided to go for assertiveness.

Iles said: 'I know you'll regret, as we all do, sir, that the sad details of this death reached the media in full, and reached the media in full when the family had not been properly informed.'

The chief rapped the display stand vehemently with the back of his hand. 'A damned disgraceful leak,' he replied, two tiny nodules of red instantly aglow on one sallow cheek. 'I've apologized personally to Goff's parents and am having inquiries made in this building as to how it occurred.'

'In *this* building, sir?' Iles replied. 'Perhaps it would have helped if *Mrs* Lane had joined you in that personal apology. The voice of a woman can do so much, including sympathy.'

'Naturally, my wife was as upset as I,' the chief said. 'But although this was in some ways a personal matter, it was also very much a police matter, of course, and she would not be totally *au fait* with the facts. She would have learned these ghastly things only from the newspapers.'

'Ah,' Iles replied.

'Oh, certainly,' Lane said.

'Ah,' Iles replied.

The chief moved to page 2 of the chart. Another colour photograph had been fixed here. It showed Lovely Mover's Toyota with its windscreen and driver's-side window smashed by gunfire. He stared at this silently for twenty seconds, his head slightly bowed, like Remembrance Sunday. 'This too on my ground,' he stated. 'Our ground. You'll understand what I mean when I say "chaos". We plummet from one unacceptable instance of violence to another.'

Iles brought out again a small notebook and gold propelling pencil and made a show of writing this down, speaking 'plummet' aloud with an awed tremor in his voice at such vocabulary. Then he said thoughtfully: 'Perhaps, though, I – speaking for myself, sir – perhaps I find this unacceptable instance of violence more acceptable than the unacceptable instance of violence on page 1, viz. Untidy. In fact, to get this fucking poisonous London lout neatly eradicated inside his own vehicle, no grunge on city structures, strikes me as towards the extreme edge of unacceptability and approaching the brilliant. I don't know what Col feels.'

This was not a question, so Harpur stayed quiet.

Lane said emphatically: 'Chaos. I make no judgement on the moral status of the victim.'

Iles yelped a minor congratulation. 'This is that glorious overview position, sir. You can take the large attitude to such things, large in spirit and scope, large in humanity. It's so very fine. Harpur and I, who may have to deal more closely with cunts of this order, are pushed, I fear, into a disgustingly practical even savage response to such lovely deaths. Would that be your feeling, Col?'

'We're trying to establish whether these two killings are related,' Harpur replied. 'Francis Garland has twenty people working on the cases.'

Lane slowly uncovered in succession pages 3, 4 and 5 on the chart. Seven more colour pictures were stuck to these three sheets, showing Lovely Mover from all angles, dead beneath the dashboard of his car.

'You know, sir, I'm not sure which portrait I like best,' Iles said. 'He looks too damned comfy in some of them. The eyes are convincingly dead in that middle one on page 4, though.'

'This is a major London figure, I believe,' Lane replied.

'Middling,' Harpur said.

The chief was in one of those suits that he had and kept on with despite everything. He wore heavy khaki socks, his shoes discarded for now. 'Yes, Desmond, you might be right in part, and from my position I do, perhaps, escape the impulses towards what one would have to call vengeance. And I must, I must. If *I* cannot, where is the proper conduct of law?' Lane flipped over another page of the chart and said: 'This is how – very tentatively I'll admit, oh, yes, very tentatively and still with the consciousness that I sit far from the nitty-gritty, unlike you, Desmond, and you, Colin – but, yes, this is how I've none the less formulated things.' The untypical now-hear-this rasp of his voice did not sound at all tentative.

Page 6 of the chart was headed in large black capitals,

INCIDENTS

Beneath this the sheet was broken into paragraphs written in smaller letters but with the same black crayon:

1. THE ETON BOATING SONG

   Deaths of: Donald McWater
                   Lyndon Vaughan Fitzhammon Evans
                       (friends of DC Naomi Anstruther)
                   Digby Lighthorn, a.k.a. Corporeal Thomas Mill-Kaper
                       (criminal enforcers)
   Escape of: Lincoln W. Lincoln, a.k.a. Lovely Mover
                       (criminal enforcer and pathfinder)

2. CARDIFF

   Death of: Esmé Carpenter-Mace
                   (friend of DC Naomi Anstruther and of L.V.F. Evans, see 1)

3. STIPEND ROAD

   Death of: (Graham Goff, a.k.a. Untidy Graham (sometime minor drugs dealer).

4. VALENCIA ESPLANADE

   Discovery of corpse of Lincoln W. Lincoln (see 1)

The chief said: 'I have to ask you, Desmond, Colin, what is, or rather *who* is, the constant in at least half of four of these paragraphs?'

Neither of them replied.

Lane folded back page 6 and showed page 7. It was headed in black capitals:

DC NAOMI ANSTRUTHER

The chief said: 'I'll tell you immediately that this chart will be destroyed by me in person as soon as our conference is over. What I have attempted here is a profile of DC Anstruther based on her documents and on the reports we received from Commander Rockmain of Hilston Manor.

The smaller black letters said:

1. Joined Force 1991.

2. Joined Drug Squad October 1993.

3. Selected for undercover work 1997.

4. Approved for these duties with special commendation by Hilston Manor. Report speaks of her 'supreme flexibility of persona'.

5. Infiltrates Mansel Shale Incorporated, suspected drugs dealers.

6. October 1997 loses partner, McWater, and other sexual acquaintance, Evans, at the Eton Boating Song (see 1 in INCIDENTS).

7. October 1997 is given sick leave and referred for counselling.

8. November 1997 loses friend Esmé Carpenter-Mace (see 2
in INCIDENTS).

9. November 1997 is deemed to be at risk of reprisals following disclosure of her role at the Eton Boating Song (see 1 in
INCIDENTS) and begins gun training.

10. Warning from Commander Rockmain that the volatility of
her disposition might lead her to seek vengeance for the three
deaths mentioned above if police investigations are not
quickly successful.

The chief said: 'I know I am not the only one of us who
sees certain frightening implications here. And she was living
in the Valencia!'

'You think Naomi did Lovely Mover?' Iles asked.

'The weapon used was not police issue, sir,' Harpur
replied.

'Oh, I think weapons are obtainable,' Lane replied. 'Since
the Wall came down, the world is awash with all sorts of
handguns.'

Iles said: 'The vengeance theme is interesting, sir, but – '

'Colin, I don't say as a certainty you're wrong in con-
sidering Lincoln's death as possibly linked to Untidy
Graham's,' Lane replied, 'but I can't really see it like that.'

The chief left the display stand and came and sat with
Harpur and Iles. To Harpur he looked serious, triumphant,
acute. The suit could not utterly wipe out a suggestion of
dignity. Lane said: 'You mentioned my wife, Desmond.'

'Sir?' Iles replied. 'Do you mean Mrs Lane believes Naomi killed Lovely Mover?'

The chief laughed for a shortish while. 'How could my wife have any views on the matter? Am I likely to discuss such things with her, or show her the contents of my charts?'

'Ah,' Iles replied.

'Never. Obviously,' the chief said.

'Ah,' Iles replied.

The chief said: 'No, I spoke of my wife because she and I dined the other night at the restaurant called Seconds. You could say, perhaps, that this was a companion visit of our meal at the Eton Boating Song. One had heard, of course, that major London dealers now look to Seconds as an alternative sales distribution centre. I wished to see it for myself. One met the other Graham – Noisy Graham, I believe he is called, the joint proprietor.'

'These are true investigative assignments you and Mrs Lane undertake, sir,' Iles said. 'I know Col is grateful for the contribution to groundwork.'

'Unfortunately one was recognized,' Lane replied.

Iles said: 'In your position, sir, you could scarcely put on a false nose and super-modish clothes.'

'I say "unfortunately",' the chief replied, 'yet perhaps not. Because he knew who we were, Noisy Graham came personally to ask whether the meal was satisfactory and I invited him to join us briefly. He was glad of the chance. Glad of the chance to talk – was instantly and surprisingly frank. This is a man full of fear, Desmond, Colin. This is a man who feels himself caught between the interests and the power of warring drugs factions. I mean, on one hand, the London people – Osprey and Basil Cope, the so-called Rt. Hon. – and, on the other, local syndicates like Mansel Shale's. He is afraid for his restaurant and afraid for his own safety and his family's. As he sees it, Seconds might become the site for a very bloody set-to. He referred to the fates of Untidy and Lincoln W. Lincoln. I'll admit I felt a kind of shame. Here was a man terrorized by recent events and immediate prospects in my domain. Our. This man was asking me, you see – asking me without actually formulating the question – he was asking me what the police could do to protect him. This was my own reading of the conversation and I was able to confirm later that Mrs Lane saw things thus too.'

Harpur said: 'People like Noisy would not normally want any link with us, sir – not for the sake of protection or anything else.'

'Don't I know this?' the chief replied. It was almost a whoop. 'That is why I see my visit to his restaurant as so useful, so fortunate. He seemed willing to reveal to me matters he might never have disclosed to . . . well, I hope I don't sound arrogant . . . might never have disclosed to someone of lower rank.'

Iles said: 'You offered protection?'

The chief laughed again, a quite lengthy, solid response. 'This was a social event. I hope I do not make major official promises in such settings and without consultation.'

'Mrs Lane was with you, sir,' Iles replied.

'It struck me we could put DC Anstruther in there,' Lane replied.

'Sir?' Harpur said.

'Undercover though with Noisy Graham's knowledge,' the chief replied. 'I believe Rockmain says he might soon certify that she can return to such work. In fact, that it would be a kind of therapy for her. Am I right, Colin?'

'Oh, Rockmain,' Iles replied. 'Naomi's probably been helping him with one of his sex trips. He'll repay eventually by saying she's fit for duty.'

'That would be unspeakable, monstrous,' the chief cried. 'Sex trips.' We are talking about a very senior officer, and a very senior psychologist.'

'He'll need more treats from her yet, I expect,' Iles replied. 'Aid with perv fantasies of some sort.'

Lane ignored him. 'As I see it, the apparently negative fact that she is known from the Eton publicity as an undercover officer can be turned to advantage here. Her presence might deter people who want to establish their base in Seconds. She is a veritable statement that we know their intentions.' He leaned forward, to emphasize confidentiality, the suit holding its own shape away from his shoulders and chest, not quality enough to respond to sudden movements. 'And if, in fact, she disposed of Lincoln W. Lincoln and the word is out, will this not be another, even more powerful, factor in frightening off other London invaders – Osprey, Cope?'

'Or they'll blast her out of the way and avenge one of their own,' Iles replied.

Lane nodded gravely. 'I concede this is a possibility, Desmond. We will be prepared for that.'

'Stake out Seconds?' Iles asked.

'That would seem only reasonable, given what we suspect of the London pair's intentions.'

'We're talking about an ambush, are we, sir?' Harpur asked.

'With Anstruther as bait,' Iles said.

'We would certainly need to look after her,' the chief replied. 'She is one of us at least until it's proven she killed Lincoln.'

'Yes, as Colin says – an ambush.'

'Well, we do know about ambushes, Desmond. Think of the Eton.'

Harpur saw that Lane's proposal was the kind of thing Iles might have devised himself. Had the chief been watching and learning? Had he come to despair of rectitude in the worsening state of things? Had his wife told him to despair of rectitude in the worsening state of things? Did he crave a sparkling victory to retire on? Did his wife crave a sparkling victory for Lane to retire on so that she might continue to respect him in old age? Had Lane undergone a conversion – was he suddenly Dirty Harry?

Iles said: 'There is not the least proof Naomi did Lovely Mover.'

'We'll see from their actions what Everton Osprey and Cope think about that,' Lane replied. 'And perceptions generally.' He stood and removed the flip chart. 'I'm going to take this home and burn it. There is a kind of narrative here which I would not want others to study. A girl's life might be involved and a girl, as Desmond rightly says, whose culpability for Lincoln's death is by no means established.'

'Might that "extreme flexibility of persona" enable her to vengeance-kill Osprey and the Rt. Hon. as well, do you think, sir, if they arrived at Seconds?' Iles asked.

'Luckily we'll be there to prevent anyone killing anyone,' the chief replied. 'Surely we have had enough deaths, Colin, Desmond. Haven't we?'

Iles said: 'Oh, I'm sure you won't expect me to answer that off the top of my head, sir.'

'Do you think his mind might have gone again, sir?' Harpur asked Iles on their way down to Harpur's room in the lift.

The ACC made some signs to indicate that they should not talk sensitive matter in case the lift was bugged. Perhaps it was a joke. In Harpur's room, Iles sat on the corner of the desk and said: 'Once in a while, despite himself, Col, and without the aid of his wife, Lane has a sound idea. I hear Naomi's been damned good in gun training.'

We're talking about what looks like a professional killing, sir.'

Yes, she's a wonderful kid and would be capable of a really first-class grudge, off and on,' Iles said. 'I'm grateful to her. As I remarked to the chief – the wonderful neatness of Lovely Mover's death. I wouldn't go so far as to say artistry, but very superior artisanship.' The ACC kicked Harpur's desk repeatedly with his gorgeous black lace-ups, a familiar reaction when he was angry or excited. 'And what reward is she going to be offered? A commendation? No, she'll be put up as a target for those other two London shits in Noisy's place.'

'We can cope with that, sir.'

'What is she – some sort of fucking Aunt Sally, Col? First the Eton, now this. *Join the police force and get your tits shot off in bars and restaurants.*'

'We'll have our best people there.'

Iles said: 'My good luck, Harpur, is that one could probably get entrée to Osprey's London place via this friend of a friend in the Met. I mentioned. Yes, I feel a very palpable debt to Naomi, you know, Col. You're probably too gross to appreciate the deftness of what she's done, but I definitely don't hold that against you.'

'Thank you, sir.'

'*Your* mother spoke to you about pictures and words. *My* mother too liked to pass on tips about life. We're indebted to our mothers, you and I, Harpur. It's one of the things that binds us unbreakably, regardless of your disabilities.'

'Thank you, sir.'

'*My* mother used to say, *Desmond, if you see trouble coming stop it at source.* Oh, yes, at source.'

'Osprey and the Rt. Hon. probably killed Lovely Mover themselves, or those operators they use,' Harpur replied. 'He'd be an embarrassment to them – someone hunted. Or he might have been trying to muscle Panicking, or even Shale. Perhaps he hoped to join up with Panicking and get him to ditch the arrangement with Shale Inc. Garland has two reports of a vehicle like the Toyota up near Low Pastures late.'

'My pal at the Yard owes me, you know, Col. I send on my wife's underwear catalogues to him. Sarah has lovely taste in all that kind of thing. Delicate colours, wonderful sheen.

Costly, yes, but . . . Why the fuck am I telling you about her underwear? It doesn't come as a revelation, does it, Harpur?' The ACC began one of his loud spells. 'Does it, does it?'

'I'll just close the door properly, sir,' Harpur replied. 'She should be careful where she hangs out clothes like that or Conrad Royston Usher the knickers nicker will have them.'

25

Gleefully Shale called: 'Here's Detective chief Superintendent Harpur, Alfred.'

At once Harpur saw Shale thought he brought a marriage offer. Shale led him into the drawing room. Harpur had visited the house before and enjoyed again now the sight of this fine space, magnificently furnished with decent stuff – probably Victorian, a lot of mahogany. So many true villains lusted for heritage, substance. Shale would most likely see himself as a flash in the pan, craved history, loved durability. Alf Ivis was seated in the drawing room on a leather sofa and near three original paintings, also Victorian. Alfie briefly stood to greet Harpur and gave a small friendly bow, his wide lumpy face sublimely attentive. Harpur sat in one of the big armchairs, facing Ivis. Shale remained standing.

'We've been expecting you, Mr Harpur,' Shale said. 'You or Mr Iles or even the chief. I mean, in view of developments.'

Ivis said: 'Recent changes impose a timeliness.'

'You're looking at the pictures again, Mr Harpur. Probably you, like myself, are a Pre-Raphaelite fan.' He moved across the room to them and gazed for a while, speaking over his shoulder. 'These were artists who knew about the colour auburn and buskin-type footwear for all sexes. What I always say is they prized closeness and fellowship. The Pre-Raphae-

lite Brotherhood. I love that term, brotherhood. Here you
have one Arthur Hughes and two Edward Prentises.'

'Manse has always yearned for a business equivalent of
that creative comradeship, a similar brotherhood. He would
definitely wish to offer a similar cooperation, Mr Harpur. In
his turn he's eager to respond to any similar offer from your
side.'

'Why, Alfie and I are so glad we could look after Detective
Constable Anstruther for you at the Cardiff funeral. We were
disgusted to witness violent intervention during such an
occasion.'

'Manse saw our small counter-effort as an excellent
expression of happy cooperation, auguring further cooperation. One hoped – knew – it was only a beginning.'

Shale stood up and went to bring from the big sideboard
what would probably be a bottle of very useful wine, most
likely claret. Ivis also rose, opened a cupboard and produced
three beautiful glasses. Shale poured. Like the chief, he lived
in what had been built as a rectory last century, and there
would certainly be cellars. One day, Shale had spoken to
Harpur about the way ownership of two former church
properties gave him and Lane what Mansel had called 'a
worthwhile link with each other and with established
religion'.

Harpur said: 'Some different pictures, Manse.' He brought
from his pocket smaller versions of the photographs used by
Lane for his flip chart of Lovely Mover dead and the Toyota.
Harpur spread them on the low drinks table in front of him 'I
need to chat to you and Alfie.'

'I've heard of this foul death,' Shale replied. 'On receiving the news I recall asking Alfred if he could explain what was happening in our previously well-ordered country. Damned unkempt.'

'Yes, Manse was catastrophically upset, Mr Harpur.'

Shale stood over the photographs and examined them slowly in turn, giving an occasional moan of horror. 'But merely hearing of something like this could never prepare me for the shock of seeing the detail now. Oh, terrible. My mother always used to say, *A picture is worth a million words*, but could she imagine I'd ever have to face pictures like these?' He finished looking and sat down.

'Lovely Mover is not someone to be easily knocked over. Getting a fine-tuned thing like Lincoln W. Lincoln in his own vehicle – that's polish,' Harpur said.

'True,' Ivis said. 'Planning. Resolve.'

'You must be very proud of her, Harpur. Mr Harpur,' Shale said.

'Clearly this development makes us on our part even more glad to have helped in an indirect way by . . . well, by preserving her life, as you know, Mr Harpur,' Ivis said. 'Oh, Manse understands why you must go through the formality of coming to see him, ostensibly investigating. Yes, *prima facie* there would be motive for us to have killed Lovely Mover rather than . . . well, rather than his being done by a gifted avenger. Some could imagine we saw him as potentially dangerous trade competition, invading our ground, and to be got rid of.'

'*Did* you see him as a business menace, Manse?' Harpur

asked. 'Was he trying to poach – poach Panicking, for instance?'

Ivis said: 'The vengeance impulse can be very, very strong, especially if someone is confronted by not just one death of a dear one but several, as in this girl's case. It is an impulse with dark grandeur to it, though, of course, also grossly illegal.'

Harpur drank his wine. He said: 'One of the very few people I can think of with the capacity to take out Lovely Mover like that is—'

'Oh, Alfie, you mean,' Shale replied, with a grand open laugh. 'I got to say that might of been possible in his heyday. The 1980s, for instance. But time, Mr Harpur. Succession. Alf's not going to mind if I talk about him like yesterday's man – but only in that type of work. He has moved to other matters more right for his age. New people come along. New people with the skill and maybe a sense of mission. Like Alf says, a wrongful, yes, illegal mission – and especially for a police officer, perhaps – yet understandable. Even to her credit, I got to say.' He drank and grew more solemn. 'And now as reward will she be put at awful risk? There's tales around. Is what I hear true – this Seconds project? She'll be set up for them London colonizers? Wise? We gather it's the chief's own scheme – why, the word's about, most probably – but I still ask, wise? Alfred and I would feel very frustrated – hurt – to have saved her for you to utilize in such a special and necessary role – as the photos show – and then to see her put on fucking toast for Everton and the Rt. Hon.'

Ivis said: 'The great thing about a woman in this kind of

work is she can get close to a target without setting off alarm
bells. A man, no. As you mentioned, this was a hit of real
aplomb.'

'In any understanding arrived at between us and the
police, Mr Harpur, I would like you to know – and all others
involved – I would like it known, we would feel thrilled to
have Detective Constable Anstruther as a colleague. This is
someone who has proved herself at topmost levels and
deserves aid in every repect. Every respect.'

26

Naomi, sleeping alone, but not sleeping, heard what she took to be someone working at the lock of her flat's front door. So, Christ, a hunter or hunters had tracked her here despite all those little precautions? Was it the same two again – the pair who located her and Esmé and killed Esmé? Naomi lay as still as she could. There was the lock but also a pair of bolts on the front door. She could remember pushing them across before she went to bed, couldn't she? Could she? And then the sounds ended. Was the front door open?

They would not let her keep her gun-training weapon at home so she slipped out of bed and quietly made her way naked in the dark towards the phone in her living room. Harpur had told her to ring him direct and at once in any emergency. If she could not reach him the instructions were to call the control room, not Iles, though Iles had given her his private number. 'The grand wish to take care of one of our people can make Mr Iles over-protective,' Harpur had said, 'especially a woman officer.'

She kept her bedroom door half open at night and she could move into the hall without noise. The front door remained closed and she stood behind it for a moment and listened. There was still no sound, but she waited for anything that might tell her how many people were out there. She was a police officer, wasn't she – a terrified police officer, but still a police officer? If she was going to scream for help the scream should try to sound like a situation report and give some measure of the hazard.

The prodding at the lock began again. Did that mean two people – *those* two? One had tried to crack it and failed, now the other? Naomi saw the bolts were in place. She moved away on bare feet towards the telephone, still silently she thought. But the sounds stopped suddenly again. Someone whispered faintly, 'Naomi, is that you?'

At first she could not identify the tiny bit of voice. Because Iles had been in her head she picked him for half a second. Then she dismissed that. The Rev. Bart? But why would the Rev. Bart try to force her lock? Yes. God, she felt relieved she had not dialled the cavalry. It would have been embarrassing and unfriendly to bring the night shift down on Iles or Bart.

'Naomi?'

She had returned and was standing closer to the door now. Just the same the whisper seemed fainter, even more designed not to rouse neighbours. 'Rockmain?' she said. She pulled back the bolts and turned the Yale knob.

'Perhaps I should have phoned first,' he said, stepping inside. 'But I thought they might have you tapped in case of threats. Could you clothe yourself, do you think?'

She shut the door behind him and refixed the bolts. She took an outdoor coat from the hallstand and put it on. 'How did you find the address?'

'You're in dossiers, aren't you, for heaven's sake?'

'You could have knocked on the door.'

'I wanted no noise on the landing. This is a confidential

visit – super-confidential and so urgent. Naomi, I heard you killed someone. Well, not someone. A redoubtable warrior.'

'Killed?'

'Please don't deny it. Don't. I drove here at once.'

She took him from the hall into her living room and switched on a table-lamp. They sat down. He had on a long, bright white raincoat unbuttoned over the chic abiding denim. Substantial, very deep excitement brightened his small features, not mere frenzy. She saw he yearned to be sure she had killed Lovely Mover: *needed* to believe it. 'Please don't deny this.' It was not him saying that her guilt was plain. His 'please' was a plea, a prayer. He meant, please don't destroy my belief in your death flair.

'You must tell me how it was done,' he said. 'The precise evil detail. And then you—'

'Must kill you again.'

'You've authenticated yourself with this,' Rockmain replied. 'I adore it. Lovely Mover's lovely movements forever beautifully fixed, like pictures on the Grecian Urn.'

'The detail?'

'Only for my personal knowledge. We are not talking police matters, I hope. We are not talking confession. We talk validation of your role. Yes, kill me, kill me, Naomi. But first the fine and circumstantial description, never to be disclosed, never to be written up, never to be squandered on mere official disclosure – all that trite forensic muck.'

'And afterwards?'

'Afterwards?' He chortled, his tiny face huge on joy. 'Afterwards, a definite certification that you may return to undercover work. I promise. That will be wholly warranted. I'll know you have freed yourself finally from those vengeance aberrations by enacting one of them. Lovely Mover's death is for you both an accomplishment and an escape into . . . into let's call it a career. But you will need to go on seeing me now and then, of course. Merely confirmatory.'

'Of course. Kill you where?' she replied.

'In your personal bed. Would you permit that? Please. Oh, please. Come upon me again in the night, myself so helpless, so poignantly a victim. Pow, pow, pow. I'll change your sheets with my own hands. Tomorrow I will write a warm testimonial from Hilston to Harpur, letterheaded paper. It will be irresistible. Your chief wholly believes in me.'

He had been sitting on her chaise-longue but stood now, needing to pace about a little and spend some of his throb. 'Naturally, I've brought a weapon,' he said. 'Brought a gun, that is. Probably the other has been discarded by you as a security matter. Well done.' He produced from his raincoat pocket what appeared to be the same Luger she had nuzzled him with at Hilston Manor. 'Fully loaded.' He handed it to her.

And so in her therapeutic role she manufactured for him step by feasible step how she might have finished Lovely Mover if someone else had not done it first. Dear Manse? Dear Alfie? Towards the end of the account he reached a stage where she saw he needed her to rush the conclusion. As his body heat soared, he took off the raincoat and his denim jacket and dropped them on the floor. His breathing grew agonized. 'Yes, yes,' he muttered, and made for the bedroom. 'Be soon, yet not hurried.' In a while she followed. His mouth was pleafully agape again and she thrust into it.

When he was stripping the bed just before leaving she said: 'You must have really impressed the high-ups on my behalf. Once I'm declared OK to return undercover they'll put me into Seconds. It's to trap Everton Osprey and the Rt. Hon. This is something devised by the chief himself, as I understand it from Harpur. Doesn't it show wonderful continuing faith in me?'

'They're going to fucking what?' he howled, that schoolboy voice jagged with fright for her. 'You'll get killed.'

'I'll have protection.'

'Balls. Think how close they went with the Eton. I could lose you, Naomi. It must not, must not be.'

'I'll be all right. They've learned from that. An all-round shield.'

He put his jacket and coat back on. 'I'll make fucking sure you're safe,' he said.

'How do you mean?'

'Why I can't leave the Luger with you.'

'Can't what?' she said.

'I've got a friend in the Met., very well placed. He's into what we call "gender variance" at quite an advanced level, so we were bound to run into each other here and there. Don't worry, he can probably help me towards those two big London sods – bastards, in their own de-luxe den.'

'What do you mean, help you towards?'

'That's right, help me towards.'

27

Ralph Ember took a call on the payphone in the Monty. It was Barney, wanting to know how far Ralph had progressed with removing opposition and turning the club into a prestige trade centre replacing the Eton. 'Rosemary, my accountant, has been badgering me, Ralph. Remember Rosemary? Talented girl, creative.' Always Barney seemed to feel that the payphone would be unquestionably safe. It did not strike him that if police put a tap on the club's listed number they would do the payphone too.

Ember said: 'There've been so many changes I thought that perhaps the pressure would be less acute now.' Despite Barney's belief in the security of this line there was a rule that Ralph must not use Barney's name in the conversation, though Barney could use Ralph's.

'Yes, the same pressure,' Barney replied. 'Greater. Maud wants a word. She's on the extension.'

'Which fucking changes, Ember?' she said. 'Nothing alters the fact that the Eton as a class depot is kaput and an opportunity therefore exists and should be grasped before the opposition establishes itself immovably while you doze.' Although there was a stool in the phone booth, Ember did not sit down. This call should not be prolonged. He said: 'But the major opposition elements no longer threaten. These appalling shootings of Osprey and the Rt. Hon. in their

London place ensure that. We have some leisure now to shape our progress, trawl for the best alternative sites.'

'You won't let the commerce into your damn chi-chi club, will you, Ember?' Maud replied. 'That's why you obstruct. What you saving it for? Camilla wants a word.'

'Inclined to agree, Ralph,' Camilla said, 'with you, that is. Inappropriateness of haste, given developments. But one is outvoted at this end. It happens.'

'Who did that pair anyway, Ralph?' Barney asked.

'This is a considerable mystery, believe me,' Ember replied.

'We hear about a vengeance cop,' Maud said. 'A girl detective. She'd have ways of getting their address. Camilla has something to add.'

'Rumour – but I don't think I'm overstating it when I say damned interesting rumour. Suggestions galore reach us here. Ability to get to them in their own West End apartment. Some inside help, Ralph? Many possibles. As ever, some say Iles, of course. Or Shale–Ivis, of course. Or, of course, a fond relative of Lovely Mover, believing he was hit by them and not the vengeance cop – or on their orders. Or likewise friends or family of Untidy Graham. Again, there's mention of some mad psychology officer, scared he might lose this girl detective who does therapeutic things for him, possibly. Maud would like to speak.'

'I suppose you think you come out of this bloody well again, Ralphy. Crowing.'

Ember said: 'There have been many violent deaths, Maud, some, admittedly, of outright enemies, but one can hardly crow, surely. I think of Churchill's call for magnanimity in victory.'

'Arseholes,' Maud replied. 'You didn't sneak up to metropoland and do them yourself, Ralphy, did you?'

Ember said: 'My main task here now is to work out exactly how the shifts in power and circumstance bear on the future. My associate, M.S., still believes we can get an accommodation with Harpur and so on – kind of self-policing, like self-assessment in tax. But I'm not sure. Perhaps we'll try to sort things out with visual aids? I have in mind to do a proper seminar presentation for my assistant and M.S. and A.I. with all factors represented on a flip chart. I shall be in touch when one can identify the most favourable route, please rely on that.'